W9-AQH-209

DISCARD

Date: 9/15/20

LP FIC GIBSON
Gibson, Rachel,
How Lulu lost her mind

HOW LULU LOST HER MIND

HOW LULU
LOST HER MIND

RACHEL GIBSON

THORNDIKE PRESS

A part of Gale, a Cengage Company

GALE
A Cengage Company

Thorndike Press® Large Print Core.
The text of this Large Print edition is unabridged.
Other aspects of the book may vary from the original edition.
Set in 16 pt. Plantin.

LIBRARY OF CONGRESS CIP DATA ON FILE.
CATALOGUING IN PUBLICATION FOR THIS BOOK
IS AVAILABLE FROM THE LIBRARY OF CONGRESS

ISBN-13: 978-1-4328-7965-5 (hardcover alk. paper)

Published in 2020 by arrangement with Gallery Books, an imprint of Simon & Schuster, Inc.

Printed in Mexico
Print Number: 01   Print Year: 2020

*To Barbara Currier, for her love of family
and devotion to Pirate's Booty*

1

This is not a good time for Mother's she-nanigans. I have a three-thirty flight to Los Angeles; my suitcases are loaded in the back, and my boarding pass is in my shoulder bag. I figure I have thirty minutes to deal with Mother and still make my flight. If that isn't enough time, I'll deal with her when I get back.

It's raining so hard the wipers can barely keep up with the drops bouncing off the hood of my Land Rover. On a good day, I'm not the best driver on the road, and this is far from a good day. Visibility isn't great and the Cranberries screaming out "Zombie" on the radio pinch the corner of my eye. Despite thirty units of Botox, I can almost feel deep elevens furrow my brow. I hit the control button, and the panel goes black. My forehead relaxes, and my eyebrows are safe.

I have to be inside the Los Angeles Convention Center by 10 a.m. tomorrow. I'm in the middle of my ten-city Find True Love in February tour. All the dates are sold out. I have to be there. I am Lulu the Love Guru, expert on finding and keeping love, but there can't be a Lulu event if Lulu is stuck in Seattle straightening out whatever mess Mom's gotten herself into this time. The administrator of Mom's senior care facility didn't go into a lot of detail, but I can fill in the blanks. Mom's been socializing again, but this is nothing new. If he'd just waited an hour, I'd be in the air and unavailable, but that would have been too easy. My relationship with my mother has rarely been easy.

My mother is seventy-four and was diagnosed with Alzheimer's four years ago, when she forgot she'd put a pan of grease on the stove and almost torched herself. She managed to escape with nothing more than some singed hair, thank God. The bad news was that we discovered she was already stage four. She'd been so good at covering it up that I hadn't noticed her decline. Looking back, there were signs, of course. She was forgetful of time and phone numbers, but who doesn't occasionally miss an appointment? Heck, I can't call anyone without looking at the contacts list on my phone, and I just turned thirty-eight.

I should have paid more attention and gotten her help earlier. Nothing will cure her disease, but things would have been different, at least in the earlier stages. I have a lot of guilt about that, and about a few other things, too.

I pull up the cuff of my black wool blazer as I turn into the parking lot. The rain slowed me down, but I still have enough time to run in and sign whatever Golden Springs wants me to sign and run back out. Mom was a card before she got sick, and now she's upped the ante. This isn't the first time I've had to meet with the administrators. This isn't even Mom's first facility — it's her third.

The first adult care residence had documented each episode of her compulsive spooning and other nocturnal infractions until she got booted. Apparently, she's at it again. Mother has never liked sleeping alone and, eyeing all the possibilities laid out before her like a senior-living man buffet, she doesn't think she should have to, either.

When I was growing up, she made me sleep with her when she didn't have a man. I hadn't minded because that meant there wasn't anyone else in our lives and I had Mom all to myself. I'd crawl into her bed, or she'd crawl into mine, and we'd laugh and talk while she held my hand. Those are some of the best memories I have of Mom and me.

Golden Springs doesn't have valet service like Mom's last facility, so I find a parking spot as close to the front doors as possible. That still leaves a few huge puddles and a stream of water between me and the sidewalk.

If I'd known I was going to take a detour halfway to the airport, I would have left earlier. If I'd known I was going to hop puddles, I certainly wouldn't have worn my Dior hobble skirt or Louboutin pumps.

With my movement restricted, I slide out of the SUV and land on a spot of asphalt that isn't completely covered in water. Rain hits my face, and I raise my shoulder bag over my head like a makeshift umbrella and skip and hop across the parking lot as best I can. Big fat drops bounce up from the ground as I pick up the pace. I'm close enough to the sidewalk that I make a daring leap at the curb. My leap is more rabbit hop than graceful gazelle, and I land in a deep puddle. Cold water fills my leather pumps, and I suck in a breath. If I were a swearing kind of girl, I'd let loose with some f-bombs right about now, but my mother raised me to be a "lady." Instead, I say, "Crap," which is hardly better by Mother's standards.

I hurry up the sidewalk and pass a golden fountain shooting a ridiculous amount of water into the pouring rain. The automatic front doors open and my shoes are squishy as I approach the front desk.

"I'm Lou Ann Hunter and —"

"Over there," the receptionist interrupts as she points to the offices down one hall. "Third door."

Yeah, I know the drill. I pass two couples sitting in the hall; they eye me like they're not really happy to be here either. Like parents being called to the principal's office.

I knock twice and open the door. My gaze instantly lands on the troublemaker, swallowed up in a puffy leather La-Z-Boy. Her long dark hair is loose and pulled to one side, and the Louis Vuitton Bumbag I got her for Christmas is belted around the waist of her velour tracksuit. Mother has always been particular about her appearance, and even with stage four Alzheimer's, she still manages to draw a perfect red lip. "Hello, Mom." She glances at me before returning her attention to a wall clock. Mother can read the numbers but has no real concept of time. Just like she can pick out words

and read short sentences, but her compre-
hension of what she's read is dicey. When it
comes to context and retention, she usually
craps out.

"Why are you here?" she asks. No friendly
hello or motherly "It's good to see you,
Lou."

"I don't know, but I'm sure about to find
out."

Douglas, the administrator, doesn't offer a
much friendlier greeting. "Ms. Hunter."

I know this drill, too. I smile and dig down
deep and channel my inner Patricia Lynn
Jackson-Garvin-Hunter-Russo-Thompson-
Doyle. Mom's been married five times and
deals in charm like Vegas deals in cards. She
discards just as easily, too. "Douglas." I step
forward and shake his hand. "I'm sorry my
hands are a little cold. The weather is horrible."

He doesn't smile, and I get a little worried.

Mother hasn't looked at me again, making me wonder if they have drugged her up.

Douglas gestures to the chair across from
his desk and says, "Please take a seat."

"Of course." I place my purse on the floor
and slide my feet out of my shoes, kicking
them upside down so the water will drain
out. "So, has Mom been wandering at night

again?" I glance at her, and she cuts me a look before returning her attention to the clock. She doesn't appear to be drugged, and I can't tell which version of her is with us today. "How'd she get out of her room this time?" Mom has what is called a passive infrared sensor, or PIR, alarm that signals the nursing station when the stream is broken. She's had different alarm systems in the past, but she's like Houdini and finds a way out. This one has worked the best — until now.

"The PIR alarms are only set when the resident is in his or her room for the night. During the day, we encourage socializing as a way to combat insolating and depression."

"So, Mom was 'socializing' during the day?" If I'm here, it means she wasn't chatting or playing board games.

"Yes." He glances at the paperwork on his desk. "Patricia was discovered in the Complete Care unit at two thirty in the afternoon."

Complete Care is in a different hub. At some point, Mother will be moved to that unit. My stomach drops. I don't like to think about it. "Today?"

"On the tenth."

That was three days ago.

"She was discovered in the bed of resident

Walter Shone."

This is not a surprise to me. "Yes. Mother is affectionate."

"Walter Shone is eighty-one and suffers from end-stage dementia. He'd been comatose for several weeks."

So if he didn't know anything happened, what's the big deal?

"Imagine his wife's surprise when she discovered Patricia wrapped around her husband like an octopus."

Again, not a surprise. Mom has always been a notorious man stealer. "I imagine that was quite shocking." I glance at the clock because it's not as rude as looking at my watch, snapping my fingers, and saying, "Chop-chop. I've got a plane to catch."

"It was horrific. His sons and five grandchildren had come with their mother to say their last goodbyes."

"That *is* bad of her." Mother had robbed a family of their private moments of grief. I feel awful about that, but she has Alzheimer's, and this is a memory care facility. She's here for a reason, and she needs help as much as any other patient. "I know Mother is very sorry." I rise to hurry Douglas along.

"He had an erection."

Gross! "With severe dementia? Wearing

Depends?" I turn my head to look at Mom. "Tell me that you did not take that man's pants off."

Mom shrugs a shoulder and continues to stare at the clock. "I have a passionate nature."

"For God's sake!" Some people are addicted to drugs or alcohol, money or chocolate. Mom's addiction has always been men, and having Alzheimer's hasn't changed that one bit. If anything, Alzheimer's makes it worse. She doesn't even attempt to hide her "passionate nature" anymore. Not that she'd ever tried very hard anyway.

"We can't have that behavior here."

No shit. I keep my smile in place and try not to lose my cool. This is her third facility. She got kicked out of the first for spooning, and the second for what I call going "Rattlesnake Patty" just one too many times — that is, threatening to kill other female patients for stealing her "boyfriends" and plundering seven bags of Pirate's Booty from her hidden stash. Honestly, who steals seven bags of Pirate's Booty?

No one.

"This is a safety issue that we cannot tolerate at Golden Springs."

Again, no shit. Somehow my mother wandered into the Complete Care unit and

15

no one noticed. Mother is very wily, and I can't blame Golden Springs entirely. "Thank God no one was hurt." Physically anyway. I'm sure the grandkids have mental scars. I shift in my seat and calmly say, "I'm sure we can come up with a better way to keep track of Mother during social hours." I even manage a little joke. "Perhaps lead shoes."

"Wynonna stole all my shoes," Mom says, and I'm just thankful she isn't blaming me this time. "My Pirate's Booty too."

Douglas pats a stack of papers. "We're discharging Patricia to your care."

"Excuse me?" Unfortunately, he repeats what I thought I'd heard the first time. Finding a different facility won't be easy. Like I said, I know the drill. Last time, it had taken more than the thirty-day grace period to find Golden Springs. I'd had no choice but to have Mom live with me in my condo. Within weeks, she made me lose my mind. It took a while to find it again, and I don't want to lose it once more. "That seems like a drastic solution to a more easily solvable problem." I'm Lulu the Love Guru. I built a multimillion-dollar empire from nothing but a legal pad. I calmly suggest a second option. "Perhaps we could tie a bell around her ankle." I didn't get where

I am today by accident. When something stands between me and my goals, I solve the problem.

"We had a staff meeting this morning, and it's been decided. We've included a packet outlining her dietary needs, medication, doctors, and appointments. You'll need to take these with you."

I take a deep breath and let it out slowly. "Okay." I slide my hand into my purse and pull out my wallet. "How much?" I grab a pen and poise it above a blank check. "How much to make this all go away and then we can all move forward with our day."

"It's not about money."

I pull up my sleeve and glance at my watch. "I don't have time to negotiate, Douglas. How many zeros?"

"It's not about money," he says again, but I don't believe him.

"I was on my way to the airport when you called." I shove my wallet back inside my purse. They probably want to charge me an arm and a leg for more sensors and alarms. "We can continue this conversation when I return." I lean to one side and grab my soggy shoes. "I have to go, or I'll miss my flight."

"I don't think you understand. Patricia has already been discharged."

"What? You've got to be kidding." That means I have only a month to come up with a solution that doesn't involve Mother driving me crazy again. Impossible. They have to reverse their decision. I slide my foot into one pump and stand. "Mother, promise Douglas you won't spoon anymore."

She continues to stare at the clock. "I'm having dinner with Earl."

"Mom!" I limp in front of her so she has to look at me, and I say firmly, "Promise you'll control your passionate nature."

"No one will believe that!" She laughs. "That's for sure!"

"If you'll sign here."

I turn to Douglas and say, as politely as possible, "When I brought her here, I told you that she wanders at night." I wave the pump in my hand at the papers on his desk. "You wrote it down and assured me that the staff would watch out for her."

"This happened during the day, when it's more difficult to watch every patient."

"I don't give a damn."

Mom sucks in a scandalized breath. "Lou Ann!"

"*Damn* isn't a swear word. How long was my mother missing before she was found in bed with that old guy?"

"A long time," admits the ruby-lipped

troublemaker.

"I don't need your help, Mom." I point my pump in her general direction and return to the desk. "Who was responsible for watching her?"

"Every one of our staff members is dedicated to the care and welfare of our clients." He thumbs through his papers. "Here's the admission agreement you signed last year."

Okay. They're not taking her back, and I need to think fast. Legally, they have to give me thirty days' written notice that they're discharging her, and I need to find an alternative memory care facility. Even if I weren't traveling, that's hardly enough time. I can't just drop her off someplace because they have an open bed. No matter how tempting, I can't do that to my mother. "I'll need more than thirty days." I have to be in LA tomorrow morning. My tour is sold out. I have to leave now.

"Perhaps I haven't been clear. She must vacate today."

It takes a few moments for that information to penetrate my skull. When it does, my mouth drops.

"I've included several brochures of qualified memory care facilities in her discharge packet." He looks at Mother. "We're sorry it's come to this."

"It's okay, Doug."

No. It's not! I want to yell at him for being an asshole, but I've learned that yelling and name-calling ends all conversation and gives men an excuse to call you hysterical. "Not as sorry as I am. You lost track of my mother, and you don't even know how long she was missing." I take a breath and intend to calmly demand at least thirty days, but Douglas says something that I wish he hadn't. The one thing that never fails to ignite my anger.

"Some things fall through the cracks."

Those words hit my forehead and shoot through my brain. I lean forward and point my Louboutin at his chest. "My mother does *not* fall through the cracks." For so many years, I was invisible. A nobody. Someone who fell through the cracks. "My mother is not so insignificant that she falls through any cracks, you asshole."

"Lou Ann!"

Douglas stands and looks at me from across his desk. "This conversation is going nowhere."

Without both heels, I am considerably shorter, but nothing intimidates me, especially when someone dismisses me or my mother. I do, however, lower my pump.

"Legally you have to give me at least thirty days."

He picks up a piece of paper and reads it to me. "This is section seven of the admission agreement titled 'Terms and Termination Rights of Care Provider,' that you signed. Paragraph three, subsection b: 'If the resident exhibits behavior or actions that repeatedly and substantially interfere with the rights, health, safety, or well-being of other residents and staff, and the facility has tried prudent and reasonable interventions, the contract may be found breached and may result in the resident's discharge and order to vacate. If the resident is found in violation of 7.03 (b), this agreement may be enforced without notice or arbitration.' "

He hands it to me, but I don't need to read it. I've seen versions of it before. The difference is that the other facilities didn't include that last sentence. "My mother isn't a threat to anyone's health and safety but her own." I don't need to glance at my watch anymore. I can't make the flight. I need to call my agent. "I know that somewhere, in some section of this agreement, is the 'reasonable care' clause, holding Golden Springs responsible for the health and safety of my mother. You don't know how long my mother was wandering around or when she found Mr. Shone. No one knew she was missing, and no one was looking out for her health and safety." I put a hand on the desk and lean to one side to put my shoe on as best I can. "You didn't contact me for three days." Then I issue a threat that I know is empty even as I say it. "I could sue you and let the courts decide who breached the agreement." I'm royally pissed off, but I'm not a masochist. I know all too well that lawsuits are emotionally draining time-sucks and that there's no guarantee I'd win. Suing would be a bigger hassle than it's worth, and what would be the point? I still have to leave with my mother today.

"You'll have to get in line behind Mrs. Shone." Douglas sighs and replaces the paper. "She's threatened a civil lawsuit against Golden Springs unless your mother is discharged immediately."

Wow, that's vindictive, especially toward a woman with Alzheimer's. "What's she afraid Mother's going to do now? The guy's practically dead already."

He looks up from his paper. "Mr. Shone has made a miraculous recovery."

I blink several times. "What?"

"He's awake and seems to recognize his family."

Mom has a little smile on her face. She's

very pleased with herself, and I suppose she has that right. Not just any woman can spoon a man out of his coma. I pick up my purse and raise my chin. There's only one thing left to say. "Tell Mrs. Shone that Patricia Jackson says, 'You're welcome.' "

2

Here she comes. My mom, the miracle worker.

A nurse's assistant wheels Mother through the big automatic doors and into a beam of sunlight slicing through heavy clouds. Her big pink Caboodle filled with lipsticks sits on her lap as if it's her most prized possession. Mom is still in good physical shape and more than capable of walking. In fact, she usually argues with anyone who tries to help her. This is the first time I've seen her in a wheelchair since her appendix ruptured in 1998. It's a little disconcerting, but maybe it's Golden Spring's policy to wheel troublemakers out the door ASAP.

I've driven the SUV as close to the big fountain as possible and opened the back so her essentials — clothes, orthopedic shoes, bags of Pirate's Booty, and Bob Ross paintings — can be loaded inside. What doesn't fit will be delivered to a storage unit until I can find a new facility for her.

The aide turns the wheelchair's brake lever and helps Mom into the Land Rover. I take her Caboodle, which is heavier than it was the last time I picked it up, and put it in the back seat. "We will sure miss you, Patricia," the aide says as she buckles her in.

"Where am I going?"

"With your daughter."

She wrings her hands, and her voice shakes like a lamb to slaughter as she says, "But I don't want to go with her."

I try not to let that sting, but it does. I tell myself she doesn't mean to hurt me. It's not her fault. Not like when I was nineteen and she told me, "You turned fat in college." Which might have been true but hurt all the same.

We head out of the parking lot, and Mom looks up at the wet leaves stuck to the sunroof. Her blue eyes have gone blank. I suspect she's been double-dosed with Xanax and it's just kicking in, thus the need for the wheelchair. I don't have a wheelchair or even a cane at home. If she can't walk, I don't know how I'll get her to the elevator and up to my condo.

"It's a pretty day," she says as the clouds grow thicker.

Yep. It's a pretty *awful* day. I've never

missed an event, and my mind shifts into crisis management mode. I have to talk to my agent, Margie, who should already be in LA by now. I need to speak to my publicist, Fern, and my assistant, Dakota, as soon as possible.

The streets are still shiny black from rain, and I hit a big pothole filled with water. I'm glad I'm not in a Smart car as I push the phone connection on the steering wheel.

"You hurt my neck."

Really, Rain Man?

"Earl's a better driver than you."

I can't speak with Margie or anyone else if Mom isn't quiet, so I disconnect. "How do you know?" I'm reasonably certain Earl doesn't have a car, let alone take Mom out for spins. Heck, I'm not certain Earl even exists.

"He has a shiny green car with a big back seat."

"Are you telling me that Golden Springs lets the residents drive on the street?"

"Yes," she insists. "It's a convertible and very fast."

The bull is getting thick now. "How fast?"

"It's the fastest set of wheels in town." She looks me dead in the eye and says, as if she's an expert in street drag, "It gets rubber in all four gears."

I believe that Mother is channeling the Beach Boys. What I don't believe is that she's been racing around town in a Little Deuce Coupe with a man named Earl. Although . . . there was the time a few years ago when she told me that her "boyfriend," a Gypsy Joker named Axle, wanted her to join his motorcycle gang and be his "old lady." There really had been a founding member of the gang at the same memory care facility, but the name on his leather jacket was Flea. While calling Flea her "boyfriend" might have been a stretch, there was some truth to the story, and it enters my head that maybe — just maybe — there's some truth to Earl, too.

"It's a pretty day." She smiles as she looks up through the sunroof at the angry sky. The Alzheimer's brain is such a mystery. Some days are better than others. Some days are good, others not so good. Sometimes her eyes are pleasant but blank, other times they're filled with a thunderstorm. Both are on opposite sides of her mental deterioration. Most of the time, she is somewhere in the middle. Thank God.

She gives me a little smile and turns her face to the passenger window. I don't know what she's smiling about, and I don't think she knows either. Warm air blows across the front of her red coat and flutters her long brown hair. She's always loved her natural curls and brags that she doesn't have one gray strand. That's still true, but she can't take care of it like she used to, so it hangs down her back or she pulls it into a side scrunchie, like today. Last year she actually told me *I* was in a hair rut.

In my twenties, I used to wear my hair in a single braid because it kept the whole mess from my face. Now the braid is part of my branding.

My gaze drops to her lap, then returns to the road. She's stopped wringing her hands, and I think she's finally settled in and is calm enough for me to attempt another call.

"Where are we going?"

Guess not. "My condo."

"I'm having dinner with Earl."

I make the mistake of telling her she's not going back, and her smile drops. "I have to have dinner with Earl or that Stella will get him to have dinner with her. She's had work done."

I'm not averse to getting a little "work done" here and there. When I was a kid, I had a nasty widow's peak like a vampire. When I got my first big check, I had it lasered off my forehead. It took almost a year of regular zapping until I didn't look like the offspring of Count Dracula.

"I have to go back home."

"Okay," I lie to calm her down. It's not like she's going to remember anyway.

Her smile comes back, and she looks up through the sunroof again. "Okay."

Margie and the rest of the team are probably at the Marriott by now, attending to last-minute details and waiting for my arrival. I hit the connect button again, and the sound of a ringing phone comes through the audio speakers. Mom cranes her neck to look in the back seat but is blessedly quiet.

"Hello, you've reached Margie Kratz at the Kratz Tolson Agency. I am —"

"Who's that lady?"

Mom looks at me, and I put a finger to my lips. So much for quiet.

"— at this time. If —"

"Where's she at?"

"— phone number and a brief message —"

"Why is she talking to me?"

— *beep.* "Hi, Margie. It's Lou Ann, I —"

"Who's that you're talking to?"

"Mom, shhh for a minute. I'm still in Seattle. Mother is staying with me at the condo. Something —"

"I don't want to stay with you."

29

The pinch in the corner of my eye is back, threatening my elevens once more. "This has been the day from hell, and I'll —"

"Take me back!" Mom is wringing her hands and her head is on a swivel. So much for the double dose of Xanax keeping her calm. Maybe next time she'll need to be hit with a tranquilizer dart.

"I'll explain what's goin —"

"Take me back! Someone help me."

I rub her shoulder to reassure her. "We can talk about —"

"Call Tony!"

Everything in me goes dark, and my hand falls to my lap. It's a good thing I'm stopped at a light. Margie's phone beeps and I disconnect. Mom hasn't mentioned that name in a while. I don't know what has triggered her memory, but whatever it is hasn't triggered her memory of what happened. "I don't want to talk about him."

"He'll take me back."

On an intellectual level, I understand why she asks about him. Tony was a big part of our lives. There were times when he got along better with Mom than I did. They had common interests that I didn't share, like painting and opera, brussels sprouts and serial cheating.

"I need Tony!"

On an emotional level, it's a stab to the heart. I know Mother probably doesn't remember what that rat bastard put me through, but her asking for him feels like a deep betrayal.

"He's like a son."

"Fuck!" I always hated when she used to call him "son," and that was when I loved the man. Now she's just twisting the knife. "He's not your son. He's an asshole."

"Don't curse, Lou Ann."

The light turns green, and I drive through the intersection. "If you stop talking about him, I won't." I turn on the radio and tune into an oldies station. Neither of us speaks, but she is the only one who seems to have calmed down. Mother hums along to the Everly Brothers while my thumbs drum out agitated beats on the steering wheel.

Mom's chaos has put me in an impossible spot. I have to be in LA in the morning, but I don't know how I'll manage it. I can't drag Mom with me, and I can't call the home care nurse, Wynonna, that I used a year and a half ago. The much-maligned nurse was actually quite good at her job and had the patience of a saint, but Mom got it into her head that Wynonna was and is the root of all past, present, and future evil. Everything from stolen shoes to Pirate's Booty theft is

31

blamed on Wynonna's malicious skullduggery.

I'm overwhelmed. I have so much to think about. So much I have to remember to think about, yet the one thing best forgotten is the one thing Mom remembers. The Tony chapter of my life was horrible, but it's over. Thank God I didn't actually marry the man. He never crosses my mind, and I feel nothing for him — except for anger when Mom brings him up, I guess.

The drive to my condo usually takes about forty minutes, but I make it in twenty-five. I want out of my wool clothes and ruined shoes. I need a glass of wine or two or maybe three.

I live in Millennium Tower and have a spectacular view of Elliott Bay on one side and downtown Seattle on the other. The walk from my parking spot to the elevator isn't far. I'm grateful Mom can manage to walk on her own, and we arrive in the apartment all safe and sound.

The condo is mostly constructed of glass and steel and filled with white marble and quartz. I love the ultramodern design, and I've covered the cold stone floors with vibrantly colored rugs to warm it up. I leave Mom standing in front of the windows and quickly change into jeans and a Lulu Sweetheart sweatshirt. When I return, she's still staring out at Elliott Bay, and I wonder what she's thinking as she looks at the vivid orange and purple sunset.

I call down to the concierge and ask for everything in the SUV to be brought to me, and I place my usual order of Thai favorites from the restaurant down the street. I'm fairly sure Mom likes Thai. It can't be worse than stuffed green peppers at Golden Springs.

"Are you hungry?"

She turns to look at me. There are deep creases in her forehead and fear in her eyes. "You live here."

I've lived here for the past five years, and for a few months she lived here too. "Yes. You bought me a flamingo oven mitt as a housewarming gift when I moved in."

Her forehead clears. "And a cow creamer."

"That's right." I look at her and smile. I'd forgotten about the cow creamer. "It moos when you pour it." She laughs, and I am reminded of the good times. The times we'd been so close there was nothing in the world between the two of us.

The phone rings and I let it go to voice-mail and take Mom to her bedroom. She stops in the doorway and starts wringing her hands again.

"What's wrong?" Mom wringing her hands is a fairly recent behavior, and I notice it's getting worse.

"Where's my happy little clouds painting?"

In storage with all the others. Mother discovered her joy of painting while in the first care facility and is a Bob Ross devotee. I still have all her paintings, but I replaced those particular happy clouds with a print of irises. "I like the flowers."

"Well, I don't! It's awful. I want my happy little clouds!"

"There are two of your paintings in the back of my car. We can put one of those up." She relaxes somewhat and plants her behind in her La-Z-Boy recliner. "Where's the clicker? Who stole the clicker?" Before she can go into her Wynonna rant, I open the compartment in the leather arm where the clicker's always been kept. I set her up with the Game Show Network and *Tic-Tac-Dough,* but she's not through with her demands. "Where's my Booty? I always have Pirate's Booty when I watch my shows." I promise her that all her things will be brought up shortly, and she calms down a bit more. I just hope she stays calm long enough for me to talk with Margie.

"Okay," I begin when I return to the living room and get Margie and Fern on the line. "I got a call from Golden Springs Assisted Living when I was driving to the airport this afternoon." I hit the high and low notes of my day for them both. Well, the low notes anyway. When I'm finished, my agent of nearly twenty years says, "Well, that explains the crazy voicemail. I thought you were being kidnapped or murdered."

"I'm not that lucky." I move to my white linen couch, and the three of us talk about my options. Margie is more than just my agent; we're friends. She's smart, savvy, and I trust her.

The conversation is short; there is only one solution. "I can't bring Mom with me, and I can't hire a nurse in time to make LA." Even if I find the most qualified nurse in the next ten minutes, leaving Mom with a stranger is out of the question. I can't do that to her. She's the only mom I've got, and I love her. Her routine has already been disrupted, and she's afraid. Mine is the only face she recognizes, and she distrusts anyone she doesn't know. Heck, sometimes she distrusts me, too. When she's upset, her emotions spiral, and she has to have a target. I know because I've looked down that barrel more times than I can count in the past few years. Mom has been an emotional yo-yo throughout her life, but she was never angry — until now.

"Realistically, what are you thinking?" Fern asks, and it really hits me that I'm canceling LA. My publicist is efficient and organized and very good at her job. I hired her to defuse the Tony chapter, and I've kept her ever since. I trust her, too.

"Realistically?" I switch the phone to my other hand. No matter how tempting the prospect, I can't leave my mother right now. "I can't make LA." My chest feels tight, and my heart pounds at the same time. "This has never happened to me." I stretch out on my back so I can breathe. I've always made every deadline and event. Like the women I hire, I'm on top of everything. I get it done. I'm in control.

Not this time. I control nothing and I hate it.

"Realistically," Margie says, "we should think about canceling the rest of the tour and rescheduling."

"All of it?" I wheeze.

"That's my thought, too," Fern says, and I can't believe this is actually happening. "It's better to make one decisive announcement than to issue four more over the next few weeks. We'll put out a statement that you need time to deal with family issues.

36

Your fans will understand, and they'll be grateful you didn't draw this out."

Even after the decision is made and I hang up the phone, none of this feels real to me. I don't pull out of commitments, and I can't wrap my head around what will happen next. The only thing that does feel real is the knot in my stomach.

This is not my life. I started Lulu in a lonely dorm room my freshman year at Gonzaga, where I'd hoped to graduate with a degree in journalism. Why journalism? Why not?

I hadn't known anyone when I arrived there, but that wasn't unusual. Mom and I moved around a lot when I was a kid. I'd gone to fifteen different schools by the time I graduated high school. I was always the new kid. Often invisible and insignificant — the kid who fell through the cracks.

I worked two jobs to put myself through school and, by my sophomore year at Gonzaga, I'd saved enough money to buy my own computer: a used iBook G3 clamshell — indigo — that allowed me to create my first blog, *Lulu's Life,* on WordPress. I carried that iBook everywhere, writing about my life as a lonely girl and commenting on the people I saw around me. Several hundred people joined my page. We chatted and laughed and commiserated, but the blog really took off when I transferred to the University of Washington my junior year and linked *Lulu's Life* with Friendster and Myspace. To my surprise, I started dating instead of hiding. I began writing more about relationships and heartbreaks and less about loneliness.

The doorbell rings and two men arrive with a cart of Mom's belongings. I show them to her room, and she smiles and flirts because she just can't help herself. She compliments their muscles and calls them handsome. While I'm used to Mom's behavior, it's still embarrassing. Of course, she keeps it up until they leave.

"Here's your Booty," I say, and hand her a bag of her favorite cheesy popcorn. As I take down the irises print, my thoughts return to my old blogs and the summer Margie first contacted me and changed my life forever.

The Diary of Bridget Jones had been a phenomenal success, and *The Edge of Reason* was about to be released in theaters. She'd said New York publishers were looking for the sort of "single girl" stuff I was blogging about, and she wanted to fly to Seattle and talk to me in person. At first I thought she was pranking me, but she actually met with me, and *A Girl's Guide to Kissing Toads,* my first book, was published eighteen months later.

Within just a few short years, *Lulu's Life* became Lulu the Love Guru, and I outgrew my simple WordPress website. I've worked my ass off and my fingers to the bone to make Lulu my own personal empire. The brand is recognized worldwide, and millions subscribe to Lulu's YouTube channel and follow me on Twitter and Instagram. Millions listen to my downloads and podcasts, buy my books, and attend my events. I can't see myself stopping for years to come.

3

"I smell like roses," Mom says as I lean over
the side of the tub and wash her back. She
is nude from the tips of her toes to her
cheetah-print bath cap. I haven't seen my
mother buck naked in a long time, and it's
equal parts disturbing and scary. Back in
the day, Mom was a babe, a real bombshell,
and she worked hard to maintain that
status, too. I remember her lunging around
the house while lifting five-pound dumb-
bells overhead to keep her figure. Mom
wasn't just beautiful; she was witty and
charming, and people were drawn to her. I
was drawn to her, too. It's sad and frighten-
ing to see just how far she's fallen, both
physically and mentally.

"Earl likes me to smell good. He likes to
smell my neck, and —"

"I've never heard you mention Earl before
today," I say, cutting her short before she
can mention other places Earl likes to put

his nose.

"He's my boyfriend. He says I put a spring in his step."

"Uh-huh." I wonder if her boyfriend knows that she put a spring in Mr. Shone's pants.

"He gave me a Christmas card with a cactus on it." She looks over her shoulder at me and smiles. "He loves me."

Yeah, because nothing says love like a cactus. "You never did say what kind of car Earl drives."

"Earl has a car?"

My hand falls to the side of the tub and the corner of my eye twitches. "You said it laid rubber."

"I never said that. Why on earth would you say I said that?"

The twitching is not good for my health. Maybe I'm about to have a stroke. I turn on the shower wand and drown out the sound of Mom's voice. I can see her lips moving but I can't hear her. Maybe it's not the nicest move, but I don't want to have a stroke. Who would take care of Mom? I reason.

Not long after I'd ended my conversation with Margie and Fern, Mom walked into the living room, wringing her hands above a wet spot in the crotch of her pants. "I need underwear," she said.

She'd wet through her Attends and needed more than underwear. A warm shower — not a full-service bath — seemed the easiest solution for both of us, but Mom's rarely chosen easy.

"My dress was blue organza." I wash her neck and armpits, and she sighs. "I was fifteen, and Daddy said I was the prettiest girl in Nashville." She chatters as if she is still a debutante in blue organza, seemingly oblivious of our mother-child role reversal. I turn off the water and pull the drain plug. I'm glad she's oblivious and can slip into her girlhood memories while she still has them.

"Robert Gaudet was my second daddy," she says, rolling her *r*'s and pronouncing it *Ro-bare Go-day* like she's sitting in Cajun country.

Robert Gaudet was the only grandfather I've ever known. I called him Papa Bob, and he called me petite boo or little sweetheart.

"My real daddy died when I was seven. His name was Louis Jackson, and he was a war hero."

"Yes." I'm named after a grandfather I never knew and, growing up, I hated that I was named after a man. I wanted to be named Jennifer or Brittany or She-Ra. I stand and sling a big fluffy towel over my shoulder. I don't hate my name anymore and prefer it over the alternative, Ro-bareta, after the grandfather I did know.

"Momma got Daddy's Purple Heart."

"Yes." But I know little else. I know my biological grandfather was from Charleston and died in Korea, a war hero. Anytime I've asked, Mom just shakes her head and says he died when she was little. Grandmother always said it was so long ago she didn't remember. I was always curious about the man I'm named after, but it's as if he never existed.

Mom reaches for the grab bar bolted to the tile on one side while I clamp a removable rail on the other. She stands up okay, but I have to help her lift one leg, then the other, over the side. I try to avert my eyes as much as possible, but there is no unseeing Mother's massive '70s bush and flat butt.

"Robert was Momma's first cousin." She wraps the towel around her and lowers her voice to a whisper. "We don't mention that."

And with good reason. Grandmother's elopement with Papa Bob broke both sides of the family into pieces and started a feud that lasted decades.

Mother dries herself while I grab a pink

jogging suit I bought her last year. She lets me help her with her soft slippers, and I hold my breath. The doorbell rings, and I practically run from the room before she can accuse me of throwing away all her "good" shoes.

Dinner is inside a takeout bag hanging from the doorknob and my stomach growls even before I get to the kitchen.

"Was that Earl?" Mom walks into the kitchen, bath cap still on her head, lips burgundy now.

"No. It's dinner." She opens her mouth to protest, but I head her off. "I know. You were supposed to have dinner with Earl."

"Where is he?"

I take utensils out of the drawer and close it before I am tempted to grab a knife and slit my wrists. "He went to Mexico," I say because she's going to forget and ask again anyway.

"Oh."

I set everything on the small kitchen table, and we eat in blessed silence. So much has happened in this one day, it feels more like a week has passed since I woke this morning. And so much more has to be done before I crawl into bed. Number one on the list is to find an experienced in-home nurse to take over Mother's medical needs and care.

I point my fork at her cheetah cap. "Do you need help getting that off?"

"No." She raises a hand and pats the side like it's the latest rage. "It's a fabulous hat."

Fabulous. My whole life, everything was "fabulous" or "amazing" or "to die for." Whether it was a fabulous hat, an amazing bikini, or to-die-for kitten heels, Mom made sure that she owned it, just as she always made sure she looked fabulous before she left the house. Waiting for her to "put on her face" just to go to the grocery store was annoying, but I loved being seen with her. She was the most beautiful and stylish mom at any of the schools I attended. While other mothers picked up their children from school in minivans, my mom rolled up in a red Mercedes 560SL convertible, a gift from husband number three, Vinny Russo, just before she divorced him.

I wrap a flat noodle around my fork tines. There had been many times she'd driven that fancy car along the poverty line, but no one ever guessed, because she looked so damn good doing it.

"We ate this in China."

I look up at Mom and smile. "Yes." It was Bangkok, but who cares? I took her with me on my first world tour ten years ago, and it was one of the best times we had together. I'm happily surprised she recalls anything of that trip and raise my fork to my lips.

"I hope I don't get the runs."

Good God. I look at my fork and set it back down on my plate.

"Pork gives me the runs."

Normally, my mother never would've talked about bodily functions at the dinner table and would have sent me to my room if I did. I guess this is her new normal and push my plate to the side. "We went to the outdoor market," I say to distract her from her real or imagined pork issues. "You bought a pointy straw hat that was painted with elephants wearing the same kind of pointy hat."

"That's silly." Her brow furrows, and she shakes her head.

"You thought it was funny." So had I. We'd laughed about it for months afterward, and I'm sad that she doesn't remember that part.

"Elephants don't wear hats."

I open my mouth, then close it again. Why try to explain? She'll just get more confused and I'll still be sad. I look at her in her cheetah cap, which apparently isn't silly, and wonder why we didn't go on more trips together after that. Was I too busy to ask or was she too busy to go? She was probably absorbed with relationship drama and I was probably absorbed with Lulu. With pushing my business, growing my success, and making a living. But neither of us has those excuses now. Her relationships are mostly imaginary, and Lulu is more successful than I'd ever dreamed it would be. I have more money than I can spend in two lifetimes, and we could tour the world if we wanted.

Now that it's too late.

After dinner, Mom takes up her favorite position in front of the Game Show Network, and I make sure she knows where to find the remote.

"That Wink Martindale is foxy," she gushes.

I glance at the TV and Mr. Martindale's pompadour. He looks more Beavis than foxy.

"Ooohh, a cassette player. That's a good prize."

"I'll be down th—" I save my breath because she's too wrapped up in Wink and his state-of-the-art cassette player to listen.

Golden Springs gave me stacks of files and paperwork I know I can't ignore, so I sit in my office looking over outlines of her daily and weekly schedules. My gaze skims the paragraphs stressing the importance of routine and the concern for sufferers when the routine is disrupted. First, I already know that Alzheimer's patients find safety in routine. Second, where was Golden Springs's concern when they disrupted my mother's routine today?

Included in the paperwork is a list of the best foods for memory sufferers. It's funny, though, I don't recall the facility feeding her an abundance of salmon or chickpeas or ginger soup.

I study pages filled with lists of doctor appointments and medications. She takes medicine to help with everything from memory loss to constipation. There's a box filled with prescription bottles and over-the-counter remedies.

I thumb to the list of memory caregivers and start dialing. The first thirteen are either already employed or work for a care service and not qualified to dispense medicine.

Like I am?

Number fourteen is Lindsey Benedict, a twenty-six-year-old from Spokane. She has a bachelor of science in nursing from WSU and provides in-home health services. I hadn't thought about having anyone actually living with us, but I call her anyway.

Lindsey picks up and eagerly lists off her credentials and accomplishments. I don't know half of what she's talking about, but it sounds impressive. She tells me that she is an independent caregiver and not associated with an agency. Then she talks about salary and acceptable working conditions, which all sounds reasonable until she informs me that I am responsible for payroll and withholding taxes. I ask myself why I would want the added headache and flip to the next page.

Down the hall, the laugh track hits a crescendo, and my eyebrows make a valiant effort not to knit a unibrow across my forehead. While Lindsey gives me her references, I look at the next name on the list, At-Home Eldercare Agency. They have several phone numbers and want me to call and schedule a consultation in their office before they'll even come and assess Mom.

"I can be there tomorrow at seven a.m.," Lindsey says.

I'd only need her until I find Mom a new care facility. Two months. Three months max. "You're hired."

I hang up the phone and realize that I didn't write down her references or anything else. She sounded young, and I wonder how long she's had her degree. I wonder if she parties like I did when I was twenty-six. I wonder if I'm inviting a wacko into my home. One wacko around here is quite enough.

I plant my palms on the desk and stand. I can't worry about that now. If she's dropped off by a prison bus tomorrow, I'll worry. Right now, I'm exhausted and want to curl up in bed, but first, I have to give Mom her sleeping medication and help her change. She chooses a leopard-print nightie to match her bath cap. "Isn't this pretty?" she asks as she pets the marabou trim around the collar. "I got it on the Google net."

She means the internet. She may have lost a good portion of her ability to read, but she knows how to get online and shop like a boss. "Yep, it's special, all right."

"It reminds me of Tina at Global Travel."

Tina worked with Mom and she'd never met an animal print that she didn't drape around her neck. "That's when we lived in Tacoma."

"Are you sure it wasn't Reno?"

"I'm sure." Mom worked at Harrah's in Reno dealing cards. I hated when she worked there, but it was better than when she worked at Daniel Law Office and Mrs. Daniel threatened to kill her at the company Christmas party.

"Oh. I thought for sure it was Reno." One thing I will say about Mom, she always had a job. From blackjack dealer to receptionist at a law office and everything in between, Mom always worked to support us. Sometimes we skated close to the poverty line, but it was never on account of unemployment.

I kiss her good night on the cheek and think about locking her in her room so she can't roam around like when she stayed with me before, and Wynonna found her in the pantry straightening cans and hiding my chef knives. The bathroom is down the hall, though, and she might need to use it. I keep the hall light on for her just in case and leave the door open a crack.

I shut my bedroom door behind me, and I pull on my favorite flannel nightshirt and let out a sigh as I slide between the sheets. I'm tempted to take something to help me sleep, but I can't with Mom in the condo. Light from the hallway falls into my room, and I fully expect it to keep me awake as my mind races over the details of the day. Much to my surprise, I am pulled into the deepest layer of sleep, the kind where you don't move or think or dream. The kind that is very hard to wake from, even when something shakes you.

"Lou Ann."

My eyes are heavy, and I struggle to crack

them open.

"Are you awake?"

"No," I mumble into my pillow.

"Wake up, Lou."

"Mom?" I blink several times before my eyes stay open long enough to see Mom staring at me from across my pillow. She's in bed next to me, and for one groggy moment, I think she is here to spoon. Instead, she reaches for my hand. Her palm is incredibly warm, and I can feel it all the way to my heart.

The light from the hall has fallen across the end of the bed, and she speaks to me through the gray shadows separating us. "I want to go home."

Her hand reminds me of when I was young and had the flu or strep throat and she used to comfort me. Or when we'd lie awake in her bed talking for hours until we fell asleep. I always felt so close to her . . . right before a new man pushed us apart.

"I want to go home," she repeats.

"You can't go back to Golden Springs."

"I want to go to my real home."

If Mom is up and talking about her town house, she needs stronger nighttime meds. "Your house burned down," I remind her through a deep yawn.

"I want to go home to Sutton Hall."

"What?" The shock of what she just said jolts me wide-awake. When I was a kid, Mom took me to visit Sutton Hall several times. Her memories of the old plantation near New Orleans are wholly different from mine. My memories are vague, faded impressions of wrinkled faces, some warm and others cold. Bright eyes or dark scowls and never knowing why some people frowned and others smiled. Never knowing who to talk to or hide from.

The whole place smelled like old rugs and faded murals. I remember the rhythmic squeaking of rotting boards and ancient rocking chairs. Bumps in the night and wind whistling through the live oaks. Long stringy veils of Spanish moss skimming the slow-moving water of the bayou and the headstones in the cemetery out back. And bugs. Lots of bugs.

I was born in Gilroy, California, the garlic capital of the world, and feel no attachment to that moldy estate in Louisiana.

"That's clear across the country." As his only direct living relative, Patricia Lynn Jackson-Garvin-Hunter-Russo-Thompson-Doyle inherited the family money pit after Great-uncle Jasper's demise. Certain branches of the Sutton family tree are no doubt still turning in their graves behind the house.

"It's our family home," she insists. *Our* home? Just last November she'd insisted just as adamantly that she would rather sell the old plantation to gypsies than let me get my hands on it. We'd been at her attorney's office signing paperwork, and I'd tried to help explain her options to her. Secretly, I'd wanted it sold now so I didn't have to worry about it after she's gone. I knew better than to say the word *sell,* so I gently mentioned that many of the plantation homes in the South have been renovated and turned into wedding locations and special-occasion venues. Mom has always been fond of "lovely" parties with real linen and a silver tea service, but you'd have thought I'd plunged a knife into her neck. She'd gone all Rattlesnake Patty, and everything got twisted in her head. She accused me of wanting her to die so I could turn Sutton Hall into a bed-and-breakfast. I love a five-star hotel, and I hate cooking, which just goes to show that Mom wasn't in her right mind.

"It's my birthright." The last thing either of us needs is a two-hundred-year-old albatross around our necks and a trust that hardly covers the taxes. "I have the front door key."

I know she does. I gave it to her after it had been sent to me a month ago. It never occurred to me that the key would unlock a nostalgic desire to move.

"Please, Lou."

I study her profile through the darkness. My life is crazy enough, and my Alzheimer's mother wants me to take her across the country to a place where the humidity lies on you like a damp towel and makes it hard to breathe.

"Take me home."

A part of me can't help but resent what she's asking. I know it may seem petty given the circumstances, but the thirteen-year-old girl in me wants to remind her that she never considered my wants and needs before she moved us from city to city because she lost a job again, or got a divorce again, or her boyfriend's wife was threatening her again. She never considered how difficult her decisions have made my life.

"I know it's a lot to ask."

Ya think, Patty? Even if I were to take her seriously, Mother's care is overwhelming, and I'm not sure the nurse I just hired is up for a cross-country trip already. "How would we get there?" After our disastrous twenty-five-minute drive across town earlier, there's no way I'm driving across the country. One of us would end up dead or found at a rest stop in Kansas with a note pinned to her coat. I'm not saying it would be Mom, either.

"Fly."

I chuckle at that. I have flight anxiety, or what doctors call "aviophobia." A more accurate term is "scared shitless" of plummeting to earth in an out-of-control plane, unable to do anything but scream before I'm incinerated in a massive fireball. Air travel is necessary for business, so to save myself from a full-blown panic attack, I usually have a few calming glasses of wine before I board. Flying with Mother, I'd have to drink a few bottles.

"I have to be near my kin."

That's the same "kin" who'd disowned my grandma Lily and my grandfather Bob — aka first-cousin-twice-removed Bob — and forced them to leave Louisiana. They're also the same kin who welcomed Grandma Lily back only after her father died. Well, most of them anyway. Her frowny-faced brother Jasper usually stayed at his galley house in the French Quarter. On the few occasions that he was at Sutton Hall, the two didn't speak. His twin, Jed, passed the same year as Bob, so no one knows if he would have been as cold to his only sister.

"That's a long way to visit your kin, Mom." I don't remind her that there aren't any "kin" left to visit. Not that I know of, anyway.

"I don't want to visit. I want to live there."

"What?" That's insane. So insane I'd have to be out of my mind to agree to it. "We can't move there." The thought of actually moving Mom clear across the country is so daunting, my mind recoils with horror. "My life is here. Your life is here. What about Earl?" Suddenly, a visit doesn't sound so bad. "We can vacation there for a few weeks. Stay at the Ritz, where it's nice and air-conditioned, and drive to Sutton Hall as often as you'd like. We'll get a two-bedroom suite with a balcony that overlooks the city."

"You have to bury me with Momma and Grandmere," she persists.

"We don't have to worry about that for a long time." I know the disease that has taken her memory will take her life, but I don't want to think about burying my mother.

"I need to rest in Sutton soil."

Technically, she wouldn't rest in soil but in an aboveground vault.

"Suttons always return to our soil." This is the first time I've heard of Sutton "soil," but it would explain why Grandmother chose to be buried in the Sutton cemetery rather than in Tennessee next to the man she'd married over her family's objections. I've always thought that the man who smiled and laughed and overfed anyone in his vicinity deserved better than an eternal blank spot under BELOVED WIFE on his gravestone.

"Please, Lou. I have so much left to do."

There is fear in her voice, and we look at each other across the pillow. Through the darkness, her eyes are shiny with tears, and she isn't smiling. Sometimes she cries out of confusion. Other times her mind is clear enough that she knows what is happening to her. I don't know which is worse.

"You have to help me with my final resting spot."

That is the last thing I want to do with my mother. No matter her shenanigans, I can't imagine a life without her. I want to dog-paddle in the river of denial for as long as possible. "Mom, we have lots of time before we have to think about that."

"You have time. I don't."

I let that sink in. Lower and lower until panic twists my stomach in a knot. If she doesn't have time, I don't have time with her.

"I can't get there on my own." She

58

squeezes my hand, and it feels like she's crushing my heart. "Promise to take me home before I forget. Please, Lou."

"I promise." Because what else can I do? My heart is crushed beneath the weight of my sadness. I want to make new and lasting memories before time runs out. I want to write them all down so I won't forget.

"Mon mouche a miel, cher," Mom whispers, and rolls to her other side.

She hasn't called me her honeybee love since I was a child, and I raise a palm to cover the thumping coming from my heart. I can't imagine my life without my mom, and I take a deep, shuddering breath. I've always known the time would come when I needed to focus less on work and more on my mother. I've known since her diagnosis that I needed to have plans in place for this eventuality, but I don't. Maybe because planning for it would make it too real.

Memories are more important than ever, and I know I'll deeply regret not writing them down once she is gone, but I also know myself and know I won't. I'll start out with great intentions, but I write for a living almost every day. Writing in a journal or diary will feel like a lot of pressure and I'll put it off. Horrible guilt will add to the pressure, but if I give myself permission to skip days, I know I'll be less likely to let weeks and months slip by. If I don't place expectations on myself and keep it as simple and as easy as jotting a little something in my day planner on my cell phone, I can do this.

I'm Lulu the Love Guru and I can do anything.

Except move to Louisiana. I can't imagine life without Mom, but I can't imagine living in Louisiana, either. The last thing I want to do is move to the land of stifling humidity and attack bugs and live the next few years in a musty plantation house. Mom will have to adjust to a new routine just as she's settled in and adjusted to living with me in my condo. I feel a little panicky until I realize that there is a real possibility that Mom won't remember this conversation by morning.

4

March 16

Alaska flight 794. I lost my mind.
Mom lost her mind.
Hell in a handbasket.

My biggest fears in life are all related to control. More specifically, loss of control. When I fly, I control nothing but the peanuts I chomp and the wine I swill. I try to control the fine line between a few calming drinks and a few too many, but sometimes the line blurs. Things quickly go from Calm Town to Delusional Drunk-ville.

Running a very close second to my fear of flying is my fear of fainting. I've never fainted in my life. Sure, I've felt lightheaded, but I've never actually blacked out. I've never fallen like a bag of laundry. I've never opened my eyes and looked up at people staring down at me. I am disoriented

61

and confused, and it seems like everything is moving at a slower speed than usual. Someone calls my name, but I don't answer.

"Goodness, Lou Ann. What are you doing down there?" Mom peers at me from her aisle seat.

"What happened?" My voice sounds weird, hollow and distant. I try to sit up, but my shoulders are firmly weighted to the floor.

"You fainted."

I roll my eyeballs toward my brows. "I don't think so. I've never fainted in my life," I tell Mom's nurse, Lindsey Benedict. She's put a blood pressure cuff on my arm and is listening to my heart rate.

"I guess this is your first time."

What are the chances that the first time I experience my second-biggest fear happens when I'm enduring my first? Or something like that. My head hurts. "Why now?" I ask.

"Might be Wild Turkey," Mom speculates. "That'll lay ya out."

Looking up makes my eyes hurt and I close my lids.

"Is she dead? She used to play dead all the time."

More like sometimes, and only on days when Mom was busy with a new man and I had to do something to get her attention.

62

"She's not dead."

"Sure looks like death."

More like I'm embarrassed to death. "How can I be dead? I'm talking to you right now."

"Then quit playing around down there."

I open my eyes and look up at Mom's red lips. I can't think of anything nice to say and am saved the effort by Lindsey ripping the cuff from my arm. "Your levels are still a little low, but you'll be okay."

"My forehead hurts."

"You smacked it fairly hard on the floor."

"I fell forward?"

"Like a ton of bricks."

A whole ton? "I'm on my back."

"The male steward and I rolled you onto your back." Great. Lindsey helps me sit up and my gaze travels up the legs and torso of the steward Mom's been flirting with since we boarded in Seattle. My right arm has been pulled from the sleeve of my St. John jacket and my skirt is up around the tops of my thighs. Thank God I'm wearing black hose. One black Manolo is still on my left foot while the other is MIA.

"You're lucky you didn't hit your face on the way down," says the male flight attendant, whose arms are so buff and his bald head so shiny that he's probably gay.

No, he is gay, no probably about it, not that Mom would stop even if she noticed. I write about love and finding love, and those topics are universal. For the most part, gay men and women want the same thing as straight men and women. Love and happiness with a person who returns love and happiness. After a couple of decades in the love business, my gaydar is finely tuned, an invaluable tool when it comes to Love Guru advice.

"How are you feeling?" Mom asks.

Groggy and disoriented. "Okay."

Before I can grab onto something to help myself stand, Lindsey hauls me to my feet. First class breaks out in applause, and I'm so embarrassed that I think I just might pass out again.

"Scoot over, Pat," Lindsey says, and dumps me in the aisle seat.

I knew Lindsey was strong the moment I opened the door a month ago. She's tall and big-boned, like a Valkyrie — the kind that sings opera and wears a big iron breastplate and horned helmet. Instead of golden braids, her hair is different shades of fried blond that she pulls back in a stubby ponytail. She towers over Mom and me and is a little rough around the edges and some of her manners are a bit raw.

"We'll need some water and juice," she tells a flight attendant as she takes her own seat across the aisle from me.

I didn't think she was going to work out at first, but I was wrong. Lindsey's a godsend. Mom really likes her, and they have several things in common. One, they talk about Mom's daily bowel movements. While I understand that Lindsey needs to know if Mom's insides are working properly, it's not a proper topic for discussion at the dinner table. Two, they both think it's necessary to announce when they're "feeling bloated and gassy," any time of the day or night. Like anyone wants or needs that information. It's like they have a membership to the same bad-manners club, and I am the odd man out.

Which is fine with me.

My pump appears from over the top of the seat in front of me. "Thank you."

Mom grabs it by the four-inch heel as I thread my arm through my jacket sleeve. I push my skirt to my knees and re-tuck my white blouse as best I can.

"You're getting your color back," Mom says, and puts the shoe in my lap.

"I'm tired." I open the vents above my head and let the recycled air blow across my face. Normally, I close the vents because

I don't want recycled germs and cold air freezing me out, but nothing about this day is normal.

Before leaving for Sea-Tac this morning, I'd braided my hair and given Mom a side ponytail. She'd pulled on a cozy jogging suit while I'd pulled on my wool suit and four-inch heels. I could have left the house in cozy, warm sweats, but I am Lulu the Love Guru. I always have to look my best in public because the one time I don't will be the one time I am recognized. The one time I have a big zit on my nose and bags under my eyes and I run into the store to grab a box of tampons and a Snickers will be the one time I hear someone behind me whisper, "That looks like Lulu the Love Guru — only uglier."

A female flight attendant returns with a little bottle of cold water and a glass of orange juice and hands them to me.

"Where's that foxy man?" Mom asks her.

Not foxy man again. This is getting embarrassing.

"Greg? He's making coffee."

"Ohhh . . . coffee."

"Would you like me to bring you a cup?"

"No, but I would like Greg to bring me that snack basket so I can have another look at it."

This will be her fourth go-round on snacks, and I suspect her hunger has more to do with "that foxy man" than with biscotti. I'm drinking the juice and holding the cold plastic bottle against my forehead when Greg returns with the basket.

"You're so big and strong," Mom coos as she plays with her side pony. "I like a big strong man. You make a girl feel safe." The steward doesn't know what to say to this old woman who keeps coming on to him. Some men look at my mom and just chuckle, while others look like they just want to run like hell. Greg falls somewhere in between.

"Mom, just pick a snack."

"What do you suggest?"

"Biscotti, same as before," I tell her.

"I wasn't asking you," she says without looking at me.

"You can't go wrong with the biscotti," he says.

"Ohhh, biscotti sounds wonderful."

He hands it to her along with a napkin, then beats feet up the aisle.

"I wonder if he has a girlfriend."

"He's gay, Mom."

She pauses for a heartbeat, then says, "Well, some men just haven't met the right woman."

I have to laugh. Mom's never suffered from low self-esteem, but lately I've wondered what she sees when she looks in the mirror. Does she see a faded beauty with lines on her face and age spots on her cheeks? Or is she seeing the reflection of a girl in the bloom of youth? Or does she even give it a thought?

I buckle myself in because it gives me the delusion of safety and lean my head back and close my eyes. I fainted. For the first time in my life, I fainted. Apparently like a ton of bricks. I recall using the bathroom and looking at my face in the mirror as I washed my hands. I remember walking toward my seat — then nothing until I looked up into Mom's face and she was asking what I was doing down there. I don't remember feeling dizzy or light-headed. Nothing more than my usual flight anxiety. I've white-knuckled it before and not fainted. The only difference between those times and now is I didn't have someone next to me wringing her hands during takeoff and wondering out loud if we were going to "make it." No one looking out the window and saying, "We sure are really high now," or "We're so high in the sky, I can't see the ground." Even after I made her switch seats with me and closed the window shade, she still made comments like, "I sure hope we can get back down."

Mom is the variable. It's the Pat factor, and the Pat factor has been working overtime, tripling my anxiety. We have about two more hours before we land, and I know she's not done. Beyond a ball gag, there's nothing I can do about it. My head rolls to the side and I let out a groan.

"Hey, you. Hey, you," Mom calls out. I open my eyes and she's waving her hands in the air. "Hey, you, woman with the basket." Oh God, more snacks while she's still working on her last. "My daughter needs some ice for her head."

And just as I'm thinking of ways to shut her up, she says something that warms my heart. "Thanks."

"That's what moms are for." She smiles and leans her head back against the seat. "I'll take care of you, Lou."

It's nice that she thinks so.

The attendant returns shortly with a little baggie tied at the top. The ice is heavenly on my forehead and I close my eyes and run through my mental checklist.

I put my satellite assistants to work coordinating everything at Sutton Hall, from making sure the pantry and refrigerator are stocked to hiring a cleaning service to knock down the cobwebs. We had boxes of our belongings and loads of Mother's care needs sent ahead. The vehicle Lulu Inc. leased will be delivered tomorrow morning, and the local cable company should arrive the next day to hook up cable and high-speed internet. I'm sure I've forgotten something, but I'm not too worried. Most anything can be replaced.

"I know Earl will come to visit. He'll take me to dinner."

"Uh-huh."

"He gave me a Christmas card with a cactus on it."

"That's nice."

"He loves me."

"What's not to love?"

"I have a passionate nature."

"Mmm."

"I hope we don't run out of gas."

Well, that didn't last long. "We won't run out of gas," I tell her without opening my eyes. "Maybe you should take a little nap. We have a very busy day ahead of us."

Mom yawns and seems to take my advice. I don't hear a peep out of her for the next hour. The ice in my bag melts and cold droplets slide down my cheek. I hand it off to the flight attendant and try not to think of hurling through the atmosphere at five hundred miles an hour at thirty-five thousand feet. My mind turns to the perplexing face-plant in the aisle of a 737. Except for my headache and the red mark above my left eyebrow, it doesn't seem like it really happened. I don't know if it's a sign of something serious or just a convergence of stressors. I think it might be the latter.

My MacBook is in the overhead compartment. I should probably use the next hour to get some work done. I need to start a blog post, but I just don't feel like it. Once we're all settled and Mom's new routine is established, I'll sit down and get into my own.

Shortly after I canceled the rest of my tour, I set up a conference call with my Lulu Inc. management team to discuss the best course for moving forward, and in the end we agreed that hiring bimonthly guest bloggers and inviting smart and savvy women to host the online events should keep the site current and interactive. Fern will post on my Instagram, and I'll continue to make podcasts and video messages. Those changes cut my workload in half and give me more time with Mother.

A few short pings draw my attention upward as the "fasten seatbelt" light flashes on. My bottle of water tips over and rolls off the tray. It lands by my foot and I leave it there. I know what those pings mean.

"Ladies and gentlemen, we are experiencing light turbulence and the captain has turned on the 'fasten seatbelt' sign and asks that you remain seated. For those passengers who are not seated, please return to your seat until the captain has determined that it is safe to move about the cabin. Thank you."

Shit. Turbulence. I hate turbulence. I hate it even more without the calming aid of alcohol. We're going to be fine, I tell myself as the plane bumps through the rough air. The wings are not going to get ripped off and we're not going to plummet to the earth and face certain death.

"What's that?"

Shit. Mom's awake — just what I need. "Nothing," I manage. The cabin rattles and dips and I try to swallow my fear.

"Are we falling from the sky?"

I turn my head and look at her wide blue eyes. "No."

"I think we're falling from the sky."

"No, we're not." I feel sick. I think I'm going to be sick.

"Yep. We're falling from the sky, all right."

"Please stop," I say, but she's wringing

72

her hands and I know she's just getting started.

"Did we run out of gas?"

"No."

"I think we ran out of gas."

"Please stop," I beg once more, even though I know it's useless.

"Yep, we ran out of gas."

"We didn't run out of gas, Mom."

"We're going to die."

I put a hand to my throat and feel my pounding pulse. "Don't say that."

"Yep, we're going to die, all right."

I think I might actually faint again. I need water. I need a paper bag to breathe into.

"Lou Ann."

"I think we're going to crash."

I need one of those little bottles of vodka.

"Yep, we're going to crash."

"Lou Ann!"

I turn my head and look at Lindsey. "Here," she says, and I release my grip on the arm of my chair and lean across the aisle to take a prescription bottle from her hand.

It's Xanax. The plane shudders and dips to one side. God bless that girl. I need Xanax.

"We're going to crash, all right."

I'm so tempted to just say, "Forget it," and numb the pain with booze or Xanax, but I can't. I have to keep white-knuckling it, and I try to hand the bottle back to Lindsey. "No, thanks."

"That's for Patricia. Put two under her tongue."

5

Mom needs glasses. I need a drink.
She swears she's in heaven.
I swear like a lunatic.

"I'm home." Mom sighs. "Isn't that just a sight for sore eyes?"

I slap the insect feeding on my jugular instead of answering her. I'm afraid of what might happen if I open my mouth. The drive from the airport sobered Mom up somewhat, but she's still a bit blissed out on Xanax, and I'm still wound so tight that I'm fighting to keep it all together. I don't want to come apart. It could be ugly.

The airport limo pulls away, leaving us in the yard and our luggage lined up on the porch.

Mom's sigh is drawn out this time. "It's so beautiful and grand."

I've been to Louisiana many times. The Windsor Court Hotel in New Orleans is a

75

real favorite of mine. Its architectural details are stunning, and it's close enough to the French Quarter that I can grab a café au lait and a beignet in the morning, but far enough to allow me to escape the craziness of Bourbon Street at night. Another favorite is the Hilton in Baton Rouge with its magnificent views of the Mississippi River, but those beautiful views are a world away from the patchy lawn beneath my feet.

While Mom sees grandeur, all I see is a massive money pit with missing green shutters and a row of dirty Grecian pillars surrounding the house and holding up a balcony and dormered roof. The wrought-iron railing looks okay from here, but I wouldn't lean against it.

"It's just like I remember."

Yeah, and that's the problem. One of the dormer windows is boarded up, there's an old television antenna on top of the roof, and the stained glass in the transom above the double doors is cracked. Veils of Spanish moss fall to the uneven cobblestone walkway from the bent and twisted limbs of live oaks and towering cypress trees. While Mom hears Dixie, all I hear is the incessant buzz of cicadas and God knows what else. In Seattle bugs aren't a big problem, but this is the South, where insects grow bigger, live longer, and breed more. Where creepy-crawlies invade at night and where my mother wants to live out the remainder of her life.

"I'm so happy. I love you. You're a good daughter." And that's why I've been killing myself for the past month to make it happen. I want to make Mom as happy as I can for the rest of her life, and I want to make new memories to last me the rest of my life, too. I can work here as well as in Seattle, and I can spend my free time with Mom, instead of paying her visits at memory care facilities that often get postponed because of my work.

"Did you see *The Skeleton Key*?" Lindsey asks.

"No." Beyond potty language at the dinner table, I've learned several things about Lindsey. She rarely wears anything but nurse's scrubs and she listens to loud country music in her room. She hates peas and loves horror movies almost as much as Mom loves '70s game shows.

"This looks like that house." Then she whispers, so Mom doesn't hear, "Super creepy."

Mother reaches for my hand and squeezes. Her touch helps calm my overworked nerves and takes my tension down from level ten to about level eight. "It's a good day." She lifts her face to the sky and breathes deeply as if she's sucking in heaven.

Beside me, Lindsey shrugs out of her cardigan and hangs the sweater over one arm. Her scrubs have clouds and rainbows on them today. Yesterday it was safari animals. "Are you sure it's only sixty-three degrees? I'm sweating like a pig."

I've never really understood why anyone would compare themselves to a pig. I swat away a bug in front of my face and say, "Humidity always makes it seem hotter in the South." Which is true. The few stray hairs that have escaped my braid are stuck to the back of my neck. "You'll get used to it," I lie, in case Lindsey is thinking about bailing on me. She's taken care of all the paperwork that ensures Mom's medical records were transferred to a local GP as well as to a neurologist. She set up appointments and spoke with the nearest pharmacy. She's done all the big and little things involved with Mom's care. We could not have made this move without her.

"Yeah, probably by the time we go back home."

I shrug because I don't know when we'll return to Seattle. Could be one year or five years. It depends on the progression of

78

Mom's illness.

"I'll have to use extra deodorant to make sure I don't stink."

And I'll buy her any deodorant she wants. I'll buy her a gross of deodorant sticks and throw in a pony, too. We need her. Mom likes her. And she loves to cook.

When I'd realized that Mom hadn't forgotten my promise to bring her to Sutton Hall and wasn't giving up on the idea of living out the remainder of her years in Louisiana, I'd feared we'd lose Lindsey, but she'd jumped at the chance to get out of Washington. In fact, she'd jumped so fast that I wondered if she was wanted for robbing banks or spree killings.

I am so relieved to have her, I don't care.

"There used to be a rain barrel over there." Mother drops my hand and points a finger to the corner of a wraparound porch. "That's where Grandmere got the water to wash her hair." Funny she can remember her grandmother catching rainwater sixty or seventy years ago but not spooning Mr. Shone last month.

"I know," I say as we head up three wooden steps to the porch. The boards beneath our feet creak; some have been replaced here and there, but it's just as I remember. Our luggage sits next to the double doors, painted the same green as the shutters, and just as faded.

"I don't know what Earl will do without me." Mother doesn't remember the incident that got her booted from Golden Springs, but she remembers her boyfriend.

The front doors are locked, and I dig around in my purse in search of the key. When I'd given Mom the key a few months ago, she'd put it somewhere "safe" — so safe we couldn't find it within her personal belongings, though we did find a secret money stash and a hoard of credit cards. Only one of them belonged to her. I don't know how she got away with stealing so many, but I assume she never actually used them, or I would have been informed of her credit card fraud by now.

It took several long hours filled with hand-wringing and worry. "Wynonna stole it. She hates me and loves to steal from me," she'd said over and over, accusing the poor woman until we'd finally found it wrapped up inside a purple Crown Royal bag.

I raise the key to the lock, but it doesn't fit. I wiggle it this way and that, cajole and plead and curse under my breath. God, I miss the Millennium Tower concierge already. I shove the weight of my body into the door, but it doesn't even rattle. From the moment we set foot in Sea-Tac this morning, the day has gone from bad to worse. My head hurts and I'm sweaty. My nerves are shot, and my sanity is barely hanging on. I stomp one foot in frustration, and the four-inch heel of my Manolo sinks into the old wooden porch. It sinks so far that it won't come out when I scrunch my toes and lift my foot. I look over my shoulder at my mother, who is so close that she's almost on top of me. "It's not the right key."

"That's the key, all right."

The humidity. The key. My shoe stuck in the porch. The flight from hell. I don't know how much more I can take. "You try." I shove the key at Mom, who hands it off to Lindsey.

I step out of my black pump and allow the strongest woman I know to take my place. She pushes and pulls on the door as she shakes the handle and tries to fit the key into the lock all at the same time. She slams a shoulder into it, and, for several hopeful moments, I think the hinges might give out, but the solid old door doesn't budge. "Wrong key."

"Wynonna must have stolen the good key. She stole my pink nightie and framed picture of Rowdy Yates."

I feel a tiny twitch in the corner of my eye

— never a good sign.

"Maybe it's to the back door," Lindsey suggests, and she and Mother turn and walk around the right side of the porch. They just leave me, but I'm okay with that and bend down to retrieve my shoe from the hole I've created. I pull at it four times before it comes free, and I stumble back a few steps. The heel is a little loose, and the leather is stripped like an inside-out umbrella. This is the second pair of ruined pumps in two months. I only packed three others. At this rate, I'll be out of shoes by May. Well, except for four pairs of boots, six pairs of sandals, and a pair of Nikes I threw in at the last minute.

It's getting hotter and more humid by the second, and my silk blouse is stuck to my skin. The heel of my shoe feels a bit wonky, and I put as little weight on it as possible as I follow Mom and Lindsey. I could take my shoes off and go barefoot, but I'm wearing pantyhose, and the fear of splinters is real enough to keep them on my feet.

By the time I limp my way to Mom and Lindsey, they're standing at a door that looks very much like the one in front. In fact, the back of the house is almost as grand as the front. Or was grand at one time.

"How's it going?" I ask as I limp toward them.

Mother is smiling, but Lindsey isn't. Not a good sign.

"I swear, it's just so beautiful back here," Mom gushes.

Clearly my mother and I are not on the same planet, let alone in the same clumpy yard in Louisiana. It appears that someone has recently attempted to mow the lawn and weeds, but beyond that, the shrubs are a nightmare. Cypress trees tower over a roofless garçonnière and what is left of the original kitchen. Kudzu has nearly swallowed most of the older structures and crumbling chimneys at the far end of the yard where the bayou meanders along, filled with creepy critters. I know that somewhere behind the converted garage to my right is a cobblestone lane that leads to the old family cemetery where my mother expects to be buried.

"Why are you walking funny?" my mother wants to know.

"I broke a heel." If I am careful and keep my weight off my shoe, I think it can be easily repaired. I might spend a lot of money on clothes and shoes, but I take good care of them so they will last.

"The key fits but the door won't open,"

Lindsey tells me.

The sun beats down on us, and I feel myself sweating like a dog, which I much prefer to pig. I shrug out of my blazer and pull the front of my blouse from my damp skin. "Let me try." Lindsey hands me the key, and I confirm she's right. It fits, the handle turns, but nothing. I'd put a shoulder into it, but I've learned my lesson. To my right, I hear a clicking sound from the overgrown shrubs that shoves my heart up into my throat. Like someone with a camera is hiding in the shrubbery, or a giant insect is preparing to launch an attack on my clammy neck. The first possibility isn't likely, and the second makes my sweaty skin crawl and raises my shoulders to my ears.

"The doors won't open." Mother states the obvious. "Call someone for help."

I close my eyes and take a deep, cleansing breath to keep my head from exploding. "There's no one I can call." I don't want to explode. I don't want to yell and scream and act crazy, but I can feel it bubbling up.

"Call Tony."

I press my fingertips to the seam of my lips. I know Mom isn't purposely trying to make my head explode, but she's standing next to a powder keg with a box of matches in her hand.

"I don't think he's coming," Lindsey helps me out. Over the past month, she's heard Mom drop his name, forcing me to explain my reaction to the jerk.

"Sure he is. He'll get the real key from Wynonna. Then she'll be sorry."

My foot wobbles, my ankles twists, and I slowly list to one side. "Fuck!"

My mother gasps, and I drop my hand from my mouth. She hates the f-word as much as I do. Maybe a little more. "Lou Ann! Don't be trashy."

She's right. Swearing is trashy, and a bad habit best never picked up. "Sorry." I'm sinking starboard — then *snap,* the heel of my Manolo shoots off into the clicking shrub. One leg is suddenly shorter than the other and sweat is running down the side of my neck. "Great! My shoe just broke."

"Wynonna stole my shoes." Mom shakes her head, and the ends of her side pony brush across her shoulder. "Tony will make her give them back. The key too."

"Stop talking about him." Stop flicking lighted matches in my direction. "Don't even mention his name to me."

Her red lips purse as she stares straight ahead at the locked door. She's mad, but hopefully she'll stop talking about Tony.

"Maybe we can find a screwdriver or

something in the garage," Lindsey suggests. "Or a hacksaw," I add.

Lindsey one-ups me. "Chain saw. This door would definitely require a chain saw."

"He's like a son."

Boom — red flashes behind my eyes and I explode. "I hate that fucker!" I put a hand on top of my head to keep it from flying off into the shrub after my four-inch heel. Pain stabs my temples, and my inner trashy nature takes over like a demon possession. A torrent of filth gushes from my mouth, and I couldn't stop it even if I tried.

Mom gasps and clutches the front of her jogging suit, but I don't seem to care that I'm giving her heart failure. Words I've never used spew forth like a fount of profanity and my crescendo is so glorious, so spectacular, teenage boys from around the world must be writhing with envy. "Tony's a rat bastard, son of a bitch, fuck-fucking-fucker, squirrel-dick shit taco!" I take a deep breath and slowly blow it out. The demon has been exorcised.

Mother's lips are pursed even tighter. Lindsey's eyes are wide.

Did I really say "squirrel-dick shit taco"?

One side of the back doors swings open and a man, looking every bit like he's straight off the cover of *Men's Fitness*

86

magazine, drawls in a smooth, Southern voice, "How can I help you, ladies?"

87

6

Rattlesnake Patty and Lay's potato chips.

My heart skips a beat and I can feel heat
flush my sweaty face. Gross. Did he hear
my tirade? Probably. This is payback for
yelling trashy words in public. "The door
was locked," seems to be all I am capable of
saying.

"It sticks." He's tall and broad, and his
T-shirt is stark white against the shadows in
the house behind him. His dark brows are
knitted in a disapproving scowl, and his
green eyes look down at me as if he doesn't
like what he sees. That's okay. I'm not looking for a date. "You have to pull while you
turn the knob."

Gee, why didn't I think of that?

His attention turns to my mother and he
smiles. His teeth are as white as his T-shirt,
defying the old Southern stereotype. "You
must be Ms. Patricia," he drawls.

"Yes." Mother pushes past me and takes his arm. Some things never change. "And you are?"

"Simon Broussard."

"Arcadian."

"My father's people are Broussards."

Beside me, Lindsey whispers like she's found religion, "Praise the Lord and the beauty of the earth."

Has Mom's health care worker suddenly found God here on this porch in Louisiana? I look at her out of the corners of my eyes. "What?"

"That's a handsome man." Lindsey's smile is huge and makes her brown eyes light up. "Handsome man with big muscles."

"Never let a handsome face cloud good judgment," I say, before I realize I've inadvertently slipped into Lulu mode.

"Huh?"

She's obviously never read my rules or listened to Lulu podcasts. Which she should, so she can avoid the traps of good-looking men.

"Did you see his eyes?"

Now she's starting to sound like Mom.

Lindsey follows me into the house and shuts the door behind us. The boxes we sent ahead are stacked in the center of the room, and Mom's latest Bob Ross painting sits on a table in the breakfast nook. The smell of old appliances and even older wood brings me back to the last time I stood in this kitchen. We'd come for my great-uncle Jed's funeral, and the scowls on grown-up faces had made me uncomfortable. Even at ten, I'd known we were personae non gratae, but Mother had acted as if we were welcomed into the warm bosom of our family. Although to say we'd been welcome might be overstating things. It's more like we were tolerated because Mom's real daddy had died a war hero and was possibly related to Stonewall Jackson. And of course, her stepdad wasn't also her second cousin by blood.

From the front of the house, I hear my mother's giddy voice and Lindsey brushes past me. I toss my blazer on a box marked LINEN and take a deep breath filled with dust and family history. Mom wants to be buried in the backyard next to my grandmother. I don't understand either woman's attachment to this overgrown plot of land in southern Louisiana. It must be the Scarlett O'Hara gene that I didn't inherit.

The central hall runs from the kitchen straight to the front of the house. The worn rugs covering the wooden floors do nothing to muffle my lopsided footsteps, so I kick off my shoes. If my memory serves, each room is a different color and is framed with white molding, cornices, and the occasional Grecian column. Most rooms have a fireplace with grand mantels. A few have pocket doors that disappear into the walls to create more open spaces for family gatherings.

Generations of Suttons stare down at me from white plaster walls as I pass. I know it was the style in previous eras to appear somber, but they look downright angry. Perhaps they're not smiling because they're missing teeth. I wouldn't smile either if I had missing teeth.

Oral hygiene is important to me.

The man in the white T-shirt is setting our luggage inside; I already don't recall his name. Mom is sitting on an overstuffed chair next to a mahogany sideboard and giving him her signature Patricia Jackson-Garvin-Hunter-Russo-Thompson-Doyle sassy smile. A portrait of a disapproving woman in a black dress and white bonnet stares down at Mom as she flirts outrageously.

"You're a foxy man."

Why am I embarrassed by her when she's not and has never been? She used to flirt with my high school boyfriends so much that I quit bringing them around her.

"I love a big foxy man around the house."

Does she think Mr. Foxy Man is going to jump at the chance to be her new boyfriend? An Earl replacement? She doesn't know what day it is, but she knows how to corner a man. It's instinctual. Like breathing, it's hardwired into her primitive lizard brain.

"It's time for your medication, Patricia."

Mom looks at Lindsey as if she's just been reminded that she's seventy-four and not twenty-four. It's a look of sadness, and I feel bad that my reaction to her flirting was a wince of horror. I blame it on *my* lizard brain.

Mom places a hand on the sideboard. Mr. Foxy Man and Lindsey move to help her to her feet, but she shoos her away. "Are you married?"

"No."

"Serious girlfriend?"

"Not at the moment."

"That's good. I'll come back in a minute so we can get better acquainted." She puts a little sass in her walk, but the effect is not quite what it was when she lived in heels. She can't get the same sway of her hips in orthopedic shoes. I wish she'd give it up before she breaks a hip.

"If you tell me where these bags go, I'll

put them in y'all's rooms and be on my way."

"I don't know, actually." Mom and Lindsey disappear into the kitchen and I turn toward him. "I was ten the last time I was here." He sets my carry-on next to Mom's large suitcase and closes the front door. Lindsey is right. There is no denying he's a big, handsome man, but I've dated a lot of handsome men. Handsome men are vain and have entitlement issues. And if I'm being honest with myself, I'll admit that I haven't quite gotten over my "men are assholes" phase since Tony.

"I'm Lou Ann Hunter." I stick out my hand toward him. "Remind me of your name again?"

His gaze rests on my forehead and I think he's going to ask about the red mark the size of a silver dollar above my left brow. "Simon Broussard," he says, and gives my hand one quick shake before dropping it.

I'm still waiting for him to explain why he is in my mother's house.

"I'm going to assume you want Ms. Patricia in Jasper's room. We turned the front parlor into Jasper's bedroom about six years ago when the stair railing got too loose."

Of course it's too loose. I look at the grand staircase curving downward against the wall, with its intricately carved balusters and railing. It doesn't look as big and ominous as it did when I was a kid. "Mom sometimes wanders at night." I have her alarm mats, but I think I'll need several more just to be safe, and I put them on my mental to-buy list.

He points to the wall of wood paneling on this side of the stairs. "We converted the trunk closet under the stairs into a bathroom."

"We?"

"I."

"Are you a handyman?"

He chuckles. "Among other things."

When he doesn't elaborate, I give up and point to Mother's big suitcase. "That's hers." Boxes of her things are also stacked in the kitchen, but Lindsey and I can go through those later.

Simon picks up the large bag instead of lifting the handle and wheeling it down the hall like a normal person. His muscles flex, and I'm glad Mom and Lindsey aren't here to fawn and coo or break out in prayer. "I thought you said front parlor."

"I did."

I point to the green room on my right. "The front parlor is at the front of the house."

94

"You're right."

He's obviously confused about the front and back of the house — not that it really matters. I follow him. The door handles are lower than normal, and he has to bend down to turn the knobs. Across the threshold, he flips a switch and an old crystal chandelier spreads weak light across the room. From what I can see, about half the bulbs are burned out. The walls are red, which makes the room creepy and drab at the same time. This won't do for Mother. "Do you know if there are replacement bulbs around here?"

"The bulbs don't need to be replaced." He drops the suitcase on a wrought-iron bed shoved up against one wall and covered by a patchwork quilt. "They just need to be screwed back in." The heels of his boots thud across the polished wood as he moves to a floor-to-ceiling window and pushes open the red drapes. Sunlight pours over him, and with his hands clutching the heavy drapes like that, he looks like he's being crucified. The image fits with Lindsey's religious experience.

"Why are the bulbs unscrewed?" I sit on the bed next to my mother's suitcase.

"Respect." He drops his hands and turns to face me. "It's more peaceful without all

95

that light."

"Was Great-uncle Jasper a vampire?" He doesn't laugh but I crack myself up.

"The bulbs should still work," he says, as if he didn't hear my funny little joke. "No one's been in here since Jasper's wake."

I stop mid-chuckle and squint my eyes. "His wake was in this house?" Sure, it took place six months ago, but it's still disturbing.

"Funeral too." He points to the bed. "We laid poor old Jasper out right where you're sittin'."

"What?" I jump up like someone lit my tail on fire. Now *he* laughs, a great big shout of laughter.

"He was ninety-seven, and we couldn't lay him out in the front parlor on account of him looking like death." He laughs even harder, and his accent gets thicker. "And scarin' young'uns."

"Who does that?" It's a rhetorical question, and I glance at the bed as if I might see Jasper still lying there. "Haven't you people heard of mortuaries?"

"You're white like you've seen the rougarou."

I don't know what that means, but I'm going to take a wild guess that it's not a compliment.

"What happened to the parlor?" Mother asks as she walks into the room. She slowly spins around, confused. "Where's Grandmere's furniture?" She points to the intricately carved fireplace. "Where's the screen with the beagle painted on it?" Her confusion turns to agitation, and she wrings her hands. "Why's it so dark in here? I can barely see."

"It's going to be all right, Patricia," Lindsey assures her in a calm voice.

"The lightbulbs just need to be screwed in." Simon walks across the threadbare rug. "We needed to get rid of all the clutter and —"

"I hate it."

"— we moved the furniture to the attic," Simon continues as if Mother hadn't interrupted.

"Why the heck did you do that?" Mother's tone gets harsher, even with her new boyfriend.

"Mais, we had to move it so Jasper could sleep in here. Getting up and down the stairs was a problem for him."

"Well, not for me!"

"The banister is loose. I'd hate for you to fall."

"I'll use the back stairs."

"Those are piled high with a hoard of

Sutton treasures."

"Put the furniture back in here," Mother demands as if she doesn't hear him. "Who stole the fireplace screen?"

Please, God, don't let her go on a Wynonna tirade.

"I'll screw in those bulbs before I leave." Simon's voice is calm but firm, like he respects his elders but not enough to take their bullshit.

"This will be your room, too," I tell Mom as Simon exits. "We'll decorate any way you want."

"No." Mom crosses her arms and looks like she's ready to pitch a fit. "I want my grandmere's bedroom upstairs."

"If you pick this room," Lindsey joins in, "you won't tire yourself out from walking up and down the stairs all day."

"This is the parlor."

"Mom," I cajole, "you heard Simon. The handrail isn't safe. I don't want you to fall down the stairs. We'll make this into the grandest room in the house."

"This room is red." Her eyes start to water even before she sits on the bed. "Grandmere's room is blue."

"We can paint it any color you want."

"You won't even let me have a real bedroom!"

"I just don't want you to hurt yourself." I don't like to see her cry, but I don't want her to take a tumble on the stairs, either.

"You don't care. You want me to die."

I take a calming breath and say, "If I wanted you to die, I'd set you up in Great-grandmother's room so you could fall down the stairs and break your dang neck."

"Why are you always mean to me?" she sobs, and covers her face with her hands.

So much for being a good daughter. Of course, this is the exact moment Simon enters the room with an eight-foot ladder.

"Lou Ann gave away all my shoes."

I guess God heard me and she isn't going on a Wynonna tirade. I'm in her crosshairs instead. "Not all your shoes, Mom."

"All my good ones."

When she says "all," she's talking about an old pair of marabou mules with three-inch kitten heels. Obviously, fuck-me pumps aren't allowed in elder care facilities. I donated them to Goodwill three years ago, but that bee is still in her bonnet. I look sideways at Lindsey, who hasn't heard the marabou mules complaint, but that's one of the things I really like about her. She doesn't need to hear it to figure out the backstory.

Lindsey sits next to Mom and rubs her

back. "What can I do to help you?" It should be me comforting my mother, but I'm her target now, and she'll likely push me away if I try.

I glance up at Simon, who is pretending not to notice the scene below him. At least he's not scowling again, like he suspects me of elder abuse.

"Make her give me my good shoes."

"Those are good shoes," Lindsey reassures her.

I turn back as Mom points to her orthopedic sneakers. "They're ugly."

She's right about that, but at least her feet don't hurt and her ankles aren't broken. The day will come when she'll have to use one of those walkers with tennis balls on the front feet and she'll still be complaining about those stupid mules.

"She hates me."

With the hope of a new beginning, there's always the danger of rejection or failure. Over the past few years, I've gotten used to her changing moods and her anger, but we've had a good month, and that makes this rejection much harder to take. I bite the inside of my lip and suck it up as Rattlesnake Patty takes over.

"She kicked me out of her place with Tony. She stuck me in a nursing home to get rid of me."

"That's not true," Lindsey assures her.

Actually, it's partly true. She was staying with me when I got engaged to Tony. He and I didn't live together, but that was just a technicality. He was at my condo so much he might as well have lived with me. And I hadn't "stuck" her anywhere. I'd found a nice place equipped to take better care of her than I could. I couldn't take time off back then like I can now. And if I'm being honest with myself (which is twice now and totally annoying), I'll admit I couldn't hack it.

"You can buy new shoes."

"No, I can't." Mom points a finger at me, and her eyes are black with anger. "She cut up all my credit cards so I can't go on the Google net!"

"Your *stolen* cards, you mean." She has access to money in the joint account I set up for her, and I'm still baffled by the how and why. "Credit card theft is a felony, Mom. You wouldn't like prison. The food's bad, the shoes are worse, and there aren't any men. No flirting or spooning or miracle healing." I feel myself getting angry and press my fingertips into my skull. Mom drives me to feel as crazy as she is, but she has an excuse and I don't. "I'll go unpack your bedding." I have to remove myself before my potty mouth takes possession of my body for the second time in an hour.

The wood floors are smooth as glass beneath my feet as I make my way down the hall, passing a sampler with a depiction of Sutton Hall stitched on it. The slate floor in the kitchen keeps the room cooler than the rest of the house. The cleaning crew I hired was here recently, but no amount of their scrubbing could turn the now-pink 1970s counters back to red.

The harvest-gold refrigerator appears to have seen better days, but when I open it, cool air brushes my throat. It's stocked with fruits and vegetables and pudding. I grab a bottle of cold water from the fridge and a knife from a drawer.

I use it to cut the tape across the box labeled LINEN. The scent of freshly washed sheets and comforters rises to greet my nose and reminds me of my home in Seattle. There is a world of difference between Millennial Tower and Sutton Hall. One is my home and the other will never feel like home.

I hear laughter from the parlor/mortuary, but I don't return. I feel as out of place now as I did when I visited as a kid. I want to make Mom happy. I want to be there laughing and talking with her, but there's no talking to Rattlesnake Patty. I'll just have to learn which words trigger her — besides *shoes, Wynonna, credit cards,* and *Pirate's Booty* — and avoid them at all costs.

My gaze falls on two doors on the other side of the kitchen, and I realize I have hazy memories of them both. I set the knife down and walk past the stack of boxes. The first door is stuck, but with a little determination, I open it to the back stairs that used to scare the crap out of me as a kid. I guess a lot of things about this house scared the crap out of me, and these dim, narrow wooden steps rank alongside the mausoleums in the cemetery. Still spooky, they're now stacked with books and newspapers and even a bed frame on its side. Simon referred to this mess as Sutton treasures. All I see is junk.

The second door swings inward to an old butler's pantry, where I vaguely remember hiding once upon a time with tins of shortbread cookies and praline patties. On the other side of the pantry is another door leading to the dining room. Light from behind me pitches my shadow across cabinets and shelves on one side and a floor-to-ceiling wine rack on the other. I could use a nice red blend about now, and I'm a bit disappointed that the rack holds bottles of water instead. I turn my attention to the shelves stocked with groceries: bread, pasta, and soup. Boxes of crackers and cans of tuna. Canned fruits and veggies and a bag of potato chips.

What? My attention returns to the bright-yellow-and-white bag almost hidden within the variegated shadows. I walk forward, and the pantry door swings closed behind me. Junk food was not on the grocery list! The grocery list *I* made was filled with nutritious food — with the exception of Mom's Pirate's Booty, of course. I certainly never would have requested an ultimate bag of chip perfection, and I wonder how it got in here. I shove a box of crackers in front of all that salty goodness. Out of sight, out of mind, but the Lay's potato chips know my weakness and seem to taunt me.

Lou Ann. Lou Ann. You know you can't resist our salty yumminess.

I tell myself to back away slowly, not to reach for the bag, definitely not to rip it open. That's what I tell myself, but of course I don't listen, and the scent of greasy potatoes fills my nostrils as I tear it open.

"Just one," I whisper. Crunching fills my ears, and my taste buds experience nirvana. I haven't had an orgasm in a long time, but this is close. "One more, and that's it."

I need to unpack my clothes and set up my office in the library. I need to make beds, put up the monitors, and lay down the sensor mats. I have so many things I need to do, but I lean back and slide down the cabinet until my butt hits the hardwood floor.

I shove another chip into my mouth without bothering to lie about having just one. It's been so long — years of dieting myself into a size 4 so I'd look like a size 6 on TV — and the chips taste even better than I remember. They even come with a quality guarantee right on the bag. It would be nice if men came with a SUPREME SATIS-FACTION stamp on their foreheads, although at this point, I'd settle for somewhat satisfy-ing.

I like sitting in here in the dark, just me and the disappointing wine rack. I can lick my salty lips and fingers, burp like a beer-bellied trucker, swear like a parolee if I want, and no one will know.

I unscrew the bottle of water and take a big swig, then smash more chips into my mouth. I have to let Mom's cutting words roll off me. I have to learn a better way to deal with the insanity she creates in my head. I can't continue to hold it all inside until I blow and start yelling the f-word in public. Especially not when a certain person opens the back door and looks down at me as if he smells something bad. As if I'm a monster yelling at my poor, sick mother.

Not that I give a fucking fuck what he thinks.

I need to work hard on my involuntary reactions to Mom. My automatic responses took root decades ago, but I can change. From now on, I'm going to smile and bite my tongue. I'm not going to argue with her even if it kills me.

I shove more chips in my mouth and lean my head back. It's cool and quiet here in the pantry — well, except for the crunching. I can breathe. No one knows where I am, and I find an odd comfort in that.

Until, that is, the door swings open and almost hits me. "Are you hiding in here?" My gaze travels up long legs and worn-out jeans.

I shake my head and swallow. Simon isn't scowling this time, but he does look at me like I'm crazy. Not that I care. "How did you find me?"

"I heard your crunching."

I lick my salty lips once more and brush crumbs from my chest. "That loud?" I struggle to my feet, and he doesn't offer a

hand. I thought men in the South were supposed to have some manners.

"I figured a swamp rat got in here."

Guess not. It's obvious that Simon and I
are not going to be friends.

7

March 17

Mom *flips* me shit.
Simon gives me the bird.

The day from hell continues past midnight.
Mom's earlier potshots were nothing compared to the howitzer aimed at me now.
We'd all gone to bed, or so Lindsey and I
had thought, but Mom had different plans.
Around one in the morning, she broke the
infrared stream we'd placed across her door.
Three hours after I said good night, we had
to coax her back into bed and reset the
alarm. Lindsey and I barely made it to the
top of the stairs before she set it off again.
No amount of coaxing and cajoling works
this time. For over two hours now, she's
wandered the house, wringing her hands
and wreaking havoc.

"You're an ungrateful child!"

Rage has changed her face and glazed her

108

eyes, but she still looks like my mother.

"What can I do to make you feel better, Patricia?"

"Nothing!" She turns her attention to Lindsey. "Who are you?"

"I'm Lindsey and I'm here to help you."

"I don't need your help. I need my shoes!"

"Here we go," I mutter a little too loudly and she looks at me. "You want to get rid of me so you can keep everything for yourself." She's still worked up about the furniture, and no amount of reasoning on the part of either me or Lindsey has gotten her past it. "Grandmere will tan your hide for the way you treat me." I know she's anxious and afraid and will calm down once she gets into her routine. I should be grateful that she recognizes me at least.

I'm tired, my forehead hurts, and I don't want to do this with Mom. "Let's please go to bed and we'll talk about it in the morning."

"You're going to kill me in my sleep." She points at the door and yells, "Get out of my house and take that fat girl with you!"

"Mother! That's horrible." I turn to Lindsey and apologize for my mother.

"I've been called worse."

Mom keeps it up for another hour before Lindsey finally manages to double-dose her with nighttime medication. I wish I was so lucky. I'm too hurt and wound up to sleep now, but even if I was calm as a millpond, my mattress is bumpy and lumpy as hell. I suspect it's a Civil War survivor. Well, maybe it isn't that old, but it's as thin as toast — and this is the good one. I know because I pulled a Goldilocks and tested them all.

I do manage to doze off for half an hour here and there, and I wake in the morning with a back- and neck ache. I am tired and my head hurts. There's no coffee to be found, and I grab my chest as a palmetto bug scurries across the kitchen counter and drops to the floor. God bless her, Lindsey smashes it beneath the heel of her tie-dye Croc.

I can still hear the crunch and now this:

"Can you say hello?" Mother pushes her face closer to the birdcage. "Polly wanna cracker?"

"Be careful," I warn her, and pull her away from the cage and the African parrot inside. At least that's what we were told he is, but at the moment it's hard to say. He's got red and green feathers on his head and wings, but the rest of him looks like a plucked chicken.

"I feel like I should knit it a sweater." Lindsey scrunches up her nose and shakes

110

her head. "It looks so pathetic."

Its name is Raphael, or, as Simon pronounces it, Ray-feel. He'd belonged to Jasper, and, according to Simon, it was Jasper's dying wish that the bird live in the only home he'd ever known. "I couldn't leave him here by himself," Simon told us as he set the cage on a big brass stand in the front parlor. "I had to take him with me, but he got so depressed from Jasper's death and leaving his home that he quit eating and started pulling out his feathers."

"Depressed?" If I'd known he was saddling me with a pitiful bird, I wouldn't have opened the front door. I'd been expecting someone from Cadillac of New Orleans to drop off the shiny Escalade I leased. Instead, I opened the door and got a naked parrot.

He'd pulled a business card from his breast pocket and left it on the side table next to Mother. "I've written his vet's name and number on the back."

"That's kind of you," Mom said as she picked it up.

"You can't leave that bird here."

"He won't cause you any problems. Y'all will hardly know Ray-feel's here." Then he'd turned to Mother, who was carefully reading the white card. "It's nice to see you again, Ms. Patricia."

"Thank you." Mom smiled up at him, all sweetness and light and nothing like the she-devil of the previous night. "Can you stay for coffee or tea?" she asked, though we don't have either.

"Next time," he'd said as he walked back out the front door. "Have a nice day, ladies."

I chased after him. "I can't take care of a sick bird!"

"He's doing a lot better already." He jogged down the steps and practically ran to his truck. "Don't stress him out, though."

Don't stress *him* out? A *bird*? What about *my* stress? The last thing I need is a self-harming parrot with an eating disorder. I watched Simon practically peel rubber out of the driveway. "Jerk," I muttered, and returned to the parlor. Number thirty-five of Lulu's Rules of Love: Avoid the jerk who shirks responsibility, leaving others to deal with his problems.

"If he's thirty-two now . . ." Lindsey skims through a care-and-feeding book Simon thoughtfully left behind. "I'm assuming this is human years . . ." she continues. "African parrots can live to the age of seventy." She's wearing smiley-face scrubs today, but the corners of her lips turn down as she looks over at me. "That's as old as dirt."

I glance at Mother, who doesn't appear to

be insulted by the comparison. Her hair is coiled into a thick bun on the top of her head today. She looks pretty in lavender pants, a paisley blouse, and pink lipstick that is almost neon. It's way too bright for anyone over the age of sixteen, but I'm not going to tell her. Rattlesnake Patty has retracted her fangs, and Patricia is in a good mood. Thank God. I just hope it lasts through tonight.

" 'Green parrots can be affectionate and highly amusing, but if left untrained can be very annoying and irritating. If they are frightened or bored, biting can become a problem. Do not poke your fingers in the cage, as that can seem threatening and may result in a painful bite.' "

Mom leans close to the cage, but not close enough for me to risk upsetting her with another warning.

She turns her face toward me. "When's your wedding to Tony?"

Her mood might be good, but she just took a big dump on mine. I smile patiently and answer, "We broke up a while ago."

"I didn't know that. Why?"

"He's a cheating bastard."

"That's too bad." She returns her attention to the cage, and I don't know if she means it's "too bad" he's a cheater or it's "too bad" I didn't overlook that minor detail.

"Polly wanna cracker?"

Raphael flaps his wings and shrieks like someone is chasing him with an axe. Mother screams, I suck in a startled breath, and the book falls from Lindsey's hands. Evidently, Polly did not want a cracker.

"Maybe we should leave him alone." Lindsey's brown eyes are wide as she backs out of the room. "It's like in *The Witch*." I suspect *The Witch* is a horror movie, and Lindsey confirms my suspicions when she adds, "Pure evil."

So much for hardly knowing "Ray-feel's here."

Raphael flaps his wings, hops the short distance to the side of the cage, and wraps his talons around the wire. He's one of the ugliest things I've ever seen, and as if he can read my mind, he lets loose with another shriek. Mom and I both jump.

"That thing is giving me heart flutters!"

One thing I know for sure is that Mother's heart works just fine.

Nevertheless, she puts one hand on her chest and shoves the white card at me. "Call the doctor."

"Who?"

"Simon."

"Really?" I guess it's possible, but his truck has the name of a construction company on the side. I grab the card and read for myself:

Broussard LLC
House Doctor
Renovation and Restoration

There are two different addresses and three phone numbers on the card. He's a busy guy but, "He's not a doctor."

"I saw it on the card."

"It says, 'House Doctor.' Not like a doctor doctor. Not like a heart doctor."

Her brows pull together. "He comes to the house."

I'm not calling a construction contractor because Mom thinks she's having heart flutters, but I don't want to get into an argument that could turn our good day rotten. "He can't come right now."

"Why?"

"He's operating and saving lives."

Her forehead clears: Rattlesnake avoided. "I always wanted to marry a doctor," she says through a sigh. "But I've been married several times already."

Yeah, five. "Who's counting?" I laugh and grab my left shoulder and roll my head from side to side. "The doctor's a little young, don't you think?" I have aches all over my body that two Advil haven't knocked out.

"Some men like mature women. Earl does. He's seventy."

I could point out that there is a considerable age difference between Earl and the House Doctor. The old me — the me of yesterday — would have cringed and covered my ears. The new me — the patient me of today — pushes up the corners of my mouth and forces myself to say, "You're a cougar."

She likes that and smiles. Not a fake smile, but a real Patricia smile. At seventy-four, she still has teeth that are white and perfect. Mostly because she goes to regular dental visits so she can flirt with her dentist. "Lord, Lou Ann." She waves away the notion with false modesty. "What would I do with . . ." Her smile wavers, and she points to the sideboard again. "With him?"

She's forgotten his name. Normally, I'd breathe a sigh of relief and take the opportunity to change the subject, but the new and improved Lou Ann pretends I've forgotten, too. "I think it's Simon."

"Yes, Simon."

To prove to myself that I am turning over a new leaf, that I can get beyond Mom's mood swings and embarrassing man-prowling, I put my arm around her shoulders and choke out the words, "I'm sure you'd figure out something to do with the House Doctor." The mental pictures make me want to stab my eyes out, but she laughs, and I tell myself it's worth the pain to see her real smile.

"Well, I have a passionate nature."

"That true." She's happy now, so I test the waters and ask, "How do you want to decorate your bedroom? We can paint it any color you like."

"It's always been red." I help her to her feet, and she actually lets me. I'm surprised and worried at the same time.

"We can paint it blue like Great-grandmother's room upstairs." Usually she'd tell me she can stand on her own and shoo me away with her hand. I don't know if she forgot she doesn't like my help, or if she truly needs it. Neither is a good sign, but at least she's forgotten that she hates me.

"I don't want it painted at all." She shakes her head and says, "I want Grandmere's bed and all the other stuff in her room."

I slept in that horrible, lumpy bed last night. It's made of ornate walnut and has a golden damask canopy and faded tassels.

"I remember naked-lady lamps with red velvet shades." The naked ladies in question are on the fireplace mantel upstairs. The white porcelain is faded, and the shades are indeed red velvet with long red tassels. Clearly, Mother is going for a bordello theme like her grandmother.

I leave Mom with Wink Martindale and Banko and take a shower in the handicapped bathroom beneath the stairs. There are five bedrooms and four bathrooms upstairs. Each bedroom is painted a different faded color, with varying degrees of damage to the walls and moldings. The bathrooms have claw-foot tubs and ornate pedestal sinks. Each is in some form of disrepair and, according to Lindsey, the water is tepid at best.

Mom's shower stays warm the entire time, and I suspect it's because the hot water doesn't have to travel as far through the old pipes. There are clean, fluffy towels in a warming drawer in the small vanity, and I make full use of them as I take out my hair dryer and defog the mirror. I lean closer and touch the bruise on my forehead. It may not look like much, but it hurts like hell.

For a split second I wonder if the hair dryer will blow a fuse, but it doesn't. This bathroom looks like it could be original to the house, but it's an addition that was meant to accommodate Jasper in his final years. It's cleaner, nicer, and more functional than the other bathrooms. The "fancy toilet," as Mom calls it, has handles on each side. The seat automatically lifts up and down, and all it's missing is a cup holder. The door is mounted flush with the original wooden panels beneath the stairs and practically disappears when it's closed. It swings inward with just a slight touch, and the floor looks like real wood but is actually heated tile.

The whole house seems to be a juxtaposition of maintenance and disrepair. Everything in the library, from the walnut bookshelves and ornate fireplace to the cream-colored walls and velvet conversation couch, is in remarkable shape. At the same time, the stair railing is loose like Simon mentioned, and the bedrooms need paint and attention. The crisp fleur-de-lis wallpaper in the front parlor perfectly coordinates with the mint-colored walls and emerald marble fireplace. The formal dining room has warped floors, cracks in the white plaster walls, and an old shoofly hanging from the ceiling on rusty hinges. It's like time stood still in some parts of the house while other parts deteriorated with age.

At noon, the three of us sit at a table that can accommodate twenty-two and eat tuna sandwiches. We eat off blue-and-white china that's so old the glaze is dulled, and we drink our bottled water out of heavy crystal goblets. It seems silly to eat sandwiches from 150-year-old china that has to be carefully handwashed, but if it makes Mom happy, that's what we'll do.

"John had horrible stomach pains, but after a few nights of my snugglin', his pains went away." I'd close my eyes to block the visual, but I have to keep at least one eye on the shoofly. "I have a passionate nature that works miracles."

Sometimes Mom's memory reminds me of a jukebox with only a handful of selections. Earl. Tony. Miracle worker.

I'm trying to block out the pain of the "snugglin' " stories, but Lindsey doesn't seem to notice. She puts a palm beneath her chin and one on the top of her head and snaps her head to one side like she's trying to pop her neck. She's chosen the yellow bedroom at the top of the stairs, and I know she didn't get much sleep either. The feather mattress on her sleigh bed is even harder and lumpier than mine. Mom's mattress — Jasper's old one — is just as

120

bad, but she seems neither discomforted nor grossed out by it. If she did, she certainly would have let me know by now.

Mom pauses in the second recounting of her miraculous healings and her brows scrunch together with confusion. "John had horrible pains," she begins all over again.

After lunch, Lindsey and I measure the beds in the house and get busy on the Google net — good Lord, listen to me — searching for the closest mattress store. I don't know how long we'll be in this house, but it doesn't matter. We can't sleep on bad mattresses while we are here. The nearest furniture store is a half hour away. Unfortunately, a mattress isn't something I can just click and enter a credit card number for, nor can I hand off the task to someone else. Lindsey and I both have to go, and Mother needs to choose a mattress for herself. I know she'll argue with me, but I just can't let her sleep on a lumpy mattress that, as recently as six months ago, displayed Uncle Jasper's corpse. Maybe she's not disturbed by that, but I am enough for both of us.

Mom takes a nap, and Lindsey and I measure bed frames. Thank God they all fit a standard queen and I don't have to order anything custom. We'll need extra bedding, too, but that's an easy problem to resolve, and I put it on my mental to-do list.

Setting up my office in the library should be just as easy. The desk looks like something out of the Oval Office, but the Empire chair is as lumpy as the mattresses. Easy, the desk stays, the chair goes, but I run into a big problem with the electric sockets that only fit two prongs. I know there are three-prong sockets in the kitchen, and I'll need to run an extension cord all the way to the back of the house until I can figure something else out.

I have to write a blog by the end of the week, and that can't happen without power. I try to imagine where I'll find a long cord and head out to the garage. Of course, the door doesn't open right away. I shove my sore shoulder into it, but unlike the front door of the house, it swings open and bangs into a wheel of the big horse-drawn carriage parked where I'd planned to park the Escalade. It's a surrey with the fringe on top. I've seen carriages like this in museums and old movies, but this is longer, with three rows of seats. I imagine it was the family station wagon of its day. Mom would love this, but I don't think I'll tell her about it. No doubt she'd want to take it out for a spin, and I don't trust the cracked wheels. Not to mention, I haven't the slightest desire to rent carriage horses.

I flip on the light and move to the other side of the garage, where I find two cords: an orange hundred-foot extension and another fifty-footer. I grab both to be on the safe side, but the orange cord is more than I need. I spend the next few hours working and take a break from my writing long enough to sign up for weekly food delivery from Rouses and hire the Cajun Maids to come twice a month.

When the Cadillac is delivered, I find Lindsey in Mom's room, insisting that she continue her daily exercise, which mostly consists of Mom doing arm and leg lifts with a big rubber band while seated.

"I already did this one!"

"We have to do three repetitions, Patricia."

Exercise used to be part of Mom's daily routine, but that was a while ago. These days she prefers watching TV and eating Pirate's Booty. "No," she says, and throws the big rubber band across the room. Both women have their arms folded across their chests in what appears to be a stalemate. Lindsey's jaw is set, and my money's on her. She's bigger and more determined, and I've seen her battles with Mom about drinking enough water. She usually wins.

"We need to get going to the mattress

store," I say. I know I shouldn't undermine Mother's health care, but this could go on for hours. "It's five already, and the store closes at six."

Lindsey glances at me and relents. She wants a new mattress as much as I do. Mother, however, wants to continue the battle. "I'm not going."

"You have to go and pick out a new mattress."

"I don't want a new mattress."

"All the mattresses here are bad, Mom."

She points to Jasper's bed. "That one is good."

I sat on that mattress and I know better. "Uncle Jasper died on that one."

"I don't care."

She's being stubborn, and I'm forced to think up a quick lie. "It won't fit the bed frame you want."

"Bring down the mattress with it."

I said it was a "quick lie," not a good one. "It was thrown out years ago," I fib again, and don't feel the least bit bad. I expect her to argue, but she rises, and I quickly usher her out the back door before she can change her mind.

"What a waste," Mom says as I help her down the wooden steps. The overgrown shrubs make the same clicking sounds as they did the day before and I say a prayer for my Manolo heel, in there somewhere but as good as gone. No way am I crawling into those bug-infested bushes. "When Grandmere couldn't have kids right off, she had a voodoo queen cast a fertility spell on that mattress. After a few years and a whole lotta practice, she birthed Jed and Jasper and Momma right on that mattress. I was born in New Orleans, where Momma and Daddy lived before he left."

"Uh-huh."

Mom sucks in a breath and lets out a dreamy sigh. "But I did practice on it a time or two with Jean Oliver and his cousin . . . What was his name?"

That gets my attention and I turn to Mom. "At the same time!" Gross. I slept — or tried to sleep — on that mattress last night. Lindsey's eyes are filled with horror.

"He sure had a big —"

"I don't want to know!"

"— mustache," she continues.

Thank God.

"That mattress had magic powers." She stops as I open the car door and the lighted running board slides out. "Now you'll never have magic powers like me."

"Bummer." And yet, somehow, I'll find the strength to live on.

125

8

Mom's a horrible back-seat driver.
Raphael's a horrible bird.
Lindsey's a horrible chicken.

The "Passion Red" Escalade was the shorter option, but it's still bigger than my Land Rover. I would have preferred a smaller SUV, but Mother loves a Cadillac. The center console is so loaded with buttons and gadgets that it takes Lindsey and me a good ten minutes to figure out the GPS. Once we enter the information correctly and don't have to delete it ten times, we buckle ourselves into the beast and take off. Not so much like a racehorse, but more like a turtle.

I've been in Escalades more times than I can count, but always in the back, with media escorts at the wheel. Everything looks a whole lot wider and longer from the driver's seat. I feel like I'm driving a short bus with touchy gas and brake pedals. I turn corners too wide and at the best of times I am horrible at gauging distance. Three miles always feels like five to me, and ten feet might as well be fifteen. I have a hard time with measurements, too. I don't know how many centimeters are in an inch, nor do I care. Tony used to tell me he was six inches, but even I knew that wasn't true.

Yuck. I'd blocked out Tony from my head for quite a while. Now he's back, thanks to Mom.

"You're kinking up my neck!" Mom complains.

"It's called whiplash," Lindsey piles on.

I do not appreciate her help and momentarily take my eyes off the road to glare at her in the passenger seat. She doesn't seem to notice.

"Would either of you ladies like to drive?"

"I will," Mother volunteers.

"I don't have a driver's license."

I look at Lindsey, who shrugs at having left this vital information off her résumé. I'd just assumed that she always took the bus in Seattle because she didn't own a car. "Since when?"

"Since never. My parents don't think women should drive."

"You're kidding me."

127

"No. My dad and brothers have licenses, but Mom and I and my sisters don't."

"You could have gotten your license when you moved out."

She shrugs again. "I only just moved out, and I knew the Spokane bus system like the back of my hand."

This is all news to me and reminds me of how little I know about Lindsey.

"Turn left in three hundred feet," the guidance system directs. I turn too soon and end up in an Arby's parking lot. The soothing female voice tells me to make a U-turn, and I whip the big SUV around.

"You're kinking my neck," Mom says again, but I ignore her.

"You have to learn to drive, Lindsey." I have to work and can't always chauffeur Mom around or pick up prescriptions.

"I said I don't have a license. I didn't say that I don't know how to drive."

"Rebel."

She smiles. "The girls in my family live at home until we get married."

This explains why she'd accepted a job four hours from her hometown, but it doesn't tell me why she'd jumped at the offer to move across the country.

"Turn left." I turn left.

"Earl's a better driver than you."

"I know, Mom."

Mother's complaint gets a chuckle from the twenty-six-year-old with no license. "I'm the first girl in my family to move out."

"How many in your family?"

"Counting my parents, nine. I have three older sisters and one younger, and two younger brothers."

To me, as an only child, that's a lot of people. Her parents must be insane to want them all to stay at home long after they should be on their own. Then I remind myself that they couldn't be too bad if they let Lindsey go to college. "You do have a bachelor's degree from WSU." Just for good measure, I add, "Right?" because, at this point, I'm not sure of anything.

She nods. "I was supposed to find a husband there like two of my sisters did."

"Women have a hard enough time finding a good date in college. For God's sake, how can you be expected to find a good husband?"

"I don't know. I never did."

"Turn left in six hundred feet." I guesstimate the distance and am shocked when I actually get it right. "You know that saying about kissing a lot of toads before you find true love." I pull to a stop at a red light and step on the brakes only a little too hard.

"It's true, but keep in mind that finding true love isn't about the pool of toads, but rather about the toads in your pool," I quote myself. "So, date broadly but be selective, and you'll find your prince."

"Why haven't you found yours?"

God, I hate that question. The answer is that I've dated broadly and selectively. That's one of the big differences between Mom and me. She dated broadly but wasn't very selective.

The one time I thought I found Mr. Right, everything blew up in my face in a very horrifying and public display of greed and dishonesty that threatened to destroy my company. Thank God it didn't. "I'll find my Mr. Right."

"Sounds to me like you need different toads in your pool." Lindsey tries not to smile as she leans forward and tunes in to a country music station.

Smart-ass. I don't have any toads, and I'm not searching for any, either. Which is another difference between Mom and me: she's still on the hunt to restock her pond.

Even though the love guru business is booming, I've privately taken myself off the market. No one knows that quite a few of the "dates" I've written and spoken about for the past three years have been fictional

— not even Margie. I'm thirty-eight, and a lot of men my age want younger women. Men older than me have baggage that I don't want to deal with. Fiction is easier than real life.

The trip to the mattress store that should have taken thirty minutes takes almost an hour, and I'm worried it'll be closed by the time we arrive. An hour of Lindsey singing along to the radio (I've heard better noise coming from a pissed-off cat) and the backseat driver yelling, "You're kinking up my neck!"

Patience, I tell myself. Mom doesn't mean to annoy me.

"Turn right," the navigation system directs, but I'm busy trying to make out the names of streets and almost overshoot the intersection.

"Where are we going?" Mom asks, her tone growing more agitated by the minute.

I don't blame her. I'm agitated, too. "To the mattress store," I remind her so patiently I should get an award.

"I already got a mattress."

"You need a new one to fit Great-grandmother's bed."

"I want the mattress that's on it."

I repeat my earlier lie. "It got thrown out." I glance at her in the rearview mirror and feel like her parent. "If you want that bed, you have to get a new mattress."

Our gazes meet and her eyes are sad. "Momma was born in that bed."

"Turn right in three hundred feet, then proceed one mile to West Gonzales." I return my gaze to the road, slow down, and manage the right turn. "Maybe you can find one that massages your back."

"Or I'll get one of those adjustable mattresses like Earl has," Mom says, kind of grumpy.

Earl's Craftmatic isn't a memory I want stuck in my head for the rest of my life, and I quickly change the subject. "We have to let Raphael out of his cage for a bit when we get back."

"Earl's mattress was perfect for spooning."

Well, it could be worse.

"And sweet love."

Damn it. I jinxed myself.

Lindsey's screechy-cat singing comes to a sudden halt, and we look at each other, eyes bugging out, ears ringing from the trauma we've just endured. Mom might wear lipstick and the latest in jogging couture, but under it all, she's sporting a big droopy bra, black-lace thong over her Attends, and geriatric compression shocks. Lindsey makes a distressed sound and shakes her head. I just shrug.

"Make a U-turn, then proceed to the route." Crap, I overshot the turn like before, but this time I hear a hint of judgment in the navigator's sugary tone.

"Earl's a better driver," Mom says again, as if trying to see if I'll snap.

"Make a right turn, then proceed to the route." I'm in the wrong lane to turn. "Proceed to the route."

"Why does that woman keep saying that?" asks the other woman in the car who likes to repeat things.

"We're lost," Lindsey piles on.

"We're not lost." I point to the map. "We're almost back on the blue line."

We make it to the mattress store as the manager is locking the front doors. I yell at him through the glass to please open, and I promise to buy three mattresses if he lets us in. Luckily, greed rules the day.

The store is like a warehouse, and Mom has to check out practically every mattress. She lies on her back and stomach, then flops from side to side like a fish before moving to the next one. I don't tell myself things could get worse. I try not to even think about it.

After much flopping by both Lindsey and

Mother, I make an executive decision to order three Sealy queen-plus Posturepedics. I love a good pillow-top, and, just as important, they are in stock and can be delivered tomorrow.

We buy a bunch of bedding and load up the back of the Escalade. I figure if we put the new duvets and pillows on the old lumpy mattresses, we'll be able to get through the night.

But I figured wrong. The duvets and bedspreads aren't thick enough to compensate. At least not for me, and I find myself not being able to sleep again. For the second night in a row, I stare up at a cracked ceiling medallion and a chandelier that's missing a few crystals.

Another crappy night on a crappy mattress. I am hot and sticky but at least Mom is asleep. Lindsey double-dosed her early enough that her huge snores practically rattle the monitor on my nightstand.

I move to the side of the bed and peel off my flannel nightshirt. I've packed five of them, along with my shearling robe. It isn't that it's too warm for flannel at night; it's too humid and sticky. I toss it onto the floor and turn on one of Mother's naked-lady lamps that sits on a side table. I remember this room from my childhood. It is even more faded now than it was then, but at one time it must have been truly stunning. The walls would have been a deep blue, the moldings and cornices a stark white with gold leaf. The white marble fireplace is flecked with gold and carved with angels.

The sitting room was converted into a big bathroom, and as a kid, I remember thinking the pink toilet, sink, and tub were fabulous. As an adult, I think the room looks like a time capsule from the 1920s or '30s.

Mom's snoring gets even louder, and I tell myself that I will miss the sound of her snoring one day, but I am tired and today is not that day. I stand and wrap the duvet around my bare shoulders. The old wood floor creaks as I move across the room and throw open the double doors to the veranda, feeling like the mistress of the manor. Perhaps there's an ounce of Scarlett in me yet.

I start to shut the doors behind me but pause with my hand on the cut-glass knob. Raphael is on the lam. For a few seconds I ponder the likelihood of him surviving on his own. How long could he last before a heron snapped up his naked little body? Would I hear his scream?

Probably. I shut the door and lean back

against it. When we returned from our mattress-store adventure, I'd discovered the cage door open and Raphael across the entrance hall in the library, swinging upside down from a chandelier and chewing on the crystals. Getting him down from the chandelier had been fairly easy, but getting him to return to his cage was a whole different story. I'd chased him around the house for an hour, trying to shoo him toward the front parlor, but he was having none of it. He squawked and flew from spot to spot, his bright green wings carrying his naked bird body until I lost sight of him somewhere near the dining room. For the rest of the evening, Lindsey walked around as if the damn bird might fall from the sky and peck out her eyes. Mom kept insisting on calling the "doctor."

Neither happened, and Raphael is still hiding somewhere in the house like a prison escapee. The plaster is cool beneath my bare feet and the moist, scented air brushes my cheeks. I haven't examined the balcony in the light of day, and I hope it doesn't give way under my weight. If it does, I'll probably break some bones and end up in the hospital. The prospect doesn't sound too bad, like a vacation maybe, complete with turndown service and intravenous pain medication.

I find an old rocking chair to my left and carefully sit, waiting for it to fall apart. When it doesn't, I tuck my cold feet beneath me. The air smells different here than it does in Seattle, sweet magnolia and jasmine blending with the earthy high notes of the muddy Mississippi.

The sky is filled with streaks of purple and orange, and if I look really hard, I can see long strings of lights. They blink and disappear as a riverboat paddles up the Mississippi.

I know things got a little stressful during the drive to the mattress store, but I have to say that Mom and I had a relatively good day. She randomly asked about her fifth husband, Buzzy Doyle (I don't know why he was called Buzzy when his real name was Lester), and brought up Tony only once. I didn't leave the room or lose my patience or yell the f-word.

I push my braid from my shoulder and wrap the duvet tighter around me. I think I made progress today, and I'm going to continue to change even if it kills me. I can't expect Mom to change. Change has never been a priority for her, and it's less than likely to happen now.

Light from the front porch spreads out

across the patchy grass and up the foot of a live oak. I'm not just going to *try* to get along with Mother. I *am* going to get along with her. I have to remember she can't help her attitude and behavior. Not when she accuses me of stealing her shoes and all her money. Not when she screams about falling out of the sky or when she tells me I'm a lousy driver.

Not even when she mentions that rat bastard Tony. Obviously, her mind retains the good and forgets the bad. She remembers that she often called him when she needed something but forgets that he tried to destroy me. She remembers that she was included in our wedding plans but forgets that I called it off three days before I was supposed to walk down the aisle at St. James. She remembers that she loved him like a son but forgets that he'd cheated on me — her actual daughter — the entire two years we were together. She has no recollection of the day I dropped by his house to show him a copy of the wedding vows that Father Nick had given me and found him in bed with a barista from the Starbucks where we'd first met. Evidently, he'd never stopped schmoozing women over his triple-shot soy espresso macchiato.

As if the cheating itself wasn't devastating

enough, he monetized it for the sleazy talk show and tabloid circuits. Tony is a lawyer in private practice and knows how to give interviews that barely skirt slander laws. He tweeted and Facebooked just enough truth to make his side of the story seem believable. He Instagrammed photos of me in colorful lingerie that I'd sent for his eyes only. At the time, when the photos were being consumed exclusively by the man I loved, they'd seemed artsy and chic, but when posted publicly, they just looked tawdry. He removed them after my lawyer contacted him, but the damage was done. I was publicly humiliated, and people called me a hypocrite for not following my own rules. Specifically, the rules from my 2016 book, *Inner Sassy, Outer Classy,* in which I dedicated several chapters to the dos and don'ts of selfies, sexy pics, and nude photos.

Fern issued several statements on my behalf, but there wasn't a lot I could do to stop his media assault — especially not after he wrote an article for a women's magazine titled "The Truth about Lulu the Love Guru," in which he blatantly lied about every aspect of my personal and professional life.

He was sent a cease-and-desist letter by my attorney, but he ignored it and shot off his mouth to *TMZ*. Finally, I had enough to prove defamation.

From the time I called off the wedding to the day Tony settled out of court, my life was a daily hell. Thirteen months of trying to salvage my reputation and keep Lulu and myself from taking a dive off the deep end.

I don't know how I could have known Tony but not seen him for who he really is: a narcissist who hates to lose at anything. What might make him a good attorney makes him a horrible person.

It took me six months after the nightmare was finally over to relax, and another year to forget him completely. Now Mother reopens the wounds each time she mentions his name. Taking Mom to the condo triggered her memories of him. I hope living at Sutton Hall will encourage her to forget Tony so I don't explode and swear like a teenage boy again.

Still clutching the duvet about myself, I return to the bedroom, praying for a few hours of calm.

Mom's the queen of chaos, the high priestess of shenanigans, the executive chef of fruitcake — calm is not on her menu. Finding calm in the center of chaos is up to me, so I download a meditation app Lindsey suggested. It's called Out of Your Mind:

Meditation for Beginners.

The house is nice and quiet. No yelling or crying, and Mom has stopped snoring like a hibernating bear. I strike a meditative pose in the middle of the lumpy bed and take in a deep breath.

The session starts with soothing music until a man begins to speak in a sedated tone. "Find a comfortable position."

That's easy for him to say because he's not on his family's "practice mattress."

"No cell phones or outside noise."

But without my cell phone, how would I listen to the app?

"Let your eyes close and observe your breath. Observe if your breath flows in your belly."

Doesn't he mean lungs? Okay. Okay, I'll stop overthinking and observe my breath in my belly.

"Imagine filling your belly like a balloon —"

Balloon belly? I take Midol for balloon belly.

"As you exhale, allow your breath to leave your belly in a gentle way. Observe how that feels."

Oh, I didn't listen and already exhaled.

"Go with it. Allow it to be a pleasure. Let it quiet your body. Let it quiet your mind and let go of the counting."

I was supposed to be counting?

"As we begin our journey, imagine yourself in a white room. The walls are white. The floors are white. The ceiling is white. You are surrounded by white light. You are wearing white flowing clothing. Breathe into your belly and imagine you are a part of this white place."

This guy sounds extremely beta.

"Allow the white surroundings to fill your center."

The kind of beta who can't figure out why he never gets the hot chick of his dreams. Men like this guy usually never get married and are very difficult to coach. They insist that women want beta men, but they don't listen when I tell them that beta shouldn't mean wimpy. Wimpy attracts wimpy. Not hot chicks. They need to step up and grow a pair or they'll never attract the woman of their dreams. Too bad they usually don't listen.

"You are walking past a smooth-flowing stream."

Wait. How did I get to a stream?

I give up and toss my phone on the nightstand. I consider trying a meditation app by a woman next time as I search for the least lumpy place on the mattress. Without Mom yelling and snoring, the house is so quiet and still. I would say "like a tomb" if I weren't haunted by the presence of the actual tombs right outside in the Sutton cemetery. I know Mom wants to "visit" her kin, but I hope she forgets about it for a while.

The creaking sound of footsteps draws my attention to the closed door. It can't be Mom because no alarms have gone off. I wait for Lindsey's knock, but she's pacing up and down the hall. The creak of her footsteps is followed by slow squeaks and groans of the old wood floors. I'm wondering if she has restless legs or something when a sudden thump has me out of bed and heading for the door. I am afraid she's fallen, but the hall is so dark I won't be able to make out the outline of her body on the floor.

"Lou Ann," she whispers.

I look toward her bedroom and think I see her head poking out the door, looking back at me. "Yeah," I whisper back, although I don't know why we're whispering.

"Was that you?"

"No. I thought it was you."

"No."

The creaky footsteps continue from the bottom of the long, curved staircase now.

"Is that Mom?" God, I hope she isn't up and raring for round two. I'm exhausted and afraid I'll break my vow of patience. "Did you set her alarm?"

"You were the last one out of her room."

Crap. Maybe she just wants to spoon. Not ideal, but I'd rather do that than get yelled at again.

There's a scraping sound like someone is dragging a shovel in the foyer. "That's not Patricia! Someone's in the house!"

I might have forgotten to set Mom's alarm, but I made sure all the doors were locked before I came upstairs. It's possible someone's come through a window, but I need to stay calm and not give in to my fear. Scared shitless is not my best look. "Hold on," I whisper just in case, and run to the mantel to grab at the outline of a candlestick. It's heavy in my hand and could deliver a lethal blow to the head. Of course, that would mean I'd have to swing at close range in the dark and I'd rather not. I turn around and let out a startled little scream as Lindsey runs into me. I almost fall backward into the fireplace but catch myself in time.

"It's headed up here again," she whispers, and I can see the fear in the whites of her eyes. I tiptoe into the hall with Lindsey close behind. She puts her hands on the back of my shoulders as if I'm a human shield.

"Why am I first? You're taller and stronger."

"I have a lot more years to live than you."

A lot? I'm only twelve years older than she is, and it makes more sense for *her* to be the shield. Over the sound of Lindsey's breathing and my own heart palpitations, I hear the creak-creak-squeak of footsteps coming up the old steps. "Mom?" There's no answer and I'm formally scared shitless now. I raise the candlestick over my head.

"Ouch."

"Sorry," I whisper as I run my free hand along the wall and flip on the lights. I can't see anything and call out, "I've got a really big gun. I'll shoot a really big hole in you if you don't get out of this house."

We don't hear anything in response and move closer to the top of the stairs to meet our fate. I peek over the banister, my heart in my throat. There's nothing there. "Hand me the sawed-off," I say really loud, just in case. I keep still and listen. Nothing but the sound of Lindsey's breathing. "I think they're gone," I whisper over my shoulder.

"Are you sure?"

Not at all. "Pretty sure. I don't see anyone."

Lindsey drops her hands and moves out from behind me to take a look for herself. "I don't see anyone either, but we both heard it. Right?" I take this as a rhetorical question until she repeats herself like she's frantic for confirmation. "Right?"

I lower my candlestick. "Right." I grab her arm as she leans out further. "Be careful. The banister is loose."

"I don't think anyone is down there."

"Right."

"They must have left."

"Right."

"We're safe now."

"Then why are we still whispering?"

"Ghosts."

My legs feel weak, so I take a seat at the top of the stairs. My heart rate is dropping to normal, but I still have a healthy grip on the candlestick. I can't explain what's just happened. I know what I heard, but I don't believe in haunted houses or spooky stuff in general. I'm sure there's a rational explanation, like the old house is settling or wind or, God forbid, an actual swamp rat. "You watch too many horror movies," I say, at a normal volume this time.

"I'm never watching another scary movie as long as I live." Lindsey sits next to me and shakes her head with conviction. "I'm done with ghosts and witches and demon possessions."

This is southern Louisiana. The heart of voodoo queens and hoodoo curses. "You didn't mention zombies."

"Oh, I love zombies. Zombies aren't real. Not like chainsaw massacres and evil birds."

9

March 18

Mom's DNA and man buffet.

How many men does it take to move a four-poster bed made of solid walnut?

Five. Four to do the work and one to tell them how to do it. That one person is Simon. "When you boys are done passing a good time," he hollers down the stairs, "these old mattresses aren't going to haul themselves out."

Apparently, I'd paid the mattress store for delivery but not for setup and removal, and no cash bribe could induce the two delivery-men to haul the new ones up the curved stairs or take the old ones out. They'd dumped them in the middle of the parlor and said, "That's not part of the job," as they'd walked out, practically slamming the door in their haste, leaving me and Mom and Lindsey staring at the mattresses and box springs. Sleep-deprived and on the brink of an emotional breakdown, I couldn't think of a solution.

"Call the doctor," Mom suggested, as if the man who'd called me a swamp rat and saddled me with an obnoxious bird was going to do me any favors.

I ignored her and looked to Lindsey, who still seemed a little pale after last night's creaking-house shenanigans. "Suggestions?"

"This is above my pay grade," she said, like I was going to tell her to haul the mattresses upstairs on her own back.

"Call the doctor."

Too tired to argue, I dialed the first number on Simon's business card and handed the phone to Mom. To my shock and Mom's delight, Simon arrived within an hour with three beefy men and a red-headed guy so skinny his wrists and elbows poked out of his skin.

"This isn't a debutante come-out party," Simon hollers down again, sounding like a drill sergeant with a fresh crop of soldiers. "We gotta lot of work before you get your cucumber sandwich and Sprite."

"Ohh." Mom sighs. "I wore blue at my come-out party." She stands next to me near the bottom of the stairs, transfixed by the buffet of men before her. She's wearing her yellow velour tracksuit and white sneakers, and I fixed her hair in a braided bun. She painted her lips a bright flamingo pink in anticipation of "our guests."

"Our guests" are charging me a hundred dollars per man, and because I am more my mother's daughter than I like to admit, I pulled on a pair of fabulous black jacquard pants with just a hint of dark-blue plaid. My blue silk blouse could use a touch-up with an iron, but I didn't pack one so I'm out of luck. I "put on my face" and braided my hair and shoved my feet into ankle boots with a modest two-inch heel. A lifetime of Mom's warning to "always look your best just in case" is embedded in my DNA.

"Don't lean on that rail. Y'all'll be in a world of sufferin' if it gives out," the drill sergeant warns. "Where's Jim?"

"Sure hope no one breaks a neck," Mom says.

"Comin'." The skinny guy with fuzzy red hair runs from the parlor and grabs the tail end of a mattress.

"Someone might break a neck."

The last time I glanced into the parlor, Lindsey had set herself up in the corner of the couch, where she was texting while keeping an eye on the empty birdcage as if

Raphael might materialize like it was an intergalactic portal.

The stupid bird is still at large, but he did leave evidence of his continued existence: a clue dropped on the white table in the breakfast nook. A disgusting bird-poop clue that made Lindsey gag and run for the bathroom.

"That skinny fella is gonna break his neck."

"He's stronger than he looks." I glance at Mom and see she's wringing her hands as she watches the "skinny fella."

"Yep, he's gonna break his neck, all right."

Before I am tempted to break someone else's neck, I follow behind the mattress. By the time I reach the top of the stairs, Simon is in Great-grandmother's room, pointing and barking out orders to the two men staring at the bed. He's wearing a black polo shirt and has a ball cap stuffed in the back pocket of his jeans. I sneeze from all the dust in the air, and he looks over his shoulder at me.

"You sure you want to keep the canopy?" he asks.

"Mom wants it." I sneeze again and grab a tissue from the box sitting atop the delicately carved dressing table. Two more sneezes and I grab the whole box. The slender heels of my boots tap across the room and I slip outside onto the balcony. I debate whether to close the doors. I doubt Raphael is hiding in the bedroom, and there's a hundred years of dust that needs an outlet. I leave it open and when the men fire up their drills, I figure another hundred years' worth is about to get stirred up, too.

I blow my nose and stuff the tissue in my pocket. If the bird wanted to escape, he would right about now, but his naked bird body is nowhere in sight.

Simon pokes his head out the door. "I hear Ray-feel is on the loose somewhere," he says as if he read my mind. "If he gets out, a heron will get him for sure."

I look across at him. "If you're worried, find Ray-feel and take him with you when you leave."

He walks across the balcony and shakes the wrought-iron-and-wood railing like he's testing it. "Solid," he says.

"Are you trying to change the subject?"

His hair shines like black coal and a filigree shadow cuts across his wide chest as he turns toward me. "What subject?"

"The bird."

"What bird is that, Ms. Lou Ann?" His grin is full of cool charm and hot intentions that reach the corners of sun-creased eyes. I have to wonder how many times he's practiced that lady-killer smile in the mirror. I'm immune, but even I have to fight the urge to check my breath and reach for a Tic Tac just in case.

I decide to let the subject of Raphael go — for now. "I need to talk to you about the staircase railing. Obviously, it's a safety issue." Dust rolls out the door and I sneeze and grab a tissue.

"Bless you."

"Thanks." It settles on my silk blouse, reminding me that I need to find a laundry service. "Do you also repair stair railings?" I ask, and toss the Kleenex box onto the old rocker.

He nods. "What do you have in mind?"

"A railing," I answer slowly because I don't know exactly what he's asking. "With wood . . . and nails."

He cocks his head to the side and squints one eye against the sunlight. "Thanks for clearing that up. I thought you might want peppermint sticks."

"No." I shake my head. "Wood and nails are fine."

Simon grabs the hat from his back pocket and slides it onto his head. "Do you want to replace it completely? Or do you want it repaired or restored?"

I understand the first option. "What's the difference between repair and restore?"

"At least ten grand." I stare at him, waiting to hear that he's joking. Instead, his green eyes stare back at me from beneath the bill of his cap. "We can repair it for about four thousand. A full restoration takes quite a bit longer and costs a whole lot more."

"Ten thousand more?"

"At least," he repeats himself. "It'll look beautiful when we're done, but it won't match the oxidized varnish on the stairs or floors. I recommend you have those done at the same time."

"Are the stairs and floors included in the ten grand?" I rub the kink in my neck and wonder what to do.

He laughs. "No, ma'am."

Somehow, I thought that was going to be his answer. If I replace it, Mom will complain that it's not the same and she'll want the old one put back. If I have it repaired, she'll notice something's different and want the old pieces put back. If I have it restored, it'll cost me a lot of money. "Where can I get a second opinion?" On the upside, all three options will make Mom happy because she'll get to see Simon more often.

"I'm in the business of giving *my* opinion,

but you're free to find someone on the internet."

I guess that means he's unwilling to suggest anyone else.

"If I were you, I'd get a plumber out here first, before some of those pipes rust out."

The plumbing definitely needs repair. The knot in the crook in my neck gets tighter and it's so humid my dusty silk blouse starts to stick to my skin. "I'm afraid to ask, but what about the electrical wiring?"

"I noticed the hundred-foot extension cord." He chuckles as he shoves his hands into the pockets of his jeans, his thumbs hooked over the tops and pointed at his fly.

Not that I look.

"There are two outdoor power posts, one on either side of the house. One's about ten feet out from the library window." He takes a hand from his pocket and points. "Making that one there about thirty feet closer than the kitchen."

Yeah, I know. I'm bad with measurements.

"You should probably have an electrician come out, just to be on the safe side."

I half-jokingly ask, "Are we going to burn to death in a fiery inferno?"

One corner of his mouth kicks up. "I doubt it will be an inferno."

That's about as reassuring as his smile,

and I've gone from half joking to half panic.

"Y'all should be fine." His smile turns to a grin, the same one he wore when he told me that I was sitting where "we laid poor old Jasper out." He rocks back on the heels of his boots and adds, "The outlets will likely blow a fuse before throwing sparks."

Fuses? Throwing sparks? "Tell me you're kidding."

"Partly."

"Which part?"

"The throwing sparks part."

What does that mean? "So, will the fuses likely blow, or are we going to die in an inferno?"

He stares at me for several moments like I'm slow in the head. "No . . . sparks. I was pulling your leg." I must look as skeptical as I feel, because he adds, "I've worked on this house for close to twenty-five years now. I said y'all should be fine."

"Twenty-five years and the house is falling apart?" His brows lower over his eyes. "No offense."

"Uh-huh." He adjusts the brim of his hat. "It was always feast or famine with Jasper and restoration. When he could afford me, he'd call, and we'd get to work on his latest project."

That would explain why some parts of the

house are more time-warped than others. "Why didn't he hire someone more afford-able and get the bathrooms fixed, too?" I know that's probably rude, but I'm genu-inely curious.

He shrugs. "You get what you pay for." He answers my next question before I can ask it. "We're standing on one of the resto-rations I did for him."

I glance up and down the veranda, look-ing for cracks and peeling paint, but there are none. In the light of day, it's in beautiful condition. The wrought iron is shiny black, and the crisp white balustrades and railing look as I imagine they did when the house was built.

"That side" — he points to his left — "fell off about three years ago."

Of course it did. "How much to get someone to check the pipes for leaks? And the electric, just to be on the safe side."

He shakes his head. "I'm not an electri-cian or a plumber."

"Can you suggest someone?" I ask before I remember he isn't in the suggestion busi-ness and I should try the internet.

"Sure." There's a heavy crash like someone dropped a part of Great-grandmother's bed. "I'll give you some names before I leave," he says over his shoulder as he walks into the house.

I follow behind him and sneeze only twice as I quickly move to Great-grandfather's room across the hall. My memories of this room are more vivid than those of other rooms. The furniture isn't as massive as I recall from childhood memory, but it does conjure visions of Henry VIII. The focal point is the imposing half tester bed with leaping stags carved into the head- and footboards. The half tester is held up with two carved posts and adorned with a big set of antlers.

By the time I was born, Great-grandfather was long dead, and this is the room Mother and I always used when we visited. I remember being terrified that the two posts would snap and the tester would smash me flat in the middle of the night. Or that the antlers would fall off and run me through. Mother used to laugh and tell me stories of when she used to jump and roll all around on the bed as a kid.

That did not reassure me.

This room is the mirror opposite of the one across the hall but is definitely more suited for a man. The walls are covered with faded murals portraying men hunting everything from deer to ducks. Over the black marble fireplace hangs a big painting of a white horse named General, according to the writing on the dusty frame. No portrait of a wife or family. Just a horse.

I move to the windows looking out at the backyard, overgrown hedges, and the garçonnière beyond. The glass is wavy and in dire need of a cleaning, but I can catch glimpses of sunlight like tiny pieces of tinfoil bobbing in the lazy bayou. Here and there I can see remnants of the past that have yet to be completely taken over by kudzu and honeysuckle. At one time, Sutton Hall was a working sugar plantation with all that implies — but, of course, we don't talk about that. There are a lot of things we Suttons don't talk about.

A white wrought-iron bench tilts to one side in the overgrown garden below, and a tall rusted pipe sticks up from a crumbling fountain. All that's left of the original kitchen, to my right, are a big iron pot and a decaying brick foundation.

As I look out, I feel neither the familial pride nor the longing that Mother feels about this place. I see a sad past gone to ruin, and I wonder why someone would leave a bench to rust in the elements.

Behind the garage I can see the cobblestone path that leads to the cemetery and towering white tombs. Mother will want to go to those tombs and pay a visit to the glorious dead. I'm not a scaredy-cat like Lindsey, but I'm not looking forward to it. I don't want to think about Mother dying or get into a discussion about what she wants engraved on her tombstone. I don't want my memories of our time at Sutton Hall to be overshadowed by the talk of death.

"The boys tell me you're a love expert."

I turn toward Simon as he enters the room. I knew it was only a matter of time before the news got out.

"They want to ask about your tips for impressing women."

"They or you?"

One corner of his mouth turns up. "I got that part covered."

I'll just bet he does. I hold up three fingers and count off the basics. "Take a shower. Bar nuts aren't a dinner date. Don't call your ex-girlfriend a bitch until at least the third date."

"You get paid for that?" he scoffs as he shakes his head. "Shoot, you need to come up with something that their mommas didn't teach them a long time ago. No offense."

"Uh-huh." I raise my fingers once more. "Brush your teeth," I count off. "Squirrel is not a protein choice. Don't date your sister."

He raises a brow. "Or marry your first cousin."

He got me on that one. I laugh and raise a fourth finger. "Never swim in your own gene pool."

"I'll let the guys know your expert tips." He points to the room across the hall and changes the subject. "The furniture is ready to go downstairs. Do y'all want to paint the room before we set it up?"

"Mom says no." I don't feel like an expert on anything anymore. Least of all on dating. "She wants to keep everything the same as she remembers."

"I should have guessed." He chuckles. "Y'all Suttons cling to your clutter. At the end of the day, you can't take your hoarded treasures with you to the grave."

"I don't really know my family." The room is filled with oversize furniture, but I wouldn't call it cluttered. Not like the back staircase. "But they don't seem to be hoarders."

"Have you been in the attic?"

"Never." As a child, I was scared shitless just looking at the closed door. Coming back as a savvy, well-traveled, educated adult, I still find it spooky as hell. I don't believe in spooky stuff, but after last night, I'm not a *non*believer either. "Is it bad?"

"I wouldn't recommend going up there without a pith helmet and camp shovel."

I look up at the ceiling, and I think I can safely predict that I won't be climbing the stairs at the end of the hall anytime soon.

"Jasper had a running catalog in his head of every last thing crammed up there. That fireplace screen Ms. Patricia's asked about is probably hidden in a chest or hanging from the rafters."

"Maybe she'll forget," I say, even though I know Mom will forget what she had for breakfast before she forgets about that screen.

"Some folks say the Suttons are short on common sense but have long memories. That was true with Jasper."

"What folks?" Did I just say "folks"? I never say "folks." It sounds so . . . folksy. Then again, I never thought I'd say the f-word either. Welcome to my new life.

"The old families still living in the parish. The Guidrys." His boots stir up dust as he moves to the windows and looks out. "The Browns at Roselea. My folks are still in the big house at Sugar Hill." He looks off in the distance and places his hand on the window casing. "Ms. Patricia probably remembers my maman, Mazie Landers. They're about the same age and Maman remembers every

162

one and 'em."

I lean a hip into the footboard and cross my arms beneath my breasts. "Mom has Alzheimer's. Her long-term memory is better than her short-term, so she might remember."

He drops his hand and slowly turns toward me. "I'm sorry to hear that."

"That's why we're here." I unfold one arm long enough to point in the cemetery's general direction. "She wants to be buried next to Grandmother."

"Of course," he says, as if I'd told him water is wet and money is green.

"I hope that isn't for a while, but no one knows. She could live for five more years or pass away in six months." I drop my hands to my sides and shake my head. "This house will fall down around our ears if we last more than five years."

"Nah. The wood rot isn't that bad."

"Tell me you're pulling my leg again."

"You're in bayou country. Can't get away from wood rot." He points toward the hall with his chin. "It's just about empty over there. Do you want some of this furniture moved into that room?"

My brain is still on wood rot, and I mentally shake my head. I hadn't thought about moving things around up here, but the windows are better in Great-grandmother's room, and the view's better too. I like throwing open the double doors and walking out onto the veranda. Especially now that I know it's not going to collapse.

We stand side by side, his shoulder on the same level as my ear, and stare up at the half tester. One of the men could get an eye poked out, and I don't even know if I have homeowner's insurance. "It's heavy."

"Several hundred pounds, for sure."

"Do you want to move it?"

"Do you want to sleep on it?"

I glance at him. "If it's moved, will it fit back together, solid like it is now?"

He shrugs. "Sure. Why not?"

"I don't want to get impaled in the middle of the night." What if it has wood rot or the screws are stripped? I'd be alone, pinned to the mattress or smashed like a pancake, Mom's snores cracking the plaster walls and reverberating from the monitor, and no one to hear my screams. "Will bolts fall out if I roll around and shake the bed?"

"Mais." He looks at me out of the corners of his eyes, which seem to turn deeper green when he asks, "What're you planning, tee Lou Ann?"

10

Mom says periwinkle. I see red.

Sometime during dinner, Raphael re-appeared in his cage. I wonder where he's been hiding out and if he's responsible for the shredded roll of toilet paper in Mom's bathroom.

"Where have you been?" I am very careful not to startle him as I slide my hand inside his cage and place his water crock in the brackets. His eyes are closed, and I gingerly pull my hand back out. "It took half a bottle of Lysol kitchen cleaner to get rid of your little gift in the kitchen." He yawns and sticks out his creepy pink-and-black tongue. "If you do it again, no more tasty seed sticks for you." His beady eyes open and stare right at me. "Pretty bird," I lie, so he won't get uppity before I can finish feeding him. Down the hall, Mother's television is blasting out game shows; Lindsey is in her room upstairs. Once again, I am left to deal with this crazy bird on my own. He watches me as I hang his food bowl. "Such a nice boy." To prove me wrong, he screeches like I've plunged a knife into his naked breast.

My wrist bumps the cage as I jerk my hand out. "You're an asshole, Raphael." I firmly close the cage door and make sure it's shut tight this time. No more nocturnal flights for him.

I follow the sound of Mom's television, hoping to spend a little time with her before saying good night. She and Lindsey set up her room earlier while I worked. And by that, I mean Lindsey set up her room earlier while Mom pointed and ordered her about.

Mom sits on the side of her four-poster bed wearing a lacy black nightgown; her hair falls down her back in rich brown waves. A rumpled bag of Pirate's Booty is next to her right hand. Minus the popcorn, the room looks like an old bordello with rich red-and-gold bedding and fancy pillows. "The House of the Rising Sun" plays in my head as the scene is indelibly burnt in my brain.

"There is one letter *p,*" Pat Sajak announces from a big TV sitting on the walnut mantel.

"Peter Piper!" Mom yells out.

I don't tell her that's three *p*'s. "How do you like it in here?"

She shakes her head. "No fireplace screen."

After everything that was moved in here for her, she's still complaining about that stupid fireplace screen. I'm tempted to tell her Wynonna stole it in hopes she'll eventually move on. Oh wait, I'm talking about my mother, who hasn't moved on from the loss of her kitten heels years ago.

"I can't change the channel." She points the remote across the room and jabs at the buttons with her finger.

Without saying a word, I take the remote from her hand and turn it the right way. I don't want to embarrass her, so I say, "That remote is tricky." Her brow is creased as she stares at the television control, and I add, "I get it mixed up all the time."

"Do you need glasses?"

"No." I shake my head and ask through a yawn, "Do you want me to braid your hair, so it won't be tangled when you get up?"

She nods, and I grab a brush and a hair elastic from her nightstand. When I was young, I brushed her hair for hours while we watched TV together. "Remember when I gave you side buns like Princess Leia?"

"Who?" she asks, and reaches for Booty.

"No one." I slide the elastic around my wrist and brush the tangles from her long, dark hair. "Do you want me to take you to get your ends trimmed?"

"G," she calls out around a mouth filled with popcorn.

I glance at the television. "Paris is for lovers."

"What?"

"I solved the puzzle. Paris is for lovers."

I part her hair as she changes the channel to *Hollywood Squares.* I guess she doesn't like that I guessed the answer.

"That John Denver is a handsome man."

It's John Davidson, but who cares? She laughs at a joke Paul Lynde makes about a mini pig, and I wonder if she really gets it or is just laughing along. She is so engrossed in the game show and her popcorn that I wonder if she knows I'm with her, braiding her hair like I used to.

I lean to one side and smooth her hair with my hand. My neck pinches, and I slowly move my chin to my shoulder. "Crap. Ouch."

"Don't curse."

I guess she knows I'm here. "Sorry," I apologize, even though *crap* isn't a curse word. Not like *shit,* anyway. "My shoulder hurts."

168

"Call the foxy doctor," she says without taking her eyes from the television. "He'll give you something."

"Simon? He's a house doctor."

She licks a sprinkling of powdered cheese from her lips. "He comes to the house."

"He restores houses for a living."

"Yep, that's right. Not many doctors come to the house these days."

" 'Squeezed and pulled and hurt my neck.' " I mutter a quote from *Rain Man.*

"Call the foxy doctor."

"He's performing an emergency appendectomy."

"I always wanted to marry a doctor," she says as she flips through channels before settling on an old episode of *Family Feud.* "That Peter sure is handsome."

I glance at the television as Richard Dawson asks the Brown family, "Name something you blow."

"A job interview," I say, before I forget that I'm not supposed to answer.

Mom glances over her shoulder and gives me the stink eye. "Periwinkle," she yells, and returns her stinky eyes to the television.

"A red light," the contestant answers.

"Periwinkle."

By the time I slide the elastic from my wrist and finish Mom's hair, she's yelled

"Periwinkle" six more times, and I want to stab my brain.

"Periwinkle." That's seven, and I can't take any more. My head hurts, my shoulder aches, and I feel the f-word bubbling up inside me. I don't want to lose it. I recognize the warning signs, and I don't want to do anything that might provoke Rattlesnake Patty into baring her fangs. I kiss her cheek good night.

"Periwinkle!"

My eye twitches and I'm hurrying to the doorway when I remember, "Lindsey has the day off tomorrow, and I think she's shopping for clothes afterward." At least, I assume she meant clothes shopping when she said she was going to the mall.

"Why?" Mom asks without taking her gaze from *Family Feud.*

Clothes shopping is something we all need to do — at least, Lindsey and I do. Mom wears velour and doesn't seem affected. "It's her day off."

"She's fat."

"Mom!" I thought she'd said that the other night because she was out of her mind and raging. "That's not nice." I frown at her, but she isn't paying attention to me. "Don't say that to Lindsey." I see how the girl pulls at her tops, and I suddenly feel protective of her. "She's a nice girl, and I don't want you to hurt her feelings."

"She should have said 'periwinkle.'"

When she doesn't respond, I ask over the sound of buzzers, "Mom, are you listening to me?"

She tears her attention from the television, and her gaze is a little more vacant than it was ten minutes ago. "That Richard is a foxy man." Before I completely lose my mind, I leave her to gush over the game show host. Cheesy theme music follows me down the hall and up the stairs. Thankfully, I can't hear it by the time I stop in the doorway of Lindsey's yellow-and-white bedroom. She is kneeling beside the sleigh bed, tucking in her clean sheets, and I avert my eye from her plumber's cleavage. Tomorrow will be our first day without Lindsey since we arrived at Sutton Hall. Mom and I'll be just fine on our own, but I'm nervous that something will set her off and Lindsey won't be here to defuse Mom's anger. "When are you leaving tomorrow?"

"Ten thirty."

I'll have to be *extra* patient to avoid Rattlesnake Patty. "If you're near a store that sells insect spray, can you buy a few gallons?"

"Sure." She laughs, but I'm serious. "I'll

171

protect you from bugs."

I'd rather have toxic spray, but I return the favor. "And I'll protect you from Raphael."

"Deal." She walks toward me, and we shake hands. "I hate that evil bird."

"You're getting the raw end of the deal. There is only one evil bird but a million evil bugs."

"I'd rather encounter a million bugs." She drops my hand and says, "Thanks for the nice mattress and soft sheets and everything you do for me." I'm about to ask her what "everything" is when she adds, "My new health insurance is better and cheaper than my old Blue Shield."

"Actually, I'm selfishly baiting a trap so you'll never leave me and Mom."

"You're not selfish." She laughs as if I'm joking, but I'm not.

It's hard to admit, but I can be selfish sometimes. In my own defense, it's embedded in my DNA. Like making myself look good even when I don't have anywhere to go and I'm not leaving the house.

I tell her good night and turn out the hall lights as I move to the blue room. There are two kinds of selfish: the healthy kind and the unhealthy kind. I've written rules and blogs and book chapters on the subject. In speeches and podcasts, I explain the differences.

There is a trick to balancing the two, but somewhere my scales got off-balance and I got absorbed with pushing Lulu to bigger and better heights. Fighting to keep my business going during the hell years with Tony didn't help my single-minded, borderline-unhealthy focus.

I keep an eye on the chandelier and push a button switch on the bedroom wall. No sparks fall from the ceiling, but in the dim light, the half tester looks just as imposing in this room as it did across the hall. So do the few other pieces of Great-grandfather's furniture placed about the room, but at least I have somewhere to unpack my clothes now.

The wardrobe can easily accommodate a family of three, and the dresser is almost as tall as I am. The old drawers smell of cedar and beeswax and don't stick as badly as I'd presumed. Before leaving the cold wind and sleet of Seattle, I'd packed wool suits and sweaters, pink Ugg boots and flannel nightshirts, which just goes to show how chaotic my life had gotten. Boots and flannel don't go with springtime in Louisiana. At least not when you're used to March in the Pacific Northwest, where moisture comes in the form of chilly rain instead of steamy humidity. Lindsey has the right idea. I need a trip to the mall.

I swing open the veranda doors and take a deep breath of Mississippi Delta air. Even I, a woman who'd rather be at the Windsor Court Hotel, enjoying pralines and dry air-conditioning, admit that I am enchanted by riverboat lights filtered through branches of towering trees swathed with Spanish moss. I pull another cleansing breath into the bottom of my lungs and let it out. There is a stillness up here on the balcony, a quiet that allows my heart to beat without worry and calms my mind. My head is clearer and I can think about moving forward.

My business has survived the tour cancellations, and I managed to work both yesterday and today. Margie called with an offer from the publisher of my last three books. It was a good offer, but I turned it down. It wasn't an easy decision. The old Lulu would have sealed the deal with a signature and a glass of champagne in Margie's apartment on New York's Upper East Side. There is a huge part of me that misses that life, but as rough as the past few days have been, Mom is my priority. Other business opportunities will come my way, but the opportunity to spend time with Mother will not.

An insect buzzes in my ear, ending my enchantment. I shut the doors tight and change for bed. No more flannel — tonight it's just a sports bra and panties. Just in case, I shake the footboard and wait for the half tester to collapse. It doesn't move, and I'm satisfied that I won't be impaled tonight.

"What're you planning, tee Lou Ann?" Simon hadn't even cracked a smile after that. He'd just turned on his heels and walked from the room, leaving the question hanging in the air and me to wonder what *tee* meant. He'd already compared me to a swamp rat, so I'm not holding out hope that it was a compliment.

I'm still mulling it over when I turn off the lights and pull back sheets that I'd brought from Seattle. Moonbeams pour through the veranda door and windows, spilling a golden path across the hardwood floor to my feet, and I grab my phone from the side table. Beneath the covers, I settle in and plump pillows behind my back. The light from my phone flashes across my face as I Google the meaning of *tee Lou Ann.* It takes longer than I expect, especially when I get sidetracked with the meaning of Cajun sayings and slang. I also discover that Simon's rougarou is a swamp-dwelling werewolf. According to legend, I have to be careful not to get entranced and led deep into the swamp, and I should especially avoid the Honey Island Swamp Monster.

Note to self: Avoid the damn swamp altogether. That means the bayou too.

Just as I'm ready to call it a night, I find what I've been searching over an hour for.

Tee or *T:* small, little, petite.

I don't know if Simon meant it as a compliment, but it's better than *swamp rat.*

I put my phone on the side table and snuggle into my pillows. I don't remember falling asleep, but I wake feeling great for the first time since arriving at Sutton Hall. No lumpy mattress. No creepy ghost sounds. No hibernating-bear snores from the monitors. I even take a really quick bath in the pink tub. Unfortunately, not quick enough, and the water turns cold while I'm halfway through shampooing my hair. On the bright side, Lindsey bathed before me and has flushed the pipes of rust.

An Uber arrives precisely at ten thirty and Lindsey tells me one last time, "I left a list of numbers and the salmon recipe for lunch on the kitchen counter. I put Patricia's Xanax in the cupboard above the refrigerator. If she gets anxious, get her to put half a pill under her tongue."

"Okay," I call after her as she gets in the

car. Lindsey obviously doesn't trust me not to overdose Mother and knock her out for a couple of days.

I watch from the doorway as she is driven toward the road and am fleetingly concerned that she's bolting, escaping the madness, and never coming back. Then I recall how happy she was when I offered her the same health insurance that I provide for all my employees, effectively roping her in and tying her down with a half hitch. I close the front door and smile.

"Is that Earl?" Mom yells from the front parlor, where she is settled with scrapbooks and photo albums.

"No."

I grab my laptop before I join Mom on an olive-green velvet chesterfield that I'm guessing is fairly new to the house. If you consider circa 1972 reasonably new. A delicate goblet made of Venetian glass is on a side table next to her. It's pink and gold and filled with sweet tea. "Was it Tony?"

I don't answer, but Raphael makes a gurgling sound. He bobs his head as if he's the cool kid in school, listening to beats that only he can hear. "I hate to be the bearer of bad news, Raph, but you can't be cool if you look like a plucked chicken." He flaps his wings, and I warn, "Behave." He opens his beak, and I steel myself for his scream, but he just yawns.

"Was it Tony?" she persists.

"Tony's an asshole," I say, before I remember that I'm supposed to be extra patient today.

Mom does the usual gasping thing as I open the laptop, and we indulge in online therapy. We shop for everything from shorts and summer shirts to light cotton dresses and skirts. I buy respectable summer nighties, and Mom picks out stripper lingerie that I know she'll never wear. I'm still planning to go to the mall, but I can't take Mom with me. She hasn't been alone with Lindsey yet, and I have to make sure she's comfortable without me before I leave her.

When we're done, I'm all shopped out, but Mom cracks open a photo album and starts ordering from it like it's her own personal Google net.

"I want this lamp."

"Which lamp?" I'd rather skip out on old family photo time and work, but I've read that thumbing through familiar pictures helps to stimulate the Alzheimer's brain. Nothing will stop the progression of the disease, but recalling even small things is a healthy exercise and makes her feel good about herself.

"This tall one."

She points to a tintype photo and a floor lamp behind a row of dour-looking women. "That has to be an oil lamp and probably isn't around anymore."

"It's here somewhere."

I remember what Simon said about Sutton treasures buried in the attic. "You're probably right."

She moves her finger to a black-and-white portrait of a beautiful woman in a wedding gown. "And this is Great-grandmere." It's the right era, so she could be right. The picture was painted in front of potted ferns, clustered next to the fireplace in the library. At the bottom, almost obscured by a long lace veil, is a fireplace screen with a beagle painted on it.

"Look." I point it out.

"What?"

"Here, it's Great-grandfather's beagle screen."

She looks up at me. "Great-grandpere had a beagle?"

"Yes!" She's only been obsessing about it for days. "It's painted on the fireplace screen you want."

She shakes her head and her nose pinches. "That's ugly."

I'm about to ask if she still wants it but

stop myself just in time. She's obviously forgotten all about the screen, and I can cross it off my search-and-find list. Thank God I don't have to put on a pith helmet and spend my day sucking up dust bunnies in that attic.

Mom moves her finger to photos of various tables and knickknacks. "And these too."

"I think I saw those in the pink bedroom." The day started out well and is getting better. We have a great time laughing at a black-and-white of Mom standing on the front porch and sticking her tongue out at the person behind the camera.

"I was five. Momma wanted me to tap-dance like Shirley Temple."

Decked out in crinoline and curls, Mom looked like an escapee from the Good Ship Lollipop. "I guess you didn't feel like dancing."

Mom shakes her head. "I didn't like being called Shirley."

Amazing that a sixty-nine-year-old memory is still embedded in her brain.

She turns a page in the album. "I want this." Her attention has landed on a silver tea service on a sideboard in the dining room. "It's on the third floor with all of Great-grandmere's silver."

"Third floor?"

I recognize the look pulling her brows together. "Up there." She points at the ceiling. "You know."

Yes, I know. The old me would have employed my best distraction techniques. The new me closes my eyes and whispers, "The attic."

"Find me this and this here and I have to have that."

I listen to her rattle off just about everything she sees. The old me would have plotted an escape by pretending to make an urgent phone call. Or maybe I'd have brought up Earl and his Craftmatic. The old me would have suspected Mom of torturing me on purpose. The new, extra-patient me says, "I'm happy to get anything you want."

What I thought would take a few hours in the hot attic drags on until it becomes part of Mom's daily routine. I haul family treasures to the parlor for her inspection, and she looks through photo albums and orders more.

The attic is hot and musty, and I open all the dormer windows to let the slightly cooler air from the Mississippi blow through. Each time I leave for the day, I make sure to close them tight in a futile attempt to keep flying insects from taking up permanent residency. I hire a local exterminator to spray the entire house, inside and out. However, I have no doubt that the tough Southern bugs and spiders will rise again.

There are close to two hundred years of history in the attic, documented mostly by fragile newspaper articles, yellowed letters, and several family Bibles inscribed with births and deaths of members of the Sutton family. I am intrigued by them, but I remain emotionally detached from the people who lived, worked, and died here.

The huge space is almost as packed as Simon led me to believe it'd be when he was here several weeks ago. Trunks of every shape and size are heaped on top of one another, filled with everything from clothes and portraits to records for the Victrola phonograph in the front parlor. Different eras of furniture are stacked in high piles. Some pieces just need to be cleaned, reupholstered, and stuffed with foam rather than horsehair and moss. Some furniture made of wicker and rattan is beyond repair. An exceptionally creepy baby carriage leans to one side and has big holes in the bottom. It's a fire hazard and needs to be hauled out and thrown away, but I am not about to risk Mother finding out that I've tossed away family treasures and getting anxious and angry.

The attic is so eerily quiet that the slightest sound, like a floor creak or raindrops on a dormer window, makes me jump. If I were a woman with a weak bladder, I might be in danger of an accident — especially if the baby carriage rolls toward me for no reason.

I know. I'm starting to sound like Lindsey, but I still don't believe in spooky stuff. If I'm wrong, the spirits of Suttons past had better behave themselves or I'll call the ghost busters. The electricians and plumbers I've hired are starting tomorrow; what are a few more people underfoot?

Mom wants Great-grandmother's silver tea service, and I find it in one of two camelback steamer trunks, which look like they've sailed the seas one too many times. Both overflow with close to two centuries' worth of Sutton silver, and Mom wants to see every piece. It takes me several days to carry it down one armload at a time and polish it until it shines like new. Well, as new as a tray from 1850 can look.

"One more thing I just have to have," Mom says as we sit on her bed watching Chuck Woolery and waiting for Lindsey to bring Mom's nighttime meds.

"I'm happy to get anything for you," I say, imagining that she wants to add her mother's china doll to her daily list of must-have treasures.

184

11

March 28

Mini vacation at Gator's.

"Grits," she'd said. "I'd kill for grits." If Mom hadn't been so insistent that she was going to "die" if she didn't have grits for breakfast, I could've just included them in the next Rouses' delivery. If Lindsey had her driver's license, she could've run to the grocery store instead of me.

A shopping basket hangs from my elbow as I walk up and down the aisles of the closest grocery store I could find using the Cadillac's GPS. I got lost twice on the way to Gator's Grocery, and I blame it on the dimly lit vanity mirror. If the Escalade had better lighting, I wouldn't have blown past intersections while refreshing my makeup. The guidance system sounded just as judgmental as the last time I drove, but at least

185

the world's worst back-seat driver is at home, probably snoring like a hibernating bear.

It's Saturday night, and the store is busy with shoppers like me, grabbing last-minute items before it closes at ten. Unlike me, they know where to find what they need and don't get sidetracked looking at bottles of hot sauce with names like Trappey's, Bayou Butt Burner, and Slap Ya Mama.

Papa Bob used to pour Crystal Extra Hot on everything, and I drop a bottle in my basket. I look at local food staples like pecan brown rice, gumbo and jambalaya mix, and turducken stuffing — who knew? After fifteen minutes of being distracted, I finally find a box of instant grits in the breakfast aisle and drop it in my basket. Mom won't have to kill for grits now. Mission accomplished, but I don't head to the front of the store. Instead, I stop to smell coconut sugar scrub in one aisle and plumeria candles in another. In the produce section, I lift a fresh pineapple to my nose and pretend I'm in Hawaii on a mini vacation. I can almost hear "Aloha 'Oe" and feel sand between my toes.

Laughter draws my gaze from the spiky green crown. I know that deep laugh, and across rows of potatoes and onions, I recognize the back of Simon's head. Two women laugh along with him, animated and chatty, playing with their blond hair. I'm Lulu the Love Guru; I know body language and recognize their subconscious wrangling for his attention. Not that I blame them. There aren't many men who look as fine as he does in butt-hugging Levi's, but I would advise the blondes to follow Lulu's three-month rule if they want more than a one-night rodeo.

The last time I saw Simon, he called me tee Lou Ann, his voice kind of low and sexy, but I'm sure it's just a natural reflex for him and it doesn't mean we're friends. He hasn't noticed me over here hiding behind tropical fruit, and therefore a friendly hello is not required: chapter seventeen ("Keeping It Classy and Staying Sassy"), rule twenty-four.

I set the pineapple in my basket and turn toward the coffee aisle. I need to stock up on French roast and chicory so that I don't ever have to face another day without my morning jolt of caffeine . . . but I get sidetracked again. This time by ten-pound bags stuffed with live crawfish in the refrigerated meat section. I lean in for a closer look. Little antennas and claws poke out of the blue mesh as tiny black eyes stare back at me, begging for freedom. I am guilty of "pinching the tail and sucking the head" — Mardi Gras 2012. I turn away shamefaced, but I know my shame isn't strong enough to make me amend my carnivorous habits.

I move past rows and rows of exotic sausages. Some I've heard of, while others are a mystery. Behind the glass in the butcher's counter are even more sausages, along with cuts of beef, fresh chicken, and . . . "What the hell is that?"

I step closer and once again lean in for a better look. It takes several long seconds before my brain catches up with the shocking display in front of my eyes. I jump back and raise one hand to my chest as I stare in horror at alligators wrapped in cellophane. *Whole* alligators, skinned, except for their scaly heads and feet. "Gross," I whisper, but I can't tear my gaze away from the pink flesh and skeletal bones. Their feet are extremely scaly, and lethal-looking claws stick out from webbed toes. Their eyes are half-open and one of them has lemon slices down its back.

GATOR'S GATORS, the price sticker reads. $35.00. FARM FRESH.

They have alligator farms around here? Alligators live in the swamps and bayous, randomly killing animals and people.

They're a danger to society, like mountain lions, poison frogs, and scat music. The first two will kill you; the last will make you kill yourself.

"Careful you don't get bit."

I gasp and about jump out of my skin. Over the pounding of my heart, I hear Simon's all-too-familiar laugh. The one that means he thinks he's really funny.

"You scared the crap out of me." Without thought, I punch his shoulder. Somehow, that makes him laugh harder. "You're not funny."

"No?" He shakes his head. "You should see your eyes."

I shift the basket to my other elbow and fold my arms beneath my breasts. Dark stubble shadows his square jaw, and instead of his usual T-shirt, he's wearing a white dress shirt tucked loosely into his jeans. Men's magazines call this combination "classic casual." I call it business up top, party down below, and it looks good on him. I wonder if he's been on a date and where the two blondes are, but even if we *were* friends, neither is my business. I point to the glass case instead and ask, "Are there really alligator farms around here?"

"Sure are."

"They're dangerous. Why not get them

189

from the swamp?" I look up into his green eyes.

"It's illegal to hunt out of season."

There's a season? "An alligator killed a dog not far from Sutton Hall just last week." Mom and I watched it on the local news. She'd shrugged and said, "It's the circle of life." I'd gotten on the internet and ordered alligator repellant.

"That happens with animals near waterways, yes. Gators like to hide just beneath the surface out in the weeds."

I think of the chest-high grass and weeds at home. "The bayou is practically in my backyard!"

He glances down at me and folds his arms across his chest. "How fast can you run, tee Lou Ann?"

"Me?" I point to myself. I'm five foot one and until recently, I wore at least three-inch heels most days. "Not very fast."

"Gators go for the slow ones. You might wanna learn to zigzag."

I think he's joking, but it makes sense. "I don't want to zigzag. I don't want to get attacked at all!"

"Don't worry too much about it. Caimans run in short bursts." He shakes his head and tries not to smile. "He'll probably just take a few chomps out of you before he's worn out." He gives up trying and his smile creases the corners of his green eyes. I think he's about to start laughing again, but someone calls out his name.

He turns toward the cookie aisle and shouts back, "Laurent. How's ya momma and 'em?"

"Byen. Tee Larry is fixin' to leave for college and it's breakin' Shawnda's heart."

I wait for a pause in the casual back-and-forth to excuse myself, but just as Laurent says, "Bonsoir," someone else calls out to Simon.

I glance across my shoulder at a man in a Bass Pro Shops T-shirt, hoisting a bag of crawdads. "Where ya at?" he asks the obvious.

"Busy," Simon answers, which makes no sense.

Before moving to Louisiana, I'd shopped at the same H Mart for years and never ran into anyone I knew. Simon's up to four in twenty minutes; it's like he's at a high school reunion. This conversation is shorter than the last and I say, "Bye, Simon," while I have the chance. I take a few steps back and add, "I've got to get home with Mom's grits."

Simon looks down and points at my basket. "Those aren't grits."

"Really?" I stop and glance at the box next to my pineapple. "The box says grits."

"Instant grits aren't real grits. No respectable Southerner would be caught dead with instant grits."

Now it's my turn to laugh. Instant or not, Mom won't know the difference. "Good thing I'm not a Southerner." I walk toward the coffee aisle and say over my shoulder, "Au revoir, Simon."

He smiles because I'm sure my pronunciation is horrible. "On va se revoir, tee Lou Ann."

His is not. If I wasn't immune to classic shirts and party pants, the sweet words rolling off his tongue might make me play with my hair like the blondes in the produce aisle.

I grab three bags of coffee and make it home before Lindsey turns in for the night. She's in the kitchen filling Mom's pill minder. "How were things while I was gone?" I ask as I set the pineapple on the counter.

"I gave Patricia her meds and haven't heard a peep from her."

"Have you ever cooked grits?" I pick up the box and read the back.

"I've never even seen a grit. Are they good?"

I hand her the box. "No."

She reads the directions and shrugs. "Doesn't look hard. All I need is water and salt."

That sounds bland. "Maybe some butter or sugar, too." But I don't know much about it. "What you really need is a driver's license so you can go to the pharmacy or grocery store." She looks up from the box. "And there are going to be days when I can't take Mom to her appointments," I add, but it isn't Mom's appointments that I can't take. It's her back-seat driving, and I don't see why I have to be the target of torture when Lindsey is a paid victim.

Lindsey hands me the box. "Where do I go to get one?"

"Google it."

"How much does it cost?" she wonders as she grabs her phone.

"Don't know but I'll pay for it."

"Really?" She smiles and it lights up her eyes. "That's so nice. Thanks."

I shake my head. "It's part of my plan to trap you. Remember?"

"Yeah." Her smile gets even bigger. "Is the Escalade part of your trap?"

"You're getting ahead of yourself." I learned in an old Taurus. Not an eighty-five-thousand-dollar Cadillac. "Just get all the information first and we'll talk about the Escalade later."

I leave her to search the internet for the Louisiana DMV, and by the next morning at breakfast, she seems to have it all worked out.

"I need to establish residency and study for the written test."

I stare at my plate of lumpy grits and scrambled eggs, mustering the courage to take a bite.

"I'll need to practice for the driving part."

"You can practice in the driveway." I reach for an antique coffee cup and glance at Mom sitting at the head of the table. We're dining off hand-painted Dresden today. "You're not eating your grits."

"They taste like instant grits." She shakes her head. "No Southerner eats instant grits."

12

April 3

Money pit. Melvin Thompson. Boots 'N' Roots incident.

Mom has started brushing her hair "one hundred times, till it's silky." Every morning she puts on her brightest shade of red lipstick and waits for the arrival of more "family treasures" and "foxy men." At first, I'd worried that men working on the house — coming in and out all the time and dropping tarps and using loud machinery — would make Mom upset. I should have known better.

"I love foxy men with tool belts," she coos every time they enter the house. I wish she loved the Cajun Maids as much, but she looks at them like they're trying to steal her foxy men. It's embarrassing, but at least she and I have found a comfortable routine. I wish I could say the same thing about Lindsey and Raphael. They've taken a real aversion to each other, and I'm afraid Raphael delights in antagonizing her.

Mom hardly seems to notice the ongoing feud and is happier than I've seen her in years. She wraps herself up in Sutton lore and history and loves sitting at the head of the table and using old family china and crystal and silver. We listen to old records and thumb through photo albums and scrapbooks. Inevitably something taps into her long-term memory, knocking loose nuggets from the past.

"Look, that's me and Momma outside the Joy Theater on Canal."

I push her further. "Do you remember when it was taken?" She looks up at the ceiling and gives it some thought. "No." She shakes her head and returns her attention to the photo. "I'm seven or eight."

"So it was taken in nineteen fifty-three or four. Sometime after your dad died and before Grandmother married Papa Bob."

She shrugs. "Momma loved Charles Boyer."

For most of today, her mind seems clearer than it has in a few years now. She wrings her hands less and mentions Tony only twice. That's progress, but each time she does, it's like Groundhog Day, and I feel compelled to explain — very patiently, I might add — the Tony chapter all over again.

If Mom is not repeating old Sutton lore, we talk about the bits and pieces of the past that she can randomly recall. Like the time she took me to a New Kids on the Block concert and bought me Jordan Knight sheets (don't judge).

I remind her of when we lived in El Paso and she worked at an Elmer's. She'd have the cook make my favorite for me after school: a grilled cheese sandwich and fries. For dessert, it was always vanilla ice cream with hot fudge and peanuts.

She remembers that she worked at the Drunken Beaver in Portland, Oregon, and recalls every detail of the fight that broke out over her there. "They broke a table and two chairs. One man had to have stitches."

She doesn't seem to recall that I'd been sitting on a keg in the back room eating bar nuts and a pickle at the time. Funny how she can remember that fight but not that I'd been ten and scared to death.

"They were so handsome and in love with me," she says through a nostalgic sigh.

"Did either give you a card with a cactus on it, like Earl?"

"No." She shakes her head as if it's a serious question. "They were both married."

This is not at all shocking. Mom loves men of all ages and marital statuses. Men have defined her life and still do. I imagine the memories of men will be the last to fade and her passionate nature the last piece of Patricia to recede before she sinks into the final stages of her disease. As much as it has driven me crazy all my life, I will hate to see it go.

I've cut my Lulu responsibilities in half and work around Mom's naps, but it's not enough time. I try to make up the difference at night when Mom's asleep, but I'm usually too worn out. Before my decision to focus on Mom, I never realized the amount of time it took to run the business of Lulu Inc. I'd been driven and hyper-focused. Doing what I loved and loving what I did, producing creative content in hotel rooms between events. I've never taken a vacation where I didn't work, and it never felt like a chore. I never procrastinated — so why now?

Lulu is my heart and soul. The question of why now has lodged like a burr in my soul and the answer is terrifying. What if I've lost the heart for Lulu? What if I don't love it anymore? My life with both Mom and Lulu is a continual cycle of guilt and anxiety, and I don't see any resolution.

I've tried a couple of more meditation apps, but I struggle to pay attention. A glass of wine might help, but I can't have one because the wine rack is filled with water bottles, and besides, I'm afraid I might not stop with just a single glass.

We've settled into a daily routine and get more comfortable with it every day. Mom's adjusting to her new surroundings and both her anxiety and her emotional outbursts have decreased. She still has them, but they are less frequent and less explosive. I'm not a doctor, just a daughter living 24/7 with her Alzheimer's mother, but in the past few weeks I've seen a marked improvement. She's calmer and happier, and I truly believe that her environment has had a positive effect on her memory and thought processes. She's far from cured, but her mind is clearer. For longer periods of time, I look in her eyes and see the real her.

I hate bugs and spiders and flying insects. I hate that the humidity is sometimes higher than the outside temperature. Sutton Hall is an even bigger money pit than I'd thought at first glance, and I'm bleeding cash. I can't stick to a productive work schedule, but despite all that, bringing Mom back to

Louisiana was the right decision. She's doing so much better, in fact, that we are leaving the house tomorrow to shop. Nothing big or potentially overwhelming. Lindsey won't be with us, so I planned a small foray close to home.

While our daytime routine is good and getting better, our nighttime routine is the best. After Mom changes into her nightclothes, I brush and braid her hair while she chomps on Pirate's Booty, watches game shows, and yells answers at the TV.

Lindsey checks in on us around eight to take Mom's blood pressure and dispense her sleeping medication. She keeps a little notebook and pen in the front pocket of her scrubs. She's also expanded her wardrobe; on her days off, she wears flowing sundresses. Due to a kernel-related choking incident that happened a few days earlier during *I Love Lucy,* Lindsey takes Mom's popcorn with her when she leaves. If I tried to take her Booty, Mom would fight me over it, but she doesn't even argue with Lindsey. She's nicer to Lindsey, but she does talk about her weight after she's left the bedroom most nights. It's rude and I'm grateful that she at least waits until Lindsey can't hear her. Then we crawl into her bed and get cozy like when I was young. I always reach for her hand, but sometimes I wonder if she knows it's me next to her, with my warm palm pressed into hers.

Tonight, Mom and I sit on the edge of the big canopy bed as Lindsey comes in to do her usual, squeezing the blood pressure bulb and listening through her stethoscope.

"Melvin Thompson," Mom yells.

I haven't thought of Melvin Thompson in years, and I wonder why she's decided to shout her fourth husband's name. I look up from my fingers braiding her hair to *Family Feud.*

Richard Dawson is leaning toward a red-haired woman and repeats the question "Name something that has white balls."

Mom's answer is suddenly extremely disturbing.

The contestant says, "An old sweater," and a second *X* flashes on the screen.

"That was dumb," counters the woman who expected her fourth husband's nuts to be nationally recognized.

Lindsey lets go of Mom's arm, reaches into her pocket, and hands Mom her medication. "Did you hear the footsteps last night?" The question is directed at me.

I did, but I don't want to freak Lindsey out, so I say, "I heard something, but the house is old." Generations of ghosts might roam around at night, but after spending so much time in the attic, I'm fairly unaffected. "Nothing like the first night."

"Yeah, that was bad."

"Melvin Thompson!"

I suppress the urge to gag and remind myself that she can't help making me want to vomit. "No one wants to hear about Melvin."

"Here you go, Patricia." Lindsey hands her a glass of water from the bedside table and writes something down in her notepad. "Good night," she says, above the game show buzzer, and leaves with Mom's empty popcorn bag.

I barely get "good night" out of my mouth before Mom yells, "They were droopy, too."

"Mom!" She looks at me, and I can see she's mid-fade. "For God's sake, I don't want to hear about Melvin's droopy white balls."

"I don't blame you. They were practically to his knees."

I rub the veins popping out on my forehead. "Mom, stop!"

She shrugs and returns her glass to the bedside table. "Lindsey has a big belly."

I glance at the empty doorway to make sure Lindsey is gone. "Stop talking about Lindsey's weight." I remember how hurt I was when she accused me of getting fat my freshman year, and she's my mother.

She shrugs and yells, "Melvin Thompson," and I'm actually relieved the subject returns to old Melvin.

I feel veins popping inside my head, too. I'm tempted to run from the room, but I crawl back into Mom's bed next to her.

"I read in an article that birds mate for life."

"When?"

"I don't know." Mom shrugs. "That Raphael loves me."

Of course he does. I look across at Mom and see her old smile. Maybe she's not as faded as I suspected. "How can you tell?"

"He whistled at me."

I stand corrected. That bird makes only two sounds: a shrill scream when I tell him to behave or a nasty screech when he dive-bombs Lindsey. "He has good taste in women." I play along.

Mom's smile turns into a yawn as she rolls on her side toward me. "He doesn't like Lindsey."

"True, but I don't think he likes me very much either."

"Probably because you're in a hair rut." She tosses my braid out of her way and slides her arm across my abdomen to snuggle. "You're too pretty for bad hair."

"Thank you." I think. I stiffen and refuse to roll onto my side. If I don't escape now, I'm afraid she'll spoon me until sunrise. I have to work and can't play Earl tonight.

"Pretty and smart and a good girl. Not a bit like Wynonna's girl."

I don't believe Wynonna had a girl, but that's beside the point. Mom paid me three compliments in a row. I don't think she's ever done that before. Not that I can recall, anyway. My insides melt. I am reduced to putty and turn on my side. Mom takes advantage of my weakened state and molds herself against my back.

"I love a good snuggle," she says, and I melt even more at the warm breath on the back of my neck.

I tuck this evening away with the other good memories of Mom and me to be recollected and relived after she is gone.

I wait until Mom is snoring to carefully extract myself from her arms. I check on Raphael and find him asleep in his cage. If Mom wants to believe that dumb bird whistles at her, who am I to burst her bubble?

My back aches from lying so still. I'm too tired to work, but my mind is too restless for sleep. I download a new app, Powerful

Guided Meditation, Wish Manifestation. The others haven't worked, but I'm willing to keep trying. I figure I can concentrate better if I'm fulfilling some wishes, but after fifteen minutes, I think of a perfect addition to Mom's routine. She needs more than family photos and mementos to keep her mind active. I grab my phone and less than a minute into my internet search, I find *The Joy of Painting* website. I order everything Mom will need to beat the brush with Bob Ross and, because I'm the queen of swag myself, I add a pair of "Let's Get Crazy" socks. Mom's going to love painting happy little clouds again.

I think about tapping a few sentences in my day planner, but I yawn and toss my phone on the bedside table. I finally fall into a deep sleep and wake the next day feeling restored.

The new clothes Mother and I bought at Nordstrom online arrived several weeks ago, and I packed away my winter wool and flannel in favor of summer cotton and knits. I join Mother and Lindsey in the dining room wearing my black Alice + Olivia cuffed shorts and a black jersey tank.

"Why do you always wear black?" Lindsey asks as I grab one of great-grandmother's silver coffeepots.

This from the girl who wears scrubs 90 percent of the time. "I don't always wear black." Only 90 percent of the time. "It's versatile and perfect for business trips." I pick up one of the royal-blue-and-gold cups I'd carried down from the attic a few days ago.

"You're not traveling now."

I shrug. "Habit." I like black and don't see a problem.

"I like pink." Mom looks up from the matching Staffordshire plate. "It's a good color," she adds, and points to the sleeve of her pink seersucker dress. Of the three of us, Mom is the resident fashion maverick with her rebellious choice of white sandals before Memorial Day. Her hair is pushed back from her face with a flower headband and her lips are bubble-gum pink.

After she finishes her mushroom omelet and toast, we jump in the Escalade and head toward a small strip of brightly painted stores. I "kink" Mom's neck only once, but it's hard to take her seriously when her hair is flying around her head like Medusa.

"Do you want to roll that window up now?" I ask for the third time.

"Nope." She breathes deeply through her nose. "The air smells like the river."

And touches of swamp.

Monique's Chic Boutique is such a bright fuchsia that I find it without getting lost. The old stucco clothing store is sandwiched between the neon-green Lagniappe BBQ and the red Boots 'N' Roots.

Even before we pulled into the small parking lot, I didn't have high expectations for Monique's Chic Boutique. I didn't expect that we'd share the same definition of chic. I was right, but it hardly matters. Monique takes one look at Mom and me and hears *ka-ching* in her head. She masterfully herds us into separate dressing rooms divided by a pink curtain, and despite a slight language barrier, she sets about selling us everything from matching crawfish T-shirts to Mom's high-cut swimsuit with a mesh insert.

"Dis'll look fabulous on you, cher. Très bien." Monique's chubby hand parts the curtains, and she shoves a cheetah-print one-piece into Mom's side. "It's on trend dis season."

I adjust a tank top with the outline of Louisiana on it and wait to hear Monique walk away. "Mom," I whisper, but when she doesn't answer I say a little louder, "Mom!"

"Is that you, Lou Ann?"

Who else? "Yes." I pull my braid from the back of the shirt and lean closer. "You don't have to try on a swimsuit if you don't want."

"I got it on one leg already."

Monique's hand appears again and pushes a pair of jean shorts at me. "Dis is da last pair of dese cutoffs. Vonda Richard, she called and had me put dese aside for her, but she has a flat bottom like me. Dese are made fo' a woman with a pretty figure like you. Très bien. Hot hot."

"Thank you," Mom and I say at the same time.

I don't know if I even own jean shorts. I think I gave them up years ago, and so I'm really surprised at how much I like them. The hemline is raw, and the back pockets are distressed enough that they look worn-in. I'm not really a shredded-edge girl, but Mom's not the only fashion rebel in the family.

"How do dey fit?" Monique asks through the curtain.

"Good." I look at my butt in the mirror. Really good. "Too bad this is the last pair."

"Lou Ann?"

"Yes."

"I can't hook this thing. I need help."

I stare at the curtain for several long seconds before I gather the courage to push it open. Mom's back is to me and she's holding her hair aside. I quickly hook the ends around her neck and say, "There you go." She spins around and poses with a hand on her waist, and I fight the urge to throw an arm over my eyes.

"What do you think?" she asks, as if she doesn't have eyes in her own head.

The suit is cut high on her hips and shows way too much of her Attends. On the other hand, it's also cut high on the top and is tight enough to keep her boobs in position halfway to her belly button. "It's one of your favorite animal prints."

She points to the mesh in back. "How does that part look?"

It could be worse; she could be wearing a bikini. "I think Monique is right. It's on trend and you look fabulous. Très bien."

"Good. I could use a swimsuit."

I want to ask why, but I don't. At least it'll match her cheetah shower cap.

"You're not goin'a believe dis." Monique shoves a stack of shorts through the curtain. "I just got dese in."

She's right. I don't believe it.

"God provides."

I seriously doubt God's in on Monique's hustle. The only difference between the shorts I'm wearing and the three pairs she's handed me is that each is a darker shade of denim.

The last things Monique shoves our way

are T-shirts with a dancing crawfish and the words "I'm Cray Cray" on the front. I take one look at Mom and she at me in our matching shirts and we crack up. I laugh at her and she laughs at me, and we manage to get dressed without losing it only by not looking at each other.

Monique waits for us at the register, two stacks of clothes beside her. The size of the stacks reminds me that, while I like to support small-business owners, I'm clearly being hustled.

"This has been so much fun." Mom adds the crawfish shirts to the pile. "I love everything you recommended for me."

"Merci bien." I hand over my Visa before Monique can think to shove a preserved alligator head at Mom.

"Goodness gracious! I thought you looked familiar." Monique looks up from my business credit card. "My sister read your book and got herself a man. Of course, he wasn't wort' a darn."

"That happens."

"My daughter is Lulu the Love Guru, and she's a big deal," Mom says, as if she just remembers my life beyond the confines of her world. She lifts her chin with pride and adds, "She's very smart. You better believe that."

"Ahh, thanks, Mom." The backs of my eyes pinch and I blink back tears. Bragging is Mom's way of letting me know she's proud of me. I don't need her to say the exact words.

"She makes lots and lots of money and got the plumbing fixed so I can have my bathroom back."

"I never had anybody famous in here before. Well, except for if you count da wife of a Jerry Lee Lewis impersonator."

Mom gasps and clutches at her heart. "Breathless," she whispers. "I loved Jerry Lee in the worst way."

Monique hands me back my card. "Nancy's havin' a big shoe sale at da Boots 'N' Roots next door. You don' wanna miss dat."

Noooo, my mind screams.

"Okay," Mom says, and a half hour later, we are the proud owners of Saints cowboy boots. Mom's are red and mine are turquoise. I don't know if either of us will have occasion to wear "Who Dat" boots, but it could be worse. Mom could have thrown a fit over a pair of acrylic slides she'd been eyeing.

The checkout counter is near the back of the store, which is an odd place to put it until you notice the empty salon chair sitting next to a woman getting her feet sanded at a pedicure station. Thus, Boots 'N' Roots. Two seemingly incongruous businesses in one building. Like a grocer selling ponies, but I have to give Nancy credit for her entrepreneurial drive. "You cut hair, too?"

"We're a full-service salon," she says, and I hand her a personal credit card this time. "You needin' a shampoo and set?"

If Nancy's hair is any indication, she's a shampoo-and-set master craftswoman for the seventy-and-older crowd. Mom will never sit still long enough for what Nancy might have in mind.

"Cut 'n' color?"

Nice try.

"Do you have one of those hair books with pictures?"

Shocked, I look at Mom standing next to me. "You want your hair cut?"

"No, I'm not in a hair rut."

"Me?" Mom's hair has been loose and unruly all day. "You're the one who needs a trim."

"You'd look good wit' a bob," Nancy helpfully suggests.

"Listen to Nancy." Although a bob is pushing the extreme and I doubt Mom will go that far.

"I mean you." Nancy hands me the credit

card. "About an inch beneath your chin would frame your face pretty pretty."

"Ha!" Mom smirks. "Told ya."

13

Mom tests shock absorbers
for her final journey.
I'm in pieces. She puts me back together.

Never let your Alzheimer's mother pressure you into getting a twenty-dollar "trim." You'll get what you paid for, and she'll forget her role in your bad decision.

"It's not ugly," Mom assures me, sipping a Dr Pepper and eating from our huge Swamp Platter inside Lagniappe BBQ.

The worst part is, Nancy promised she'd take only an inch off the ends, and I knew better than to believe her. The most embarrassing part is, I knew better than to get a backroom haircut in a discount boot store.

Our waitress, Tana Mae, shakes her head as she refills my water glass. "Nobody round here lets Nancy near der hair."

That might have been good to know an hour ago, before she cut my hair longer on one side than the other and just kept cutting to correct her mistakes. I stopped her after her third "Darn it, your hair's curly." Now it's curlier and the right side is still shorter than the left. I'm trying not to freak out, and I just thank God I'm not on tour.

The bell above the door rings and Monique rushes in like there's a fire. "Lord, I heard Nancy cut your hair."

Good news travels fast. "How'd you hear about my hair?" I bite into a spicy hush puppy and wash it down with Diet Coke. I like hush puppies. I know what I'm putting in my mouth, unlike the rest of the Swamp Platter.

"Giselle called me after her pedicure, and I called Tana Mae and she said it's true."

"The gator's really good," Mom says as she chomps on a deep-fried hunk of meat.

I think of the skinned gators at Gator's and say, "I'll pass."

"When I told Giselle you're Lulu da Love Guru, she told Nancy, and Nancy yowled like a scalded cat and run out da back door. Last anyone saw, she was headed down da bayou."

"It tastes like chicken."

"I'll stick with shrimp, Mom." I recognize shrimp.

"Da frog legs are good and fresh," Tana

Mae tells us as she points them out.

I'm grateful. Now I won't accidently eat one. I'm not a snob, but I draw the line at amphibians and reptiles. And rodents. I had a pet rat in the sixth grade. I don't want to eat Miss Gertrude.

"Mais, la." Monique raises her hands, palms up. "Nancy's a good woman, bless her heart, but never let her near you with a pair of scissors in her hand, no no."

Again, that might have been good to know know.

"I'm sure it's trendy somewhere, très bien." She drops her hands and tilts her head to one side. "I can recommend a good stylist."

She's also the woman who recommended the shoe sale at Boots 'N' Roots. I thank her, but I'll find my own. Someone who works in an actual salon. Someone who knows how to cut thick curly hair without butchering it. Someone who can get me in asap, but that's the problem. Four-star salons are booked solid for months in advance, and I officially start to freak out. No one will book Lou Ann Hunter, but Lou Ann Hunter has an ace up her sleeve. I call my assistant in Seattle and have her book an appointment in New Orleans for Lulu the Love Guru and special guest Lindsey

216

Benedict. Lindsey has to drive to make sure I don't get lost, and she's the only person I know who needs her hair cut more than I do.

I don't like to use Lulu to get special treatment, but this is an emergency, and the owner of Shear Masters in the New Orleans Warehouse District gets us in after the salon has closed for the night. His name is Fabian LaFleur and he is a shears master. He corrects the length and thins the volume until soft messy curls fall to my jawline. It's a nice change and I like it a lot — but there's a reason I always wore it long and braided.

"When did your hair get so curly like that?" Mom calls out, her voice vibrating and arms jiggling from the plush massage chair where she sits attempting to drink tea.

"For as long as I can remember." I glance up into the mirror. "Sorry," I say, and Fabian continues to tell me how to keep my hair from looking like I stuck my finger in a light socket. By the time the three of us head home, my hair looks fabulous. Lindsey's hair is short and sassy, and she can't quit touching it or looking at herself in the rearview mirror. Even Mom got into the act and let Fabian trim several inches from her hair.

We're exhausted, especially Mom, and I

217

don't think she snores all night. If she does, it doesn't matter, because I don't crack my eyes open until ten the next morning.

I can't believe I slept so late and jump into the pink tub for a quick bath. The water remains hot and rust-free, and it cost me only eleven grand. I was told I'm lucky because it could have been a lot worse. If the pipes throughout the house had needed to be replaced, I would've had to add an extra zero to the final invoice. Which reminds me, the electrician's bill came yesterday, but I'm afraid to open it.

From the top of the steps, I can hear Simon's deep voice and deeper laughter. The last time I saw him, he told me to learn to zigzag and that instant grits aren't grits. Which I still think is ridiculous, but my Alzheimer's mom can tell the difference. It must be a Southern thing.

There's a different energy with Simon here, and I can feel it as I walk downstairs. It's more than just his being a man. I had electricians and plumbers all over the house for several weeks, but it never felt like we were being exposed to alarming levels of testosterone.

"How were your grits?" he asks Mom as I enter the room.

"Horrible. They were instant." She pre-

218

tends to spit before she adds, "I about choked to death on those lumps."

"Simon's come to take his bird back home," Lindsey tells me.

"I never said that. I'm just . . ." Simon glances my way and stops in mid-sentence. Raphael is perched on his finger and the two stare at me without blinking.

They stand in front of the fireplace, Simon in a tight black T-shirt like he's got something to prove, and the bird in a bright pink sweater like he got dressed in the dark. Raphael is the first to react and he bobs his head as if he approves of my hair and dark-red lips.

I walk across the room and take a closer look at the trendy bird. "Is Lindsey right? Are you here to take your bird home with you?"

"Mais no, tee Lou." Simon's gaze slides across my hair, stopping here and moving there. "I'm just here to give an estimate on the rail and bring Ray-feel his plucking vest."

"You work on Sundays?"

"Don't tell anyone." The marbled stone behind him accentuates the variant depths in his green eyes. "I like your hair."

I resist the urge to fluff my curls and feel sorry for the women who aren't immune to good looks and smooth drawls. "Thank you." I glance at Raphael and see that it's not a sweater but a fleece and it's Velcroed across his back. "That vest is pink."

"Magenta," Simon corrects me. "It takes a confident man to wear magenta."

"Can he fly in that thing?"

"Absolutely."

"Dang. He's been getting out of his cage."

"Tell me, are you being a handful?" Simon turns the bird to face him as if he expects a reply.

"That's a nice way to put it." Lindsey scoots back further into the sofa and turns an evil eye on her nemesis. "He screams and chases people."

"That's true. He likes to antagonize Lindsey."

"He whistles at me," Mom says from across the room.

I lower my voice and say, "He doesn't whistle."

"No?" He touches his finger to Raphael's beak to get his attention and whistles as if a hot girl just walked into the room. After two more tries, the bird mimics the catcall. I look from Raphael to Mom in disbelief. She'd been right all along.

"But he doesn't talk," Mom adds.

Simon scratches the top of Raphael's

head. "Bonjour, bon ami." Raphael closes his eyes, but Simon persists until the bird repeats the greeting, sounding very French, like he could be wearing a magenta beret to match his vest.

Mom claps her hands. "What else does he say?"

"Bonjour, mon vieux," rolls off Simon's tongue and the dang bird replicates it perfectly.

"What's he sayin'?" Mom shouts, like we're all hard of hearing.

"Hello, old man," Simon answers.

"I didn't know he was a French-speaking bird," I tell him.

"He speaks four languages: English, French, Cajun, and gambler. Shake your tail feathers," he says, and Raphael repeats it right down to the Southern drawl. "I'm feeling lucky. Call my bookie," he squawks. Next in his repertoire, he mimics the front door's squeaky hinges as it opens and shuts. He squawks random words and sentences. He bays like a hound dog, and follows it up with "Merde! Shut the fuck up, Boomer!" sounding remarkably like Simon.

"I think that's enough for now. Quiet down, Ray-feel."

Surprisingly, the bird shuts his beak. "I take it you have a dog named Boomer."

"He's a good huntin' dog, but just as hardheaded as Ray-feel." Simon chuckles. "Give me your hand."

"Why?"

He doesn't explain before he reaches for my hand and raises it next to Raphael. The bird takes a few steps sideways and wraps his talons around my finger. It feels really weird, reptilian and bony. Simon supports the bottom of my hand with his palm and warms my wrist. Raphael's black eyes stare into mine without blinking. "Is he going to bite me?"

"Probably not."

My gaze shoots upward to the heavens, and Simon laughs. Another big, boisterous laugh like when he told me about Uncle Jasper's mattress. Neither is as funny as he seems to think.

"Scratch his head."

Reluctantly, I raise my free hand to the fine red feathers on the top of Raphael's head and lightly scratch. He tilts his beak up and purrs. "He sounds like a cat."

"What?" Mom yells from across the room.

"He sounds like a cat when you scratch his head," I yell back.

Lindsey says something grouchy that I don't catch.

"He's heavy."

"He's gained some weight since I brought him back home." Simon takes Raphael onto his finger and returns him to his cage. I can almost feel Lindsey's relief. "He likes you."

"Me?" I doubt that.

"He hates me," Lindsey says while keeping her eyes on the cage door.

"Ray-feel chases you because he can smell your fear."

I picture her running from the naked bird, and me running interference. I can't help but chuckle.

"It's not funny." Lindsey has no sense of humor when it comes to Ray-feel. "Aren't you going to shut his cage door?" she asks, her brows rising up her forehead.

"Sure, but he'll let himself right back out when he feels like it." Simon closes the wire door so that Lindsey can relax. "He likes to unscrew bolts with his beak. So you might want to check your chairs before you sit."

I thought one of the dining room chairs wobbled more than it had the day before. "Do you have an estimate for the rail?" I ask him.

"I have to look at it yet."

"We passed a good time." Mom's scarlet lips turn up in a coy smile.

"It won't take me long," he says, and true to his word, he's back within ten minutes.

He spends another ten minutes saying goodbye to Mom.

"That was fast." I walk with him to the front door and out onto the porch. "Did you look at everything?"

He pauses a moment like he's going to say something, but he just shakes his head and continues down the steps. "I know this house inside and out. I could have given an estimate over the phone, but I wanted to bring by Ray-feel's vest."

I'm hoping the latest estimate is lower than the first. "How much?"

"Give or take . . . sixteen grand," he says over his shoulder as he walks toward his truck.

"What?" I chase after him. "You said fourteen."

"I said at least fourteen, tee Lou Ann." He opens the driver's door and turns toward me. "If you want the best, it's sixteen, maybe more."

More? I shade my eyes with my hand and look up at him. I've negotiated contracts for years now. "I only have your word that you're the best."

"Ask around." He shrugs. "Call down at the Historic Preservations building, then get back to me. Don't take too long. I'm busy."

The longer we talk, I know the more he'll raise his price, but I risk it. "If we agree, how long will the project take?"

He takes a deep breath and exhales. "From soup to nuts, best guess . . ." He tips his head to one side and thinks about it before he answers, "Hard to say."

"Gosh, that *is* a good guess." I fold my arms beneath my breasts. "Do you think you can be a little more specific?"

"I won't know what I'm looking at until it's down and at the shop."

"You said you know this house inside and out."

"That's right, but there are always surprises and most of them aren't good. If I have to replace a baluster, I can't predict how long it will take to find what I need."

"So you can't tell me how long or exactly how much it will cost."

"I told you the probable cost, and I imagine if I can find period mahogany . . . maybe three months."

"Three months!"

"The library restoration took two years and cost four or five times what I'm charging for the rail."

I'm starting to get a clearer picture, and it looks like a pain in the ass and mind-boggling money. "We'll split the difference.

225

Fifteen grand and a month and a half." I stick out my hand to seal the deal.

He doesn't reach out. "C'est fou."

I'm not sure what that means, but he's pointing to his head and making a circle with his finger like I'm crazy. "I think you're trying to take advantage of me because I'm a woman."

He laughs, and fine lines crease the outside corners of his green eyes. "I don't take advantage of women. I let them take advantage of me." He gets in his truck and shuts the door. "But I'll make an exception for you."

"Wow, I feel special."

"For you, I just might change my bedsheets."

"Sweet talker."

The engine fires and he adds, "You have my number, cher."

I watch him wave and drive away, and I'm not certain, but I think Mom's boyfriend just made a pass at me.

I move toward the porch but glance back through tree limbs heavy with moss as he pulls onto the road. I'm Lulu the Love Guru, and I've written books and blogs on how to read a man's body language and interpret his actions so you can gauge your reaction. When it comes to Simon, I have a difficult time interpreting or reading any-thing. When I think he's serious, he laughs. When I think he's joking, his voice lowers and he says "cher" as if he's thinking about rolling me around in those clean sheets, his hot skin sticking to mine. Or maybe I'm overthinking it.

I open the front door and shut it behind me. It's been a long time since I've thought about hot, sticky skin in a good way. Maybe I'm not as immune as I'd like to think.

"It's called a memento mori," Lindsey says as I walk into the front parlor. She and Mom are thumbing through scrapbooks.

"What are you two looking at?"

"Memento mori," Mom says without looking up.

"I saw it in *Post Mortem Mary.*"

Mom points to something in the book. "Postpartum Mary," she says, and I don't tell her that postmortem and postpartum are two totally different things.

I sit next to Mom and look at the photo she finds so fascinating. It's a daguerreotype of five siblings standing in a row, like stair steps. The two girls have ringlets and big bows in their hair and the boys are in suits. No one's smiling, but that's typical of Victorian photos.

"This is the dead one," Mom says, and

227

points to the boy who's fourth in the row.

"What?" On closer inspection, I see that the boy's eyes are closed, and his head tilts a bit to one side. The littler girl on the end looks a little freaked out, and I don't blame her.

"That's morbid."

Mom flips the page. "This one's dead," she says, and points to the bride in a Victorian wedding photo. Her eyes are closed, and she's resting her head on the groom's shoulder like she's drunk or tired and passed out while standing up. Once you look at it enough, the dead ones are easy to spot.

"This is disturbing." I close the book.

"These are kin." Mom flips the pages back open. "Look at this."

"I'd rather not."

"It was taken right over there." Lindsey points to the fireplace across the room.

Despite my aversion, I glance at the photo of a white casket draped in flowers. The photograph was taken from just far enough away to capture the silhouette of a woman in white lace. I'm horrified, and I wonder how many people in the creepy book wander the halls and slam doors at night.

"I want a white coffin like this one," Mom announces.

"We don't have to worry about that for a long time."

"With gold handles."

I can't take any more and leave the room to get Raphael a seed stick and some dried fruit cocktail. When I return, she's still at it, but now she's fixated on people in caskets and determined to talk about it, no matter how many different ways Lindsey and I try to change the subject. Even when I mention her boyfriends and remind her that Simon and his men will be back to work on the banister.

"A white one with gold handles and a blue pillow to match my eyes."

I carefully pull my hand from Raphael's cage. "Your eyes won't be open, Mom."

"I want to wear blue."

Raphael yawns like he can hardly keep awake. "Do we have to talk about this now?"

"Earl says I look good in blue."

"Earl won't be here."

"Earl loves me. He gave me a Christmas card with a cactus on it."

Yeah, I remember. "Earl lives in Seattle." I shut the cage even though I know he's an escape artist.

She points to Lindsey. "Look on the Google net."

"For what, Patricia?"

229

"One of those places." I can feel her anxiety building as she can't remember the word she wants to use. "The casket places."

"Funeral homes." Lindsey and I look at each other as she reluctantly pulls out her phone.

"We have a long time before we have to think about that," I tell her again.

"You have to take me."

I shake my head. It's morbid and unsettling, and if she picks out a coffin, it'll all feel too final.

"Before I forget."

Those three simple, self-aware words have a lot of power behind them. They had the power to make me move across the country when that was the last thing I wanted to do. Now they have the power to make me load Mom into the SUV and take her casket shopping when that's the last thing I want to do. The last place I want to go to is Bergeron Funeral Home, but I do it because of those three powerful words.

As I soon discover, it's not called coffin shopping. It's called preplanning and involves a lot of paperwork that I have to fill out while Mom and Lindsey push on the coffin mattress, testing the spring of every casket in the showroom. They *ooh* and *aah* at the "shock absorbers," and I feel sick in my stomach. Mom gives a thumbs-up or thumbs-down like she's Goldilocks, and I try to swallow past the big lump in my throat.

Mom chooses flowers and music and a guest book with a matching quill pen. Her casket has to be specially ordered with her name embroidered on the overlay, and Bergeron will store it until she "takes her heavenly journey." Everyone is acting like we're planning a party and picking out por-tieres.

I'm the only one who is broken inside. I'm the only one who wants to scream at the top of my lungs. I'm the only one who wants to cover my ears and rock myself back and forth.

I'm given a pamphlet, and we go over the instructions on what to do if Mom dies at home, and by the time we return to Sutton Hall, I'm a wreck. I've held my pain inside, mostly in the form of frustration, but as I kneel behind Mother, brushing her hair as I do most every night, I can't hold it in any longer. It rips me apart. The brush falls from my hand, and I double over. My arms cover my bowed head, and the more I try to control my stuttering sobs, the worse they get. I am a ball of raw misery. I can't do this. It's too hard. It's too much for me.

"Ahhh, baby." I feel Mother's warm hand rub up and down my back, soothing me like I'm a child again. "Baby mine, don't you cry," she softly sings. "Baby mine, dry your eyes. Rest your head close to my heart." I remember the next lines and I cry even harder. "Never to part, baby of mine." Mom always loved that movie, and I slept with a little stuffed Dumbo when I couldn't sleep next to her. "Don't cry, cher baby." My heart breaks even more than I think is possible, and I lie next to her, hiccupping and wiping my nose across the back of my hand. I lie next to her long after she falls asleep, listening to her soft breathing.

She's my mom, and I'll take care of her until she's placed in that shiny white coffin with the gold handles and blue pillow to match her eyes. I'll take care of her before and after she forgets.

She's my mother, and as difficult as she can be, she's equally easy to love.

14

May 2

Happy trees. *Moonlight Sonata.*
Mom's proposition.

I knew Mom would love to paint with Bob
Ross again. The day her supplies arrive, I
set up an art studio in the morning room
right off the kitchen. It's painted teal with
white trim and gets the most natural light.
I've seen pictures of this room when it had
fruit trees in large brass planters to scent
the air with citrus for luncheon soirees, but
it's sat neglected for decades. I had to knock
down cobwebs, vacuum out the dust, and
wash the windows. That's a lot of glass to
clean, but it's worth it. Especially in the
morning when sunshine hits all those original windows. The room sparkles and shines,
but in a wavy and otherworldly way, like
we've stepped back in time.

Mom wants the old Victrola dragged into

her new "studio" so she can listen to Bach and Beethoven and Jelly Roll Morton as she watches *The Joy of Painting* DVDs on a small TV. I often sit beside her at an easel I bought for myself, and we're quite the pair in our smocks, watching Bob and listening to "Für Elise." I do not have an ounce of artistic talent, but there is just something so peaceful about listening to classical music and making really bad art. When I should be working on Lulu business, I find myself painting or sorting through the attic for things I know Mom will enjoy. I keep pushing more and more work off my plate and onto other people. I feel guilty, but I'd rather spend time with Mom. That's why we're here, and painting is a nice start to the morning . . . but not this morning. Instead of retreating to the studio to paint with Bob, Mother announced we're visiting the dearly departed.

I knew this day would come, and I dread every part of it. I dread the heat and humidity and bugs almost as much as I dread standing next to Mom while she points to her tomb. I don't want another day like the one when she "preplanned" her funeral.

But I don't have a choice, and I accept the can of Deep Woods Off! Mom hands me. I cover every part of me and choke on the cloud of poison. I spray my turquoise "Who Dat" boots inside and out and douse my cutoffs and the vintage-looking Rolling Stones T-shirt I bought from Nordstrom online. I know it's too hot for boots, but it's too buggy for anything else. I'll risk sweaty feet over bites and stings any day, and just in case, I toss in my can of alligator spray.

Mom's wearing purple pants, a pink floral blouse, and lavender lips. Her long hair is braided, and she's stuck an old butterfly comb at the back of her head. She says it belonged to her mother and makes her feel close to her.

It's been nearly three months since Mom crawled in bed with me and asked that I bring her to Sutton Hall. She was just as determined then as she is today, and nothing can distract her from her mission. Not even the prospect of Simon and his crew coming to remove the old staircase railing and replacing it with a temporary one can sway her.

I follow her out the back door, and we make a quick trip to the garage. "We'll need these to clean up around Momma's tomb," she says as she grabs an old tin bucket filled with garden tools and shoves it at me. I toss in the can of alligator spray and we continue on.

"This is in fine shape," she says as we slide past the old carriage taking up half the space.

"The wheels are cracked," I point out.

"That doesn't matter." She grabs a wreath of plastic lilies and a small shovel. "It's not going that far."

I don't know what she means, and she hands me the flowers and shovel before I can ask. I don't expect her to carry anything, but the bucket isn't exactly light. I hang the wreath from the crook of my arm and follow Mom outside. Tools clank around in the bucket as we hit the cobblestone path.

"It's a beautiful day," she says through a happy sigh.

A big green fly circles my head, looking for a spot I might have missed with repellent. I swat at it with the shovel. A hint of sweetness hangs in the humid air, and as long as the spray does its job, I'm good.

Mom looks down at her feet as cobblestones disappear beneath wild honeysuckle and kudzu. "Please be careful, Mom." I would help her, but I'm loaded down like a pack mule. "I don't want you to fall." Lindsey took the morning off, and she has the SUV, but it wouldn't matter if she'd left it. I couldn't get Mom back to the house by myself, let alone navigate us to the ER. I'd have to call 911, and the EMTs would have to strap Mom to one of those orange boards and pack her out.

She waves away my concern and adjusts her comb. "You'll have to remove the seats when you get out the funeral buggy."

She means the surrey, the station wagon of its day. It's long enough to carry a casket. That's what she meant by it not going far, but I don't think it's even in good enough shape to leave the garage. "What's wrong with a hearse?" I ask the obvious.

"Suttons use the funeral buggy." She looks around at yellow wildflowers beneath bald cypress, and I get anxious that she's not watching her feet. "Make sure the funeral folks polish my white coffin so it's nice and shiny for my final journey," she continues as we move closer to the mausoleums. "I sure will be something in that buggy."

I know she's describing what she wants, but I just can't see putting her in a buggy that could throw a wheel and toss her out, white coffin and all. Out of self-preservation, I block out her talk of death and buggies and fill my head with happy clouds and friendly rocks.

The Sutton family graveyard is just as creepy as I remember it. Wispy curtains of Spanish moss drape the limbs of ancient cypress and live oak trees, falling like dull green witch's hair across the tops of pocked-limestone headstones and granite mausoleums that used to give me nightmares of mummy-like hands sticking out from between the cracks.

The cemetery is surrounded by an ancient wrought-iron fence, and a weathered metal plaque hangs on the gate:

Sutton Hall Plantation Graveyard
In Loving Memory of Our Dearly Departed
Any Person Who Disturbs
This Hallowed Earth
Shall Suffer the Wrath of Our Lord
1831

Undaunted by the dire warning, Mother pushes open the gate, and it gives the obligatory rusty metal screech. The scene inside looks like the setting of one of Lindsey's horror movies. All it needs is a group of horny teenagers and a six-pack to set the stage.

I'm not convinced that Sutton Hall isn't haunted, but I ignore my misgivings and follow Mom inside.

"This is so peaceful," she says as we stop in front of the first family tomb. It's cracked down the middle, and an angel leans precariously to the left. Time has eroded the face, and I can barely make out the engraving:

Sutton
John Hayward
Born May 1815
Died November 1866

Below is some scripty writing that is impossible to make out.

"This is my great-great-grandpere," Mother says, but I think there might be one or two more greats in there. "He built Sutton Hall in 1830." A slight breeze stirs tendrils of Spanish moss and picks up strands of her hair. She points at the engraving. "It says, 'Beloved father, husband, and patriot. He will live on in our hearts.' "

Since I can't make out all the letters, I'm fairly positive she can't either. Incredibly, though, I bet that is exactly what it says.

" 'Helen Davis Sutton,' " she reads the epithet on the next tomb over. The stone is so pocked I can barely make out the date of her death, 1890, but it doesn't stop Mom. " 'Niece of President Jefferson Davis. Beloved wife, mother, and daughter of the Confederacy. She is gone but never forgotten.' "

President? I look at Mom and wonder if it

really said that at one time, or if she just straight made it up like she does answers to her game show questions.

We find my great-grandparents, and Mother stops to put her hand on the smooth white marble of George Bernard Sutton and Rose Oliver Sutton.

"Maw Maw Rose. I love and miss you, goodness knows."

We continue on, making our way past rows of single and large family mausoleums, all inscribed with different names and dates, but each heavily adorned with angel statues. Live oaks have uprooted the ground, tilting stone crosses and knocking several angels off their pedestals. The bright morning sun shines down on white vaults and bounces off marble mausoleums entombing generations of Sutton relatives, and I am surprised by the genuine feeling that settles in my soul. As creepy as I find this fenced-off plot of earth, it holds the remains of one family. My family.

"Isn't that sad?" Mom asks as she points to tombs of red brick, crumbling past the point of identification.

It's a rhetorical question, but I answer anyway. "Yes." Some of the markers indicate a long life, while others memorialize infants or young men taken in wars dating as far back as 1843. Whole families were taken by floods, smallpox, cholera.

"That must be Jasper." Mom heads to a shiny new vault a few rows away.

I walk with her to a spot where the earth looks more recently disturbed. My bucket starts to weigh on me, and I switch hands with a clank.

"Remember when you dressed like a vampire?"

I wonder what sparked the random memory. "I was always a vampire for Halloween because of my widow's peak." Most of Mom's memories are connected, in one way or another, to the men revolving in and out of our lives at that time. I wait for an old-boyfriend connection, but it doesn't come.

Mom looks up at my forehead. "Oh yeah."

We make it to the grave where a wreath of long-dead flowers is staked in the ground. The black marble stone simply bears Jasper's name and the dates of his birth and death.

"Here lies Jasper Sutton, he loved his bird but hated mutton."

I look at Mom with her lavender lips and laugh. It's been so long since I've heard Mom make up little rhymes, I've forgotten that she used to do it all the time. You could say she was the OG rapper of her time.

She smiles at me. "Does it say that?"

"Yes. Of course."

She points to the gravestone next to Jasper. "Who is that?"

"Jedediah Sutton."

"Jasper's twin." Mom looks over her shoulder before she whispers, "Those boys were gay as a box of sprinkles."

Which explains why the uncles never married or had children.

"But we don't talk about that."

"It's not a crime to be gay." Not like marrying a first cousin.

"Who's that?" Mom points to another ledger stone.

I scrunch up my eyes and read, " 'Donald Aiken.' Died in 1922."

She cocks her head in contemplation. "Here lies Donny Aiken. He said he was sick, but folks thought he was fakin'."

I laugh and join in. "It says, 'Here lies Donny Aiken, he hated peas but loved his bacon.' "

Mom winces. "That wasn't any good."

So much for joining in.

"Momma's over there." She points to the far corner of the cemetery, where the Spanish moss is thickest.

I was a sophomore in college when my grandmother died. She passed during finals week, and I didn't attend her funeral. I know I should have felt bad about that, but I didn't really. Truthfully, I felt bad for *not* feeling bad.

Whenever we visited Grandmother Lily in Tennessee, she always acted so happy to see us. She'd hug me up in her perfumed linen and lace and gush, "Awwww, cher baby." It sounded so beautiful in my ear, but I was only Grandmother's dear baby on her own schedule. For an hour or two, I'd be the center of her attention, and she'd shower me with love and praise. Then it was like she was ruled by a kitchen timer that only she could hear; when it rang, she was done. No more kisses and hugs or storybooks. Just, "You run along, cher, go." I felt like a doll she put up on a shelf. Forgotten until she took me down again. As a kid, I was confused and hurt. I wondered what I'd done wrong. I wanted her to care about me. As a teenager, *I* stopped caring.

No doubt Grandmother's push-and-pull impacted Mom's life and shaped who she is. It explains Mom's relationships with everyone in her life — especially me.

I stop next to a bench dedicated to Suzanna "Sugie Bee" Verot and rock back as if I've been slammed with a big bag of *duh*. Mom's also ruled by a timer that only she can hear.

In my sociology class in college, I wrote a paper on Mom and determined that her male attention-seeking and hypersexuality, as demonstrated by her ability to fall in and out of love seemingly on a whim, was due to severe daddy issues. I'd thought I had her all figured out, but I didn't. At least not fully. Mom falls in and out of love not necessarily on a whim, but according to a capricious timer that only she can hear. When it rings, she's done.

I shift the heavy bucket back to the other hand and catch up with Mom. I understand her more than I did just a few moments ago, and I certainly understand that she's a better mother than Lily.

"You'll need to tell Earl about my passing."

"You might outlive him."

"A lot of people will want to know. We have to make a list."

I agree, but I'm all too happy when the subject turns to songs she learned as a child and she belts out, "In 1814 we took a little trip, along with Colonel Jackson down the mighty Mississip." I push a swag of moss aside with my shovel and join in the choir, our voices rising up past the high branches.

"That was fun. Your voice is almost as

good as mine."

"Thank you, Mom." That wasn't exactly a compliment, but I'll take it. Not only do I have a better understanding of her, but I feel a deeper connection with her, too.

We stop in front of the four graves in the corner, the Sutton outcasts, all of whom are women. I'm fairly certain there are some Sutton men buried around here who deserve a plot in this corner of the cemetery, if for nothing else than for the numerous paintings of their horses and dogs I've found in the attic.

I drop the bucket and shovel in front of a white marble vault with a life-size weeping angel on top.

Lillian Elizabeth Sutton Jackson
Born into This World 1921
Beautiful Daughter, Wife
Beloved Mother, Grandmother
Taken Too Soon

Too soon? She was almost ninety.

She points to the ground and sighs. "This needs to be cleaned up."

"Grandmother's last name was Cooper for over forty years. A lot longer than Jackson."

"We can't have Stepdaddy's name on

Momma's tomb. It wouldn't be right." She grabs the wreath from my elbow and places it on the angel's foot. "Lily married a Jackson, then a Gaudet; one wore an army uniform, the other a green beret."

What? "Pawpaw Bob was a Green Beret?"

"No, but he made gator gumbo."

That logic hurts my head, so I reach for the shovel and attempt to remove a clump of grass. Grandmother's vault is one of the showiest in the cemetery, let alone in this corner of sinners. Grandmother was never brash or loud and probably would have been a little embarrassed by the over-the-top angel. I understand why Mother wanted her to have one, though.

"I want to be buried here." She points to the locked door of the vault. "With Momma."

Even though I'd rather talk about anything but Mom's burial, it's part of the reason she insisted we come here. I put my boot heel into the effort and shovel a clump. "Do you want me to add another weeping angel?"

"No."

Surprising.

"I want my angel gazing up, with her wings wide like she's flying. . . ." There she is. A frown wrinkles her brows, and she points to the sky. We've probably been away from the house for an hour, and I'm sure she's getting tired and needs lunch and medication.

"Do you want to go back?"

"Why?"

Because sweat is collecting beneath the wire in my bra and the bayou smells swampy back here. My feet feel gross and the trees are buzzing with cicadas.

"I want my angel to look like she's flying to heaven."

I move to a different patch of weeds and dig in with the shovel. "Anything else?"

"Yes, she has to have really long hair like me."

The patch is determined to win, but I dig the shovel deep and jump on it with both boots. I grunt a little and ask, "You want to be remembered as an angel?"

"No one will believe that," she scoffs.

"True." She's divorced five men and broken the hearts of countless others.

"I want a simple engraving like Momma."

Somehow, I doubt that. "What do you want it to say?"

"I don't know."

Even though I'm "not any good" with rhymes, I try to think one up. Something pretty that will make her smile. I start with,

"Patricia Lynn Jackson . . ." (Since her fifth divorce, from Buzzy Doyle, she legally changed back to her maiden name, Jackson.) I rack my brain, and the only rhyme I can think up is *flaxen,* but her hair has always been dark like mine. "Patricia Lynn Jackson," I try again, "her friends called her Patty . . . she was always pretty and seldom bratty."

She tips her head back and laughs, and my heart is happy. "Remember when you stuck your tongue out at one of your teachers and I had to come get you from school?"

Yes, and I probably looked like Mom in her Shirley Temple dress. "You were mad, but when I told you she said I was a poor thing from a broken home, you took me to McDonald's for lunch as consolation."

She sits on the granite slab supporting Grandmother's vault. "You're a good daughter."

She hasn't said that since the first day that we arrived at Sutton Hall.

"I've had a good life." She gazes off into the distance like she does when she starts to sink further into her Alzheimer's. But it's only morning, and she's usually good until at least four.

"You're tired. Let me take you back to the house."

248

"I've had a good life," she repeats. "I want to die soon."

"What?"

"You have to help me end my life."

The shovel falls from my grasp. "What?"

"If you love me, you'll help me die."

I sink to the granite slab beside her. "No." This isn't the first time she's mentioned killing herself. Shortly after she was first diagnosed with Alzheimer's, she talked about Washington State's Death with Dignity Act, but she didn't meet the requirements for medical assistance to end her own life. Namely, she wasn't six months from dying of a terminal illness. I'd forgotten all about that. I thought she had, too.

She looks into my eyes, her expression as clear as it was that first night in Seattle when she said, "I know it's a lot to ask."

My face goes numb. She's serious. I open my mouth, but I can't form words. I should have known she was buttering me up for a reason. All that happy reminiscing and "you're a good daughter" were because she wanted something.

And I fell for it. Again.

"I told you I want to be buried next to Momma."

"Yeah." In disbelief, I wave my hand in the air. "Sometime in the future, and you never mentioned anything about me killing you!"

She shrugs and adjusts her hat. "I don't want to suffer and wear a bib. It's a horrible way to go."

I agree, but I'm not going to kill her.

"I help others with my passionate nature, but I can't help myself."

"Oh my God, stop with the passionate nature."

"Don't curse. That's why you have to help me."

"No, Mom. I can't." This is absurd. It doesn't feel real, but I know it is.

"Think of it as a mercy killing."

I cross one leg over the other and fold my arms over my chest. "That's still killing."

"Call it a merciful slumber."

In this alternate universe, Mother not only asks me to do the impossible, but she also puts me in a terrible situation. "What's your timeline for this?"

"I don't know."

In this alternate universe, Mother not only asks me to do the impossible, but she also puts me in a hopeless situation. I slap at some kind of green insect on my arm. She's serious, and I'm pissed. "Could you guess?"

"Soon," she answers, and doesn't seem to notice my sarcasm. "Before I forget."

There are those words again, but they won't make me give in to Mom's wishes this time. No way they're powerful enough to make me kill my mom. I take a deep breath and let it out slowly. I don't want to blow up, and I attempt to reason with her even though I know it's impossible. "Think about what you're saying."

"I've been thinking about it since that first day."

"What if I asked you to kill me? You wouldn't do it." I try to reason.

"Yes, I would."

I suck in a breath. "You'd kill me?"

"It's not killing if you want to die."

Oh, *that's all.* I point out the obvious consequence. "I'll go to prison for murder."

"Oh." Her brows draw together. "I didn't think of that."

Of course not.

"I can't do it by myself." Tears well up in her eyes. "I'll forget."

Exactly. I brought Mother to Louisiana so we could laugh and have fun for as long as possible and create a few final memories together. Helping her die is not a memory I want to create for myself.

She sniffs and wipes her nose with the back of her hand. "I guess it's okay that you don't want to get me the pills."

"Thank you." My shoulders drop with relief.

"All you gotta do is remind me," she says as if it's the perfect compromise.

"And just how often should I remind you?" Mom can still figure out how to shop online, but I don't think she has the ability to research drug-assisted suicide and shop for the right pills. Even if she managed it somehow, there is no way I'm going to remind my mother to take her life. "Once a week?"

"I'll need more reminding than that. Once or twice a day should do it."

"Is that all?"

"Yep. Unless you think it should be more."

"For God's sake!"

"Don't curse."

"I can't remind you to die. I love you too much."

She turns toward me and takes my hand in both of hers. "If you love me, you'd do this one little thing."

One little thing? I'm angry and hurt and lash out, "Ask Tony. He's the son you never had."

She lets go of my hand, and I can make out Rattlesnake Patty in her narrowed eyes. "You broke up with Tony."

Now she remembers.

"I have a right to die. You want to keep me around until I am just bones and skin and my mouth hangs open."

The backs of my eyes sting from hurt and anger. "Mom —"

"You want me to drool on a bib like a baby, and no one will come spoon me in my hour of need."

"Of course I don't want you to suffer, but I'm not going to help you kill yourself."

"You're selfish!" she shouts, and attempts to stand.

I try to assist her to her feet, but she shakes off my hand. "Don't touch me."

The mood on the walk back to the house is icy on account of Mom's cold shoulder, but I try to ease the tension. "Mom, let's get along. I love you."

"Well, I don't love you. Go away from me."

Her words plunge deep into my heart, and I stop to let her walk ahead without me.

15

Return of Rattlesnake Patty. Bob's gone.
Raphael is MIA — again.

By the time I make it back into the house,
I'm hot, clammy, and exhausted from fighting off horseflies with the shovel until I
finally gave up and ran.

Lindsey is in the kitchen making lunch
and wearing one of her flowing sundresses.
She looks young and happy and is chatting
with the skinny guy from Simon's crew. His
name is Jim Poulet and he is so Cajun, I
can hardly understand a word out of his
mouth. Lindsey smiles and laughs as if she
doesn't see me leaning against the door,
gasping for breath.

Somewhere in the house someone is bang-
ing a hammer, and my head pounds in time
with it.

Mom returns to the kitchen long enough
to announce, "I want lunch in the parlor."

Her gaze narrows and she points a bony finger at me. "I don't want to see her face."

Everything stops, and the kitchen goes silent as my face flushes deeper. My shoulders are sore from carrying those stupid tools in that stupid bucket that we never even used, my feet hurt, and I can feel tiny gnats in my throat. The day started off so good, which makes this turn of events all the harder to bear.

I want off this roller coaster. I thought I could ride it out, but I can't. I'm not as strong a person as I'd always believed. I don't have it in me to help Mom kill herself.

I grab a bottle of water from the refrigerator and walk out the back door before I burst into tears or yell f-bombs. I stand at the top of the step and open the bottle. The Escalade is parked next to several work trucks, and for a few moments, I let myself get lost in the fantasy of jumping in the SUV and driving away. I take a long drink and clear my throat of unshed tears and bugs. I don't know where I'll go. Just away. Someplace cool and dry with room service and a stocked bar.

Simon stands by the tailgate of his truck wearing jeans and a white T-shirt like the first time I saw him. One hand is on his hip, and he's having a heated conversation with someone on his phone. I don't know what he's saying, because it sounds like he's speaking French. I duck my head and walk toward the garage; his conversation grows quiet as I pass.

I don't turn on the light inside, because the cool darkness feels better. I'm living in a two-hundred-year-old money pit to make my mom happy. I made sure she had the bedroom she wanted (perhaps not in the right location), and I regularly haul family mementos from the attic to keep her brain active. I listen to Jelly Roll Morton until I want to stab my ears with a paintbrush. I braid Mom's hair and help her bathe, but no matter what I do, she's never happy for long.

I turn sideways and slide past the surrey. My tears catch up to me and roll down my hot cheeks. I'm responsible for Mom's health needs and quality of life. I'm responsible for making sure she is happy and comfortable for the rest of her life. I'm her daughter. I gladly take on those responsibilities, but now she wants me to take on the added responsibility of killing her, too.

I need a place to hide other than the hot attic. I climb into the surrey and take a seat on the front bench. The tufted velvet is worn and itchy in places, but no springs poke my butt.

My vision blurs, and I don't realize I'm crying until I wipe tears away with the back of my hand. My life is a three-ring circus with Mother's roller coaster at the center. Raphael and his bird antics share the next ring with Simon and the house restorations. Lulu Inc. fills the remaining circle like a rudderless ship in a storm-tossed sea.

I'm the circus ringmaster, jumping through hoops to control chaos, direct disorder, and manage time. I am failing at all three. Mom doesn't love me. Raphael has taken screws from two dining room chairs and hidden them somewhere. Sutton Hall is a mess. My subscriber growth is near stagnant, and Lulu merch is down. Our organic clicks have hit new lows, and people are opting out of notifications.

The release we sent out in February, asking for patience and understanding, apparently had a time limit, and followers have run out of both. Margie thinks we need to remind followers why they love Lulu with a splashy relaunch. That sounds all fine and dandy, except I don't have the time to invest in a big splashy relaunch. With everything else going on in my life, I don't even have the time to *think* about something so mentally taxing. On the other hand, I don't have the time to *not* think about it. Lulu's my baby — I'm not ready to let her die, just like I'm not ready to let Mom die either. I'll figure it out, but not right this minute. All I want to do right now is sit in the old buggy and let the world pass me by.

The back door creaks open and the light flickers on. I dry my wet cheeks on the shoulders of my T-shirt and wipe my nose for good measure.

"Are you hiding, tee Lou Ann?"

"Yes." I hear the tread of heels on concrete before Simon appears beside the carriage. I turn my face away to hide my red eyes.

"Ms. Patricia bein' a pill?"

More like a snake. "That's one way to put it."

The surrey dips to one side as Simon climbs aboard.

"Nice boots."

"Thank you. They match my eyes," I joke.

He sits next to me and lays one arm across the back of the seat. "Your hair looks good." He tugs a curl. "I like it."

"That's nice."

"It's kind of . . ."

I look across my shoulder at him. "Kind of what?"

"Well, that braid you wore made you look

258

buttoned up."

"Now I look unbuttoned?"

He smiles. "Yeah."

"That's me. Unbuttoned and falling apart."

His smile wavers. "How long's it been since you had a break?"

I laugh without humor. "What's that?"

"When was the last time you got away by yourself?"

That's easy. "The night I ran into you buying groceries. It was like a mini vacation."

"Gator's Grocery isn't a vacation. It's a last resort when the Piggly Wiggly is closed for the night. It's not my idea of a good time."

"It seemed like you knew everyone."

"Not everyone, but I was born and raised around here. Only left long enough to get my degree at Georgia Southern. I figured out real quick this is where I belong."

I guess that's the difference between living in one place and moving every few years. "What's your degree?"

"Civil engineering and construction, but we're not talkin' about me."

Simon isn't touching me, but I can feel his testosterone invading my personal space. On a normal day, I might feel intimidated by the bombardment. Today it's oddly comforting, and I lean back until I feel the length of his warm arm across my tense shoulders.

"You need a break. I took care of Jasper when he got real bad. There was nobody else and I about lost my mind."

"That's nice." My brain is filtering through the past, trying to recall the last time sitting next to a man just felt easy.

"What?"

I finally look over at him. "What?"

"He didn't have anyone else to take care of him."

Oh yeah. Jasper.

"You need to take time for yourself."

"You sound like a therapist, and I should know."

"Jasper could be cantankerous." He shrugs, and his shoulder brushes mine. "I went to some support group meetings in Terrebonne Parish."

He went to caregiver meetings for a man who wasn't family? "That's a lot to take on for a 'cantankerous' old man not even related to you."

"Not by blood. Jasper was my parrain, and he didn't have anyone else."

"What's a *pa-ra*?"

"Godfather."

"Oh." Well, that explains why he opened the house for us the day we arrived. "He didn't have friends?"

"Ray-feel was his only real friend. He ran most folks off. All the others owed him money and made themselves real scarce."

If Raphael was his only real friend, that doesn't speak well of Jasper. I'm not sure I would have stuck around. "You could have made yourself scarce."

"I owed him." He turns toward me, and his eyes turn a deeper shade of green beneath the weak garage light. "He taught me how to strip antique furniture the right way and how to make plaster casts of old moldings and cornices. Most everything I know about restoration comes from Jasper."

I let that sink in and then ask, "If Jasper restored homes for a living, why'd he let his own house fall apart?"

"Restoration was his hobby. He made his living from gambling."

That explains a lot about Raphael, too.

"And Sutton Hall isn't falling apart. I've restored homes that were actually uninhabitable."

"I bet that cost an arm and a leg."

He grins and rises to his feet. "An arm and a leg and a few other body parts, too." He grabs the pole holding the carriage top with the fringe on it. "We put Jasper in this thing and hauled him over to the cemetery." He shakes it like he did the balcony railing. "I imagine y'all will use it, too."

"That's Mom's plan, but on days like today, I'm thinking more of hauling her *behind* it." I expect him to frown at me for saying such a horrible thing, but instead he chuckles and jumps to the floor.

"Come see." He holds up a hand like he's planning to help me down, but I don't know if I'm ready to leave yet. I'm suspicious of what he might want to show me, and I look around.

"Come see what?"

"Come here." He motions for me. "I'll help you down."

"You should have said that."

"I did. Everyone knows that 'come see' means 'come here.' Just like we don't go to the store and *buy* groceries. We go to the store and make groceries."

"What? Why would you make your own groceries when they're already packaged?"

He shakes his head like *I'm* confusing. "I forget you're from the North and talk funny."

"Me?" I take his hand, even though I know I'll have to turn around and give him an eyeful of butt cheeks as I climb down. "I talk like a normal person." He wasn't a gentleman that first day when he found me shoving chips in my mouth. I guess he's reformed. "Move back so my behind isn't in your face."

He laughs and puts his hands on my waist. "As tempting as that sounds . . ." He lifts me from the surrey and I instinctively grab his shoulder. In those few seconds, several things happen all at once. My pulse jumps, my heart booms, and my skin flushes. My brain says, *Ohh, this is nice,* but my mouth says, "I'm too heavy."

He sets me on the ground but keeps his hands on my waist. "You're far from heavy, tee Lou."

I've gone from tee Lou Ann to tee Lou. I like it, and I'm not going to analyze the situation to death. With his green eyes and dark hair, and his smooth southern Louisiana accent, he could talk a girl into some real trouble.

"You don't weigh much more than the catfish I pulled down the bayou last weekend."

Or not. "You seriously need to work on your pickup lines."

His thumbs brush my stomach a second before his hands drop from my waist. "You don't like being compared to a catfish?"

"No."

He chuckles, and we walk toward the door. "You're the expert."

"I suppose it's better than swamp rat, though."

"Who called you a swamp rat?"

"You." He moves behind the carriage first and reaches for my hand. "The first day we arrived."

"How do you remember that?" He pauses at the back door and turns to me.

"It was memorable."

"Mais, I must have meant it as a compliment."

"Uh-huh. You totally blew my image of a Southern gentleman."

He raises my hand to his mouth and kisses the back of my knuckles. "Swamp rat est belle, yes?"

I look up at him, his eyes staring into mine, waiting for an answer. Maybe I make him wait for a few heartbeats longer than necessary. "No."

He laughs and lets go of my hand. "You're the expert."

I follow him out the door and raise a hand to shade my eyes against the sun. "I'm too tired to be an expert on anything these days."

"Even more reason for you to get away

and relax."

The knots of tension have eased from my muscles, and my ears no longer ring. "I'll work on it," I say as I head up the steps.

He stops at the bottom and looks up at me. "You should probably work on it before you get riled and holler 'squirrel-dick shit taco' again."

I pause with my hand on the doorknob. "You remember that?"

"It was memorable," he says as he turns on his heels and walks toward his truck.

I might be tired these days, but I still recognize the dangers of men like Simon: a smooth operator, charming and handsome, with a really nice butt. Okay, maybe I just added that last part. I turn the doorknob and walk inside.

The kitchen is empty, and I move to the equally empty hall. The temporary railing is finally up, and all the workers are gone. It took a day to put it up, but considerably more time before the old one came down. Simon's men photographed and labeled each piece, cataloging even the smallest splinters before it was taken away.

There's a settling calm after workers and guests leave Sutton Hall. The house feels languid and relaxed, practically begging me to slide into a rocking chair on the squeaky porch and sip a cold mint julep. I have a new appreciation for the evening slowdown, especially when Mom has spent most of the day shattering calm like a hammer through glass.

I hear Mom and Lindsey in the front parlor. I'm tempted to hide in the attic, but I force myself to join them. Mom is just going to have to get over her anger. I'm not going to apologize for not agreeing to kill her.

The two sit on the chesterfield looking at pictures like many times before. They smile and laugh, and I feel like the odd man out.

"Has anyone seen Raphael?" I point to his empty cage.

"I haven't seen the demon since you fed him last night."

Which means he could be swinging from chandeliers or taking apart chairs or hiding out until poor unsuspecting Lindsey walks by.

"Maybe he's gone for good," Lindsey adds hopefully.

"You're not that lucky." I laugh.

Mom refuses to look at me, and I realize this impasse could last for days if I let it. I remind myself that I'm the fully functional adult and join them as if everything is peachy.

"I like your dress," I tell Lindsey.

"Thanks. I like it, too." She touches the light fabric and smiles. "Come look at this." I hesitate, waiting for Mother to say she hates me. Instead, she just turns another page without looking up.

"We're giving captions to the old photos." I sit next to Lindsey, and she points to a faded tintype. "Grumpy woman with a doily on her head."

Mom's up next and says to Lindsey as if I'm not in the room, "Baby passing a good time in a buggy."

I look closer and stare at the buggy from the attic. It was creepy even back then.

Lindsey pokes me with her elbow. "Your turn."

I point to a black-and-white photo with the caption of Salty Joe. "Another damn horse picture."

Mom won't look at me, but at least she's not yelling. I'm good with that.

Lindsey makes up several more, and we fall into a pattern. Lindsey's captions are funny, mine are dry, and Mom's are "passing a good time" with this or that.

I point to a woman standing beside the fireplace in the yellow office. "She's a long cool woman in a black dress."

Lindsey groans. Mom points to a new

photo. "Passing a good time in a sugar field."

Lindsey and I push our faces closer to the tintype. The black men and women in it do not look like they're passing a good time in a sugar field. The men are naked from the waist up, the women have babies on their backs, and the children are barefoot. "Mom, they're not having a good time."

She scowls and sticks her chin up. "They're smiling like they are."

Perhaps there are a few smiles, but I'm not mistaking them for a good time. Mother is a seventy-four-year-old woman with Alzheimer's, and I've never heard her say anything racist. She's never looked at color when choosing a partner. All that has ever mattered is gender. So is it worth explaining the meaning of the photo? Do I risk another rattlesnake strike?

"Look at those poor little kids. They don't have shoes," Lindsey says just before she bursts into tears. I'm taken aback, and all I can do is stare. This is a side of Lindsey I've never witnessed. I've seen her all business with Mom, happy about her new driver's license, laughing with Cajun Jim, and scared shitless by ghosts and Raphael. I've never seen her this emotional. I suppose, coming from her family, it's understandable that she would have a soft spot for children trapped by the circumstances of their birth. My heart aches for her, and I wrap an arm around her trembling shoulders. "It's okay," I tell her, because I don't know what else to say.

"No one gave them shoes," she sobs through her fingers. "That's hor-rible." I rub her back and wish I could do more. "People can be so meeeean."

"What'd you do to Lindsey?" Mom is finally looking at me, and her eyes are snaky at the edges.

"Me?"

"You're always bossy and mean."

"I didn't do anything."

"Well, you must have done something."

"I didn't!" I look at Lindsey, then back at Mom. "What did *you* do?"

"Nothin'."

"Sor-ry," Lindsey manages between hic-cups.

Mom's chin goes up even further. "It's the baby."

I give her a warning glare.

Of course she doesn't notice. "Babies make women emotional."

"Mother!" She's gone from calling Lindsey fat to saying she's pregnant.

"Yep. It's the baby."

269

"You're being mean," I whisper over the sound of Lindsey's sniffles.

"It's the baby, all right."

"Stop." Alzheimer's is no excuse for how she's treated me, and now Lindsey, today. "I've had it with you."

"She's got a big ol' baby in there."

I close my eyes. Please God, make her stop.

"Might have to get her uterus yanked out like I did."

God isn't listening, so it's up to me. "No one cares about your uterus." Out of all her remaining memories, of course, that one is securely wedged in her hippocampus right next to Melvin's testicles. Two things no one wants to hear about. I hug Lindsey closer and kind of press my shoulder to her ear in hopes she can't hear what I'm mouthing to Mom. "If you can't say something nice, stop talking."

"There's gonna —"

"There is no baby!" I interrupt.

Lindsey hiccups and wipes her nose with the back of her hand. "Actually, Patricia's right."

"What?" I push Lindsey away and look into her red puffy eyes.

"I'm pregnant."

My brain seizes. No thoughts coming in.

None going out.

"Told ya there's a baby."

How'd she get pregnant? Okay, I know *how,* but in the three months she's been with me, I've never even heard her talk about a man. She hasn't talked about anyone since we've been in Louisiana either. I put a hand to my forehead in an attempt to make sense of all this. Lindsey has her driver's license, but she never really goes anywhere. When she does, she isn't gone long and she's never out at night. I drop my hand to my lap. This has to be a prank. Is it April Fool's Day? No, that was last month.

"I have a picture of my baby." Lindsey reaches into a side pocket in her dress and pulls out an ultrasound photo. She puts the small picture in my hand, and I expect to see an image like when Fern showed me the first ultrasound of her baby. I think I'm going to see something that looks like a nugget with flippers, but the glossy image in my hand is of a fully formed baby sucking its thumb.

"His name is Frankie."

I let that sink in. Frankie. A baby. A real person.

"When is this baby due?"

"September ninth."

My math skills are about as good as my

271

measurement skills. "Which makes you how far along?"

"Nineteen weeks."

"What's that in months?"

"Five."

I don't have to be in the mood for math to figure out she was two months pregnant when I hired her. I wonder if she knew. "When were you going to tell me?"

"I wanted to tell you when you called in February, but I knew you wouldn't have hired me."

That answers that question. "You were right." For the first time since Lindsey entered our lives, I'm angry with her. She lied to me by omission and betrayed my trust.

"I've been afraid to tell. I'm afraid you might fire me."

"You're right about that, too."

"I'm sorry," Lindsey says again, and tears fill her eyes.

"You knew when I hired you that I needed someone on board for the long haul." I stand and walk toward the door. I thought we were close, that we had each other's backs. Now I have three months left with her, at best. "I trusted you."

"What are you going to do?"

I look back at her and at my mother's face

still pinched with anger. This is a mess. "I don't know," I say as I walk from the room, hardly noticing the temporary railing as I climb the stairs. Lindsey's eagerness to leave Washington makes sense now. She had a baby on board and wanted to get as far away as possible.

It's still early, but I strip down to my bra and panties and crawl into bed. There have been innumerable bad days in the past few months — the flight to New Orleans, the first night in Sutton Hall, casket shopping at Bergeron Funeral Home — but today tops them all. It started with Mom thinking that I'm going to be cool with killing her and ended with Lindsey thinking I'm going to be cool with a baby named Frankie.

"Lou Ann." Lindsey knocks and pushes open the door at the same time.

I turn on my side away from her. I don't want to see her right now.

"I'm sorry. I should have done things different, but it just got crazy. When you called in February, I was staring at an e.p.t. stick, and you seemed like the answer to all my problems."

"And here I thought you were the answer to mine." I roll onto my back and look up at her. "I depend on you to help with Mom. You're my rock when everything goes insane around here. Did you think about the position your pregnancy puts me in?" Her silence is my answer. "What about your family?"

"They'd never accept Frankie." Lindsey sits on the side of my bed. "And every baby should be born into a family that can't wait to welcome it."

"What about Frankie's father? I'm assuming you told him."

She shrugs and looks away. "He doesn't want the responsibility."

Well, that makes him an irresponsible asshole, but it doesn't change the fact that she's kept this baby a secret since I hired her. It's not a small secret, either.

"It's just Frankie and me."

"No, it's not." I sit up. "It's you and Frankie and my sick mother."

"I can still give the same quality of care to Patricia that I've —"

"No, you can't," I interrupt. "If Mother falls and needs help getting up, you can't help her. Once the baby is born, you can't take care of Mom and a newborn at the same time."

"I think I can."

"Don't be naive."

She looks down at her hands resting on her round stomach. "I'm sorry."

"You never answered the question of when you were going to tell me." How had I missed something that was so obvious, even to Mom? She must have scheduled doctor appointments on her days off. "Did you think you could have this baby on your day off and sneak him into your bedroom?"

"I wanted to tell you, but I was afraid you might fire me."

It seems we're right back to the same chaos as when we first arrived at Sutton Hall. Only now a baby has been added to our madhouse.

"Are you going to fire me?" Lindsey asks just above a whisper.

"I don't know what I'm going to do." The only thing I do know is that the circus is officially out of control.

16

Mom slams her studio door and cranks up the Carmen Miranda record I found in the attic yesterday. She's behaving like a petulant teenager, blasting her music on the Victrola. Lindsey sticks her head in and leaves the door halfway open so Mom won't succumb to paint fumes, but unfortunately that means we all get to share in the pleasure of bongos and maracas and "boom-chica-boom chica-boom-boom chica-boom."

I head toward the front of the house to get as far away as possible. I hurry past the stairs and Raphael perched on the temporary railing, bobbing his head to the beat and squawking "Chica, Chica, Boom, Chic" like it's an old favorite.

"You're demented," I tell him as I rush to my office and slam the pocket door behind me. I can still hear Carmen in the distance, but I'm safe from a migraine for now.

It's been five days since the cemetery incident and Mom's anger has dropped from boiling to frozen solid. There is nothing I can do to change the situation, except maybe agree to kill her. She hasn't mentioned her "merciful slumber" plot, and I'm not sure she even remembers why she's so mad. She just knows that I've done something to her, like hidden her shoes or stolen her money. She even mumbled something about her old mink coat, which, incidentally, I mercifully killed five years ago when I found it stinking like a wet cat in the closet with threadbare elbows and ripped seams.

Mom's anger will have to run its course, but I did nothing wrong. I'm not going to act as if I did, and over the next few days I continue to search out interesting articles and photos for her, although she says little to me. We eat our meals at the same dining room table, but she mostly talks to Lindsey.

The upside of Mom's cold shoulder is I've spent more time in my office and created meaningful content for the website. I made a funny little video about my life in southern Louisiana. I showed off my new hair and

"Who Dat" boots and got over a hundred thousand likes the first hour it was posted on my website. I'm finally feeling optimistic about Lulu's recovery.

The downside is, I miss Mom. I'm sad that instead of wonderful memories, all I'm getting is the stink eye — and that's only when she pays any attention to me at all. With Mom storming around at night and wringing her hands, it seems we're back to where we started months ago. Nevertheless, I feel I've made huge changes both inside and out. I have more patience, have re-arranged my priorities, and have shifted the focus of my life. My hair is different and sometimes I only wear mascara and lipstick. Maybe it's the climate or the change in me, but my designer clothes and shoes remain in the wardrobe in favor of jean shorts and T-shirts and flat sandals or sneakers for climbing around in the attic. Today I pulled on a tank top with an angry crab holding a "Say No to Pot" sign that I wouldn't have been caught dead in six months ago.

There's a knock on my door and Lindsey pushes it open. "Simon's here. He said you wanted him to come over to talk about varnish or something."

Well, that's the cover story, anyway, but I lied. He's man bait, pure and simple. Mom won't be able to control her passionate nature around him. She'll smile and flirt and glow with giddiness. Once he's escaped her clutches, I'm hoping she'll bask in a happy afterglow for a few days and forget she hates me.

I admit it's a shameful and sexist plan. I'm a horrible hypocrite and a very selfish woman. And yet, I am quite willing to bear that burden.

I follow Mom's laughter through the hall and find her smiling like rainbows and sunshine just walked through the door. Her man bait has arrived, and he doesn't disappoint. Jim's with him, which makes Lindsey all smiley and giggly, too. She knows I'm not going to fire her, but I wonder if she's informed Jim of the baby on board.

"I'm glad you called, and I guarantee you'll love the new finish on those stairs."

I can't really blame Mom for her crush on Dr. Simon. I've always been attracted to a man in a sharp suit and tie, polished shoes, and hair cut to razor perfection, but lately I've come to appreciate a man in tight T-shirts and old-school Levi's with seams worn in interesting places. A man with finger-combed hair and scuffed work boots and a languid ease about him that misses nothing.

"It's cheaper and easier to do it before we put the railing up," he adds.

I'm sure he's right, but cheaper and easier are relative. "Easy for you," I point out. "You won't be living in a construction zone with my mother, sucking up dust."

"I don't mind," Mom says, one of her front teeth marked with red lipstick. She must have been in a real hurry to get out here and chat with the doctor.

"No dust. All our electrical sanders have dust filters, and we bring in the cyclone to clean the air. We'll be in and out in a couple of days."

"We have to be able to use the stairs while you work."

"Use the back stairs. I'll have two guys clear all that stuff out."

"That's a problem. The attic is full as it is, and I don't know where else to put all that mess."

"Landfill. Unless that's a problem."

"Not for me, but Mom's going to have a problem with it."

"No problem," Mom says to spite me.

She wouldn't agree with the plan if she understood he was talking about disposing of Sutton treasures. "I don't even want to imagine what you'll charge me for a dump run."

"I'd waive the debris removal charge."

"Wow. Generous." I look at all those wooden steps. That's a lot of sanding. "Do you charge by the stair?"

His gaze lowers past my mouth and chin, down my throat to the front of my tank top. He chuckles and folds his arms across his chest. "By the hour."

"How many hours?"

He rocks back on his heels and looks up as if the answer is written on the ceiling. "Best guess . . . soup to nuts . . ."

"Hard to say," I finish for him.

"You're learnin'."

Mom coaxes both men to stay for lunch, and she puts me at the head of the table so she can sit closer to Simon. We eat roasted chicken breasts and coconut brussels sprouts off gilded Limoges china, and I feel like a third wheel.

Lindsey and Jim talk between themselves while Mom chats nonstop about herself and squeezes Simon's arm. It's embarrassing, but I remind myself that this was my big plan. Only it's not working like I'd hoped. Mom is still ignoring me and rambling on about her "wonderful paintings" and "sexy swimsuit."

"That's where we bought our 'Who Dat' boots," I add when Mom comes up for air.

She gives me the side eye, then returns her attention to Simon. "It has little holes in the back."

I am invisible. My scheme is a bust, but more than anything, I hate brussels sprouts. You can sauté them in butter, smother them in cheese sauce, or sprinkle them with coconut, but they still taste like fucking brussels sprouts, and I flick one off my plate. It leaves a trail of shredded coconut as it rolls to the center of the table. No one notices but Simon, and he raises a brow and gives me half a smile.

"I always wanted to marry a doctor." A piece of coconut is stuck to one corner of Mom's red-lipsticked mouth, and if I wasn't invisible, I'd help her take care of that. I'd give her a subtle hint, but I push my plate to the side and rest my chin in my hands instead. Lindsey asks if I'm okay. "Peachy," I answer without looking up. I tune Mom out and pay closer attention to Lindsey and Jim's conversation. The more I listen, the more I can pick out a few words here and there, or here and dere, rather.

A brussels sprout rolls into view, and I glance at Simon out of the corner of my eyes. Apparently, I'm not the only one who hates brussels sprouts.

"You should seriously consider what we

talked about," he says.

It takes me several seconds to recall our last conversation and I sit up in my chair. "It's been so long since I took a day for myself, I wouldn't know what to do."

"Mais, dere's nothin' like a cool-a of beer and a bucket of fish." Simon chuckles and points across the table. "Axe Jim."

Jim's smile lights up his brown eyes. "Talk about."

"I think I'll pass," I tell them both.

"I got a massage at a day spa in Houma." Lindsey gives me a tentative smile, and I feel like I've been mean to a pregnant puppy.

Ahhh . . . a spa. I check out my short fingernails and let myself wish. I haven't had a manicure in months.

"I never get to go to a spa."

I look at Mom, sitting back in her chair and finally looking at me. "I'll take you if you want to go. You always liked an aroma-therapy pedicure."

She folds her arms over her chest. "I don't have money." I mentally brace for impact because I know what's coming. "You stole all my money. I never get anything."

This is so unfair.

"I can never buy anything on a card."

Now, that's somewhat true. I had to lower

the spending limit on her Visa due to her new QVC habit. I hadn't realized the depth of her addiction until a UPS truck began to show up several times a week to drop off everything from palazzo pants to a police scanner with laser detectors and voice alerts. Mom said we needed it in the Escalade to "hide from cops" like we were boozed-up moonshiners. I'm just grateful that she used her own card and not one she managed to steal.

"You bought Tova Beauty just the other day," Lindsey reminds her.

"Thank you," I tell her.

"I hate Tova Beauty!" Then Mom points across the table at me. "She hides the remote so I can't watch my shows."

Funny. I hear her shows blaring every time she's in her room.

"I think it's just been misplaced," Lindsey steps in. "We'll find it."

"My own child wants me dead."

Says the woman I refuse to kill. "That's not true. I love you."

Jim makes an uncomfortable sound in his throat, and he's looking around as if he doesn't know what he should do.

"No one wants you to die, Ms. Patricia," Simon assures her.

"Be quiet!" Mom snaps, her anger clearly

overruling her passionate nature. "You don't know anything. She wants me gone so she can make Sutton Hall a bed-and-breakfast."

I groan. Not that again.

Simon rises from his seat. Lindsey scoots her chair back and poor Jim jumps up like he can't get away fast enough.

"I'll get your meds, Patricia." Lindsey makes a quick exit with Jim on her heels.

"Are you leaving me, Dr. Simon?" Mom smiles up at him as if the past few seconds haven't happened.

"Afraid so." Simon helps Mom to her feet. "Thank you for lunch. It was delicious," he says, but I notice he hasn't eaten much, especially compared to Jim, whose plate looks licked clean.

She offers her cheek and scowls at me over his shoulder. "You don't get to watch my shows ever again," she whispers loudly, as if no one else can hear her. As if listening to her yell about Melvin Thompson's white balls is some sort of reward for good behavior.

I watch Mom shuffle from the room, madder than ever. So much for a giddy afterglow.

"Do you have a hat?"

Since Simon and I are the only two left in

285

the room, I assume he's asking me. "No. Why?"

"I want to show you something?"

For a split second, I imagine Simon ripping off his shirt to Joe Cocker's "You Can Leave Your Hat On." "What?"

"I'm not going to tell you. You'll just have to come with me."

I doubt he's going to show me the Full Monty, and I follow him into the hall because I'm intrigued and have nothing else to do.

"I parked my truck out front."

I turn toward the parlor and he heads toward the kitchen.

"This way, tee Lou."

"You said you parked in the front."

"I did."

"That's the back of the house." You'd think since he's worked on this house for twenty-five years, he'd know the difference.

He points to the front door. "That's the back."

I walk toward him. One of us fell on our head one too many times as a kid, and it wasn't me. "The kitchen is at the back of the house," I tell him.

"But this wasn't always the kitchen. This used to be a grand entry just like the one at the back of the house." He shakes his head as we walk outside. "Front of the house to you."

"What?" Maybe it *is* me. Maybe I'm the one who fell on my head and just doesn't remember.

He points to the columns and transom above the doors. "Originally, the front and back were identical."

"What?" He puts a hand on the small of my back and we walk to the passenger side of his truck. "Why?"

"River side and road." He opens the door and helps me inside. "If guests arrived by river, they had the same view of the house and grounds as guests arriving by buggy from the roadside."

He closes the door and I'm still confused. "There isn't a road back here," I point out as he gets in the driver's side. "It's on the other side of the house. The front side."

"It is now, but it used to be on this side." He fires up the truck and cool air flows from the vents. "The old road was closer to the house than the river, and both sides of the house had fountains and gardens to impress people when they arrived." We drive slowly down the old cobblestone road toward the cemetery. "A flood in the late eighteen hundreds forced the bayou this way and cut off part of the old road."

"So the front of the house became the back."

He shakes his head. "No. It's still the back."

"But the kitchen is in the back."

"When the kitchen got moved inside, it made sense to put it in front since folks arrived by boat."

No. I was right the first time. He's the one who fell on his head as a kid, but it might explain why the front-door key unlocked the back door on the day we first arrived. "Where are we going?"

"You're going to love it."

Mom's being horrible and I suppose I can use a little time away from the house. All I see out my side window is the cemetery. "I don't love the cemetery, if that's where you're taking me."

He looks across the cab at me. "Just relax."

"That's a problem for me."

"I noticed."

"I can probably relax more if I know where you're taking me."

"Practice some breathing or something."

Five meditation apps haven't helped with that. "I smell the bayou. It stinks."

"That's nothin' this time a year. Wait a few more weeks. Pooyi." We follow a bend in the road and the trees get thicker. "This'll

288

be great. Trust me."

"Mmm-hmm."

He glances across the cab. "Don't you trust me?"

"I don't know you well enough to trust you. For all I know, you're a serial killer."

"Ahh, boo. You hurt my feelings."

"I doubt it."

He pulls the truck off the road and stops in a clearing of jagged tupelo stumps and cypresses that I remember climbing up on as a kid. I was joking about the serial killer thing, but the trees are now covered in moss and the place looks weird and creepy.

Simon jumps out and reaches behind the seat. "You can get down," he says, and tosses a can of bug spray onto the seat.

I point to my loop-toe sandals. "I'm not wearing shoes for a hike."

"You'll be fine."

"I'm not very outdoorsy."

"Uh-huh." His seat flips forward and disappears from view. "Come see."

"See what?"

I hear his long-suffering sigh. "Come here."

I open the passenger-side door. "You should have said that."

"Mais la! You're a pain in the ass."

He's trying to be nice, and I don't want

289

to be a pain in the ass, so I walk around the front of the truck . . . and he's holding fishing poles. This has got to be a joke. "We're fishing?"

"Take about." He pulls a Minnie's Bait and Tackle ball cap from behind the seat and puts it on my head. "That's my lucky hat. Don't worry about the guts."

"There's guts on this thing?" My voice sounds kind of squeaky. I don't like guts, but I leave the hat on my head instead of touching it with my fingers.

"Lucky guts."

"I hate to deprive you of your lucky guts hat. You should wear it."

"It looks better on you, city girl." He laughs and holds up the bug spray. "Now close your eyes."

He sprays every inch of me, then hands me the can. "Get the back of my neck really good." I do as he says; then he grabs a cooler and hands me a tackle box that has seen better days. I don't see blood or anything suspicious, but I'm sure it too was christened with lucky guts at some point. The metal handle is loose, and I tuck the box beneath one arm as we walk down a short path to a wooden dock.

He said I would love it. "This'll be great," he said.

"Have you fished before?"

"No." And I've never had a desire to either. I like my fish the same way I like my chicken: packaged and clearly marked with an expiration date at the grocery store. The dock sways and creaks beneath our feet as we walk toward the two Adirondack chairs at the end. Simon sets the cooler between them and I ask, "What's in there?" I hope it's not live bait that might jump out.

"Water and Coke on ice." He rigs the poles with shiny lures and red-and-white bobbers as I wave away bugs flying in front of my face.

"I don't want to catch an actual fish."

He looks down at me from beneath the brim of his own lucky guts hat, then reaches into his tackle box for a big knife. "We'll both be safer this way." He cuts the line beneath the bobber and the lure falls onto the dock. "When Jasper was too much for me, I'd come back here and throw in a line." He ties a bell-shaped sinker beneath the bobber and lets go. "Nothing like it to get your head straight."

He shows me how to cast, his big arms around me and his hands cupping mine. He smells like man soap and bug spray. As it did that day in the garage, my brain says, *Ooh, this is nice.*

Simon drops his arms and takes the nice feeling with him. Which is probably a good thing. "You try now."

To my surprise, I drop the bobber behind me only twice before I whip it over my head and out into the bayou. I smile with accomplishment. I've never fished before, but I sit in one of the chairs and watch my bobber rock within the ripples like a pro. Frogs croak and cicadas sing, and a snapping turtle comes up for air. I suppress my "city girl" urge to lock myself in the truck and hope ugly beetles don't dive-bomb me. "What if there's an alligator?" I sit up straighter. How could I have forgotten my alligator repellent? "What should I do? I haven't practiced a zigzag!"

"Just watch your bobber, tee Lou. Don't overthink it."

"Easy for you to say. Your legs are longer, and you can run faster."

"True." Simon's line makes a *ziiiing* as his lure whips out to the other side of the bayou. "But for you, I'll give you a head start."

"Promise?"

"Mais la! Gators don't mess with you unless you mess with them."

"That isn't what you said at the grocery store."

"You obviously don't know when someone is joking."

"And you obviously don't know when you're not funny."

"Relax." He sits in the other chair and looks over at me. "I promise to throw myself on a gator if you promise to relax."

"Sounds fair."

A shadow slashes across his face as he opens the cooler. "What's your poison?"

"Water, please." I do take a peek inside before I lean back in the chair, though, and I'm grateful that I don't see anything in there but bottles. I stretch my legs out in front of me and stare out at trees and grasses on the far side. "Why'd you throw your lure so far away?"

"The current'll take it downstream and dump it in a hole where the fish hang out." He hands me the water and cracks a Dr Pepper. "Nothing to do now but relax and watch your line."

I doubt something so simple as watching a fishing line will help me relax, but much to my surprise, the tension at the base of my skull slowly begins to ease. My gaze is fixed on the hypnotic rocking dips of my bobber. I think of my original goal in bringing Mother to Sutton Hall. Every step forward is two steps back. I just can't make her happy. Not even when I toss man bait her way. "Sorry Mom yelled at you earlier."

"You don't have to apologize for your mother, tee Lou."

"I feel like I do. She's angry with me and took it out on you." I lift my hair off the back of my clammy neck. "She gets angry when I do something to her and angrier when I don't. Half the time, she doesn't remember why she's angry, just that I've done something to make her angry." I shake my head. "I don't know if I'm making sense."

"I understand. Jasper could be fine one moment, and the next, his vicious streak would get the best of him. One second, he'd be happy 'cause I brought him paint samples, and the next, he'd yell and throw things because the samples were only eight ounces."

"What would you do?"

"Walk out the door and go back to work." He spins his reel and takes up some slack. "Or I'd come down here and poach on Sutton property."

Sounds like Jasper had some Rattlesnake in him, too. "When Mom says she hates me, I believe her. She hates me for days and sometimes weeks, long after she's forgotten why." I feel like I'm betraying Mom, but once I start, it just pours out. "She can be very hurtful and rarely gives anyone else a thought." I let go of my hair. "But when she's not angry, she's great to be around and often surprisingly present. I love being with her. She's my mom. She's all I've got." I think about our conversation in the cemetery. "I'm not in denial about her Alzheimer's. I know she'll die, but I'm not ready for her to go. It's not time."

"Not up to you, tee Lou. It's in God's hands, and your momma will pass on his watch, not yours. C'est la vie."

"I know, but life sucks sometimes."

"When life sucks the hardest, you survive by finding someplace to sit still and clear your head. Breathe fresh air and lose yourself in life's simple pleasures. That's the beauty of fishing, or, in your case, bobbering."

The air could be fresher but sitting here in my crab T-shirt and Simon's lucky guts hat, I'm more relaxed than I've been since the day Mom got kicked out of Golden Springs. "I prefer bobbering. It's not as cruel as hooking a poor innocent fish and yanking it out of the water."

The end of his pole dips and he stands and yanks it back at the same time. "You say cruel and I say, 'Hot damn, I'm having poor innocent fish for supper.' " He laughs as sunlight pinwheels off his spinning reel.

"You're cruel *and* heartless." I bite my lip to keep from smiling. "And way overpriced."

"And you're a bossy pain in the backside. Mouthy to boot." He glances over his shoulder and his eyes lock with mine. "Make sure you don't lose yourself down here, tee Lou. I'd hate for that to happen."

17

June 13
Where's my mom?

Mom's still a little chilly toward me, but at least we're back to most of our routine. This morning, while she painted happy trees, I rummaged through the attic and came across a trunk filled with Confederate war bonds and paper currency. I thought it was fascinating, and so did Lindsey. Mom, on the other hand, was underwhelmed. After lunch I redeemed myself by hauling down scrapbooks and jewelry.

I'm back to brushing Mom's hair and watching game shows with her at night, but she doesn't want me to climb in bed with her like before. At least I'm not completely banned, and I leave when Lindsey comes to give Mom her sleeping medication. The chasm between us hasn't fully closed since the euthanasia drama. I'm not surprised, since we've maintained a degree of distance for most of my life, but I hate that — ironically — I'm the only one willing to sweep the past under the rug. It's always up to me to keep pushing forward, but not tonight.

Tonight, I'm in my office, reading over several rough outlines Fern sent for the possible relaunch of Lulu. We invited guest bloggers, but followers are confused by the differing views and are picking favorites and taking sides. I can't believe it's come to this. The business I built from nothing but a legal pad is slipping through my fingers. All I can do now is hold tight and poise myself to bounce back.

I think about what Simon said that day at the bayou: "When life sucks the hardest, you survive by finding someplace to sit still and clear your head. Breathe fresh air and lose yourself in life's simple pleasures. That's the beauty of fishing, or, in your case, bobbering."

I haven't taken his advice yet. Maybe tomorrow. I rub my eyes and push back from my desk when Lindsey knocks at the door.

"I'm sorry to bother you when you're working, but your mother has a temperature of a hundred and two."

"What?" I quickly follow Lindsey to Mom's room, where she's sitting on the side of her bed in leopard pajamas.

"I'll have hot pastrami," Mom tells no one in particular.

She's pale and her eyes are crazy — relatively speaking. "What is wrong with her?" I ask Lindsey as she whips out her stethoscope. Just a few hours ago, Mom was her normal self, angrily telling people that I want her to die, and conveniently leaving out the part about me refusing to kill her.

"And a beer!"

"I'll tell you what I suspect in a minute." She takes Mom's blood pressure, then listens to her heart and lungs.

All I can do is fold my arms across my chest to hold in my panic.

"Your heart and lungs sound good, Patricia." Lindsey hooks the stethoscope around her neck.

"Grab Tiger and Blacky." Tiger was a cat Mom had before she burned her condo down. We never saw him afterward, and I like to think he found a good home a few blocks away. I've never heard of Blacky. Mom tries to stand, but Lindsey puts a hand on her shoulder and keeps her seated on the edge of her bed.

"I don't want you to fall." She turns her

299

face to me. "I think she has a bladder infection. She drinks her water every day, but she's had three in the past few years, according to her medical records." Lindsey reaches into her scrubs for her little notebook. "I'll call the closest hospital and let them know she's coming."

Mom's no stranger to urinary tract infections. The first one traveled to her kidneys and landed her in the hospital. The pain that would send anyone else screaming to the emergency room at the first twinge of a problem, Mom doesn't feel. The first sign that anything's wrong is a rise in her temperature. "I've never heard of a bladder infection making anyone crazy," I say as I put Mom's orthopedic shoes on her feet.

"Bring me the cats. I'll wait by the saltwater pool."

"It's not unusual for a temperature spike to cause confusion and even hallucinations in people with dementia," Lindsey assures me.

With past infections, Mom's temperature had returned to normal by the time I saw her. This is the first time I've seen her like this and I'm worried and afraid.

"We're taking you to the hospital, Patricia." She sticks a file of Mom's records in a tote and hangs it from one shoulder.

"I'll need my passport and swimming suit," Mom says as we get her to her feet.

The thought of taking my delirious, back-seat-driving mother to the hospital makes my panic bubble to the surface of my skin. Mom's heart might sound good, but mine is in danger of cardiac arrest. "How far away is the hospital?" I ask as we move to the back door.

"Ten miles." Lindsey snatches the keys from a hook by the back door before I have a chance to reach for them. "I'll drive."

The spare key went missing about the same time Raphael started to go missing. "You just got your license."

"We want to get there before it closes."

Hospitals don't close, but I get it. I grab my purse, and the three of us head out with Lindsey in the driver's seat and Mom buckled in back.

"I love a good visit with Lorena and Vito. He's such a cutup."

I lower the sun visor and watch Mother through the mirror. I've never heard of Lorena, but Mom's third husband, Vince Russo, had a brother named Vito. I haven't seen Vince since Mom divorced him. I liked him and his family. He was a good guy, but that didn't save him from getting the axe.

I look over at Lindsey, and her face has a

slight green tinge. I don't know if she's sick or if it's the dashboard lights. "Are you okay? Is Frankie okay?"

She smiles and glances over at me. "We're fine. Everything's good."

To distract myself, I ask what I've been dying to know. "What about Jim?"

"What about Jim?"

It might not be my business, but I'm the only one looking out for Lindsey.

"I think he likes you."

"Obviously, we're just friends. He's nice to me, and I like him, too."

That's nice, but what I really want to know is, "Did you tell him about the baby?"

She nods. "I told him. He said it doesn't matter."

Call me insane, but I find it alarming that a single young man is interested in a woman who is six months pregnant. "You can understand what he says?"

"Not always." She laughs. "But I know what he means."

"How?"

"Cuba," comes the answer from the back seat. "We disembark in Cuba."

"I've never been to Cuba," Lindsey tells Mom as she glances in the rearview mirror.

"I visit all the time." Mom sighs as if reliving fond memories of the one place I know for certain she's never stepped foot in. "Cuban cigars are rolled on the thighs of virgins."

I turn my head and look into my mom's crazy eyes. "That's a myth, Mom."

She just gives me a blank look and says, "Connie has a fondness for scotch, Lucky Strikes, and her sister's husband."

I don't know Connie, either. She might be as made-up as Lorena and Cuba.

"I told Bill she was no good."

This is a new Patricia that I've never witnessed. It's not Pleasant Fog Patricia, with her vacant eyes and pasted-on smile. It's not Rattlesnake Patty, either. This is delirious Bat-Shit Pat. I'm not ready for Bat-Shit Pat. I turn back around. "Is she going to go back to normal? I mean, normal for her?"

Lindsey looks at me, then at the road. "A serious infection can affect the progression of Alzheimer's, but I don't think it's nearly that bad yet."

I should have seen the signs before she got this bad. I haven't been paying as close attention to her since that day she asked me to kill her. I've allowed the standoff to go on for too long. I tell myself she'll be all right. That everything will be okay. It's just a little bladder infection, and we'll get some antibiotics and be home before the end of *Tic-Tac-Dough.*

Unfortunately, I'm wrong. Mom's UTI is serious enough that she has to spend the night in the hospital. Lindsey and I leave five hours after she's assigned a bed and drive home in silence. I don't want to blame Lindsey. I know she's conscientious and methodical with Mom's care. This is Mom's fourth urinary infection, and she has always recovered. Still, I have a knot in my stomach the size of a soft pretzel and the urge to take it out on someone. Too bad Doug from Golden Springs isn't around.

My mood goes further south when I walk into the big house, which feels more like a big oven. It's after midnight, and the thermostat says it's ninety-two degrees. The air-conditioning switch is in the on position and I hit it a few times with the side of my fist. "Come on, baby," I plead. "Don't quit on me now." Surprisingly, cool air starts to flow from the vents. It's either my magic fist or my pitiful begging.

The bedrooms upstairs are almost unbearable. I open the windows, but they're heavy, and I have to wedge a fire poker in one casement to keep the window from sliding back down. Cool night air pushes through the screen as I get ready for bed.

There's a little knock on my door just before Lindsey enters wearing a purple cotton nightgown that might as well be a muumuu. Her eyes are red and her face is blotchy. "I'm sorry, Lou Ann." She blows her nose, then sticks the wadded-up Kleenex in her cleavage. "Maybe I should have made Patricia pee on a stick more than once a week."

"It's not your fault. We're both trying to figure out what we could have done differently." I shake my head. "I don't know."

"I'll understand if you fire me now, but I'm really hoping you won't."

"You're not fired, Lindsey," I say through a sigh. "Mom likes you more than any nurse she's come in contact with."

"She doesn't accuse me of hiding her shoes and stealing her Pirate's Booty."

"There you go. She likes you more than she likes me."

"No. She just takes her frustration and anger out on you more than she does on me, but she yells at me, too."

"That makes you practically family, I guess. Lucky you."

She wipes her fingers across her wet cheeks. "Sorry. I usually don't cry so much. It's Frankie." She looks down and rubs her belly. "He makes me gassy, too."

"Ahh, TMI. Even if we are practically family, we don't need to share everything."

She laughs and sticks out her hand for me. "Come here."

I frown and put my hands behind my back. "No."

"Come on."

"Why? I don't want to pull your finger."

She laughs and moves toward me. "You're so funny."

I wasn't trying to be funny.

Lindsey grabs one of my hands and places it on her belly. "Feel that. Isn't that wild?"

Beneath my palm, I feel her whole stomach move, and something pokes out at my fingers. "What was that?" Startled, I pull my hand back and watch her stomach move again, pushing up on the side of her muumuu. It looks like a scene out of one of Lindsey's alien movies.

"He's running out of room and not very happy about it." She rubs her stomach, and it moves again. "Jim says that means he's going to be a handful, but I don't think so." Then I look up at her, and her face gets serious. "I want to ask you something, and you can say no."

I never like it when a question begins that way. Usually it involves a raise or a loan.

"Would you come into the delivery room

when it's time?"

That's the last thing I expected her to ask. "Me? I don't know anything about babies."

"You don't have to. I'd just like someone to talk to and be with me when the baby comes."

"What about Mother?"

"I'll arrange for someone to come and sit with her." She laughs. "Maybe Simon."

"Mom would love that." Strangely, her wanting me to be with her touches me. "I'd be honored to talk to you and be with you when Frankie enters the world."

"Thank you, Lou Ann. You're a good friend." She breathes a sigh of relief and heads for the door. "And you're a good daughter. I know you don't hear it enough, but Patricia is lucky to have you."

I'm tempted to list all the ways she is wrong, but I say, "You're welcome, Lindsey," because the knot in my stomach is gone and I think she and Frankie have something to do with it.

I crawl into bed and shut off the lamp. I've never felt a baby move inside the womb, and Lindsey's right, it's wild. There's a real baby in there, and I can't imagine giving birth to something that size. Obviously, women do it every day, but it's not for me.

Sure, Tony and I talked about it in a

general "someday" sort of way, but never seriously. Now I'm thirty-eight. I don't have a boyfriend or marriage prospects. Giving birth looks painful and exhausting, and for all of that trouble, they make you leave with the baby and take care of it for eighteen years.

I can't think of one good reason why I'd sign up for that. I come from at least two generations of women whose maternal instincts are wishy-washy at best. Personally, I've never heard the tick of a biological clock, and I've never had an urge to push a baby out of my vagina.

At my age, if I haven't heard the clock or felt the urge, I think it's safe to say it's not going to happen.

I'm fine with that. Lulu the Love Guru is my baby. We've had our ups and downs, good times and bad, but I'm very proud. We're going through a little rough patch right now, but I'll figure it out. Mom and I are going through a rough patch, and I'm taking care of that, too. I'm the ringmaster. I can run both shows at the same time. I can do anything, and everything will be okay.

I fall asleep feeling better after my little pep talk and wake up radiating positive energy. Like I tell Lulu fans: what you project out into the world is what you will attract back to you. I meant it in terms of loving relationships, but I think it applies to life in general.

By the time I get downstairs, Lindsey's already spoken to the hospital. Mom had a restless night but is asleep now and doing okay. Lindsey and I have breakfast at the table in the kitchen off paper plates. It's a refreshing change. No formal settings or handwashing old china and crystal.

"I'll take the first shower," I say as I dump our paper plates in the garbage.

"Frankie wants the first shower."

"Tell you what, I'll race you and Frankie for it."

"No fair." Lindsey laughs. Her phone rings, and she's still smiling as she looks at the number. She holds up one finger and answers. "Hello, this is Lindsey Benedict."

I lean a shoulder in the doorjamb and fold my arms over my chest.

"Yes. Okay." She puts a hand on her belly and looks down. "When? . . . I have to look at her history to be sure, but I believe that is correct. What are you giving her? . . . Yes." She glances up at me. "We will. Yes."

"What's up?"

Lindsey hangs up and answers, "Patricia's temperature spiked again."

"Didn't they just say she was doing okay?" I push away from the door, and my hands fall to my side. "That was only an hour ago."

"The cultures just came back from the lab. The infection is worse than we thought and has spread to one or both of her kidneys." Lindsey holds up a hand before I can ask any questions. "The doctor ordered stronger antibiotics and an ultrasound of her upper and lower tract."

That doesn't sound good, and a familiar knot of anxiety replaces any optimism I woke up with.

I don't know what I was expecting when I walked back into Mother's hospital room, but it wasn't a cannula in her nostrils or another bag hooked to her IV machine. Her eyes are closed, and her dark hair starkly contrasts with her pale cheeks and white sheets. She looks smaller, older, and more fragile than when I left her last night. My heart sinks, and I grab onto the raised bed rail. "Mom." I watch her chest move up and down as her vital signs scroll across a monitor. "Mom."

Her eyes flutter open, cloudy and unfocused.

"Mom. It's me. Lou Ann."

She blinks a few times, and her eyes focus

on me. I take that as a good sign. The cloudiness is probably because of her high temperature. Lindsey is looking at Mom's chart at the nurses' station down the hall. I'll ask her about it when she comes to the room.

"Where did you go?" Her voice is scratchy. I reach for a cup of watery crushed ice. "I went home for a few hours."

"I need you to get me out of here."

She opens her mouth, and I spoon-feed her a little ice. "I will when you're a bit better."

"I'm fine."

I give her more ice. "Have you watched any of your shows?" I ask to distract her.

"I don't have a remote."

"It's right here." I show her the combo remote control and speaker hooked to her bed rail. "Do you want me to find you something?"

"No." She studies it intently, like she's trying to figure out how it works. "Don't turn it on." She might look worse than she did last night, but she is making a heck of a lot more sense. She pushes the minus sound button, then gazes up at me. "Get me out of here."

"Let's wait to hear from your doctor first."

"He's in on it. They're all in on it."

"What?" Confused, I put the ice on a bedside tray.

"Wynonna's doing their dirty work."

I blow out a deflated breath. I don't ask what "dirty work" means because I don't want to know what Wynonna is stealing now.

"That bitch is stealing my underwear."

My head snaps back. *Bitch?* Forget that she doesn't have underwear anywhere near this hospital; my mother said "bitch." No way that just happened. No way I heard that right.

"I saw her give my black lacys to that other bitch with the red hair."

Again? The woman in bed looks like my mom. Her voice sounds like my mom's, but I've never heard a curse word pass *my* mom's lips. Not once, let alone twice in the same conversation.

Lindsey comes in and tosses her tote bag on a chair. "How ya doing, Patricia?"

"Who are you?"

Lindsey doesn't seem fazed that Mom doesn't recognize her, but it reminds me of the first night at Sutton Hall and scares me shitless.

"I'm your good friend Lindsey." She takes Mom's hand and smiles.

Mom yanks her hand away. "You're in on it with the rest of them."

312

"I'm here to make sure you're comfortable."

"You're huge! Huge people are sneaky bastards."

I glance at Lindsey out of the corner of my eye. "Sorry."

"Don't worry about it. I was forewarned before I came in." She puts her hands on the bed rail. "Patricia isn't quite herself yet."

"You're sneaky like that bitch Wynonna!"

Lindsey lifts a brow and groans. Now I'm really scared. The last thing we need is for Lindsey to be the new Wynonna. "It's Lindsey. Remember?"

"There's nothing wrong with my memory!" she yells. "You're in on it with the sneaky people."

"Lou Ann is here to help you," Lindsey assures her. "We're both here to keep you safe from sneaky people."

"Then get me out of this goddamn place. They're listening." Mom points to the remote. "They hear everything."

"Is she going to be like this forever?" Last night she'd been bat-shit crazy, but in a great mood. Today she's still bat-shit, but her eyes have turned to slits like a snake's.

"Her temperature is still spiking at a hundred and two." Lindsey turns her attention to the vital-signs monitor. "The bigger issue is, her oxygen level dropped to the low eighties this morning." She points at the screen. "It's back up to ninety-three, which isn't great but is about normal for her."

"What made it drop?"

"She's not taking deep enough breaths. Her lungs are clear, so the best guess is hallucinatory anxiety."

"I need a shotgun, a carton of smokes, and some fucking jerky." Scratch what I said about making more sense.

I take a step back just in case the woman who looks like my mother levitates and spews soup. "Has she had the kidney scan yet?"

"Not yet. She's a little too riled up."

"Yeah."

"She was given Tylenol in her IV just before we got here. It shouldn't be too long before her temperature drops and she's back to normal," Lindsey predicts.

"Shouldn't be too long" translates to another hour before Mom's temperature lowers enough that she quits fighting the hospital staff. She persists in cursing her archnemesis, Wynonna, but I'm fine with it as long as neither Lindsey nor I are her target.

I sit in a chair beside her bed while she sleeps, answering emails but mostly watching treasure hunters on *Oak Island* and unsolved murders on *Cold Case Files.*

There's good news and bad news regarding the results of the ultrasound. The good: the infection only spread to one kidney and the antibiotic should clear it up with no problem. The bad: Mom has cystocele, meaning her leaky bladder sags and can't empty all the way. There are no good options for a seventy-four-year-old Alzheimer's sufferer who has nerve damage in her urinary tract. We have the choice of a catheter or nothing. Both have risks and issues, and I'm going to leave it up to Lindsey to decide what's best for Mom.

Lindsey and I leave around seven and return to a house that is even more stifling than it was the night before. This time, though, no amount of begging or pounding appeases the AC gods. My cotton sundress sticks to my back, and a bead of sweat slips down the side of my neck. I lean forward and press my forehead into the old plaster wall, bracing myself for another long night ahead.

"What are you doing?"

I turn my head and look at Lindsey. "Feeling sorry for myself." She's changed from her tight scrubs into a maternity wrap dress with yellow flowers on it. It looks like she might be wearing a little makeup, too. "Are you going somewhere?"

"Jim's picking me up, and we're going to a movie. I'll have my cell on me if the hospital calls."

Again, why is a young guy taking a very pregnant girl to the movies? It seems weird, and I open my mouth to give her my opinion, but I close it again. She's an adult capable of making her own decisions and she didn't ask for Lulu's advice. Still, I'm going to keep my eye on Jim.

"Frankie's getting popcorn with extra butter tonight."

"And air-conditioning."

She rubs her stomach. "Wanna come?"

I'm almost tempted. "What's the movie?"

"Welcome to Hell 666: The Return of Satan."

"I thought you gave up horror movies."

"I tried, but I can't go cold turkey. You should come and get out of this house."

"No, thanks. Not even for cool air."

"Are you sure?"

"Not even for popcorn."

Jim shows up in a green car with a dent in the right front fender. I don't know what model it is, but I wouldn't be surprised if it was manufactured in the last century.

I wave them goodbye and start looking around the house for an electric fan. I don't find one in any of the rooms or closets, and I've rummaged through the attic enough to know there isn't one up there. The best solution I can come up with is a freezer baggie filled with ice. I put it on the side of my neck and sigh luxuriously, when my phone rings in my dress pocket. I don't recognize the number and immediately assume it's the hospital with more bad news. "Hello?"

"Hey, tee Lou." I've never been so glad to hear Simon's smooth Southern drawl. "I got some samples for you."

"I didn't recognize your number."

"I'm at my office on the landline. I'll make a pass with those samples tomorrow."

I don't even know what he's talking about, but it doesn't matter right now. "Mom's in the hospital. I don't know when I'll be home tomorrow."

"Damn." He pauses for a few heartbeats before he says, "I'm sure sorry to hear that. Is she going to be okay?"

"Yes," I answer, because I hope it's true. I lean a hip into the counter and give Simon the short version of the past twenty-four hours.

"Where y'at?"

I slide the ice to the back of my neck. "Home."

His soft chuckle fills my ear. "That means,

317

'How are you doing?' "

"You could have said that?"

"I did."

It must be one more of those Southern things, like *come see* and *make groceries.* "The central air isn't working. I don't think there are any fans in this house, and I'm melting."

"We can't have that. Hang tight. I got something you need."

I can think of a lot of things I need. At the moment, a new air conditioner is number one on the list.

Simon brings the next-best thing: a big fan and a six-pack of cold beer. "At times like this NOLA Blonde goes down easy and hits the spot."

I laugh, but he's right. Within a few short minutes, we're sitting on the front porch, the steady squeak of rocking chairs on old wood lulling away my tension. "I never imagined that I'd one day be rocking in these old chairs. I must be getting old, too."

"You probably have a few good years left." Simon raises a beer to his lips as the setting sun washes the night sky in deep purple and orange.

Not so much as a wisp of a breeze tonight, and a scattering of fireflies twinkle and flash like tiny stars right in front of me and the depths beyond. "One or two before I get my AARP card, I suppose." The scene is enchanting, and the rhythmic creaks of worn planks fill the comfortable silence. I take a long drink and it does indeed go down easy. "Jim picked up Lindsey earlier and they went to a movie," I say as I lower the bottle.

"Hmm," is his only response.

"Did Jim tell you she's pregnant?"

"Didn't have to tell me." He raises his bottle again, and I watch as it seems to go down easy for him, too. "It was obvious the first or second time I saw the girl."

Yep. I'm the only one who didn't figure it out. "Lindsey says they're friends. I think it's kind of . . . odd."

Again, "Hmm."

"She's going to have a baby in about three months." I lift a palm inquisitively. "Why would he go out with someone who's pregnant with another man's baby?"

"I don't ask."

"It's weird."

He shrugs one shoulder. "Maybe for you."

I point my bottle at him. "Are you saying you'd date a woman who's about to pop out another man's kid?"

"No. I wouldn't, but Jim's a different kind of guy. He's lived a different life. He's had some rough patches, and I imagine he sees her as someone having a rough time too."

"That's what concerns me. Lindsey's naive for her age." I look over at his profile, bathed in increasing shadow. "Now she's pregnant and has no family to protect her. Mom and I are all she's got."

"Mais, you don't have to worry about Jim Poulet, no. He's the last person on the planet anyone needs protection from, believe me. There isn't a bad or mean bone in his body." He finishes off his beer and sets the empty in the cooler next to him. "He had a brain fever when he was a baby, and I think it burned up any meanness in him." He pulls out two bottles. "Want another?"

I chug the last sip and hand him my empty. "How do you know him?" I ask, trying very hard not to burp like a teenage boy.

"I saw him picking up cans on the side of the road about two years ago. He had a big ol' garbage bag full, and I thought if a man works that hard for cans, he's likely to work hard for real money." Simon screws off the top of the two bottles and hands me one. "I stopped and asked if he wanted to come and sweep up my shop, and he's been with me ever since." He drops both caps in the cooler. "He lived in Terrebonne Parish, and I didn't know he walked to and from work for the first six months."

"Well, he has a car now."

Simon laughs. "He loves that Malibu. It looks like hell, but it runs good."

"My first car was a '96 Ford Focus I bought off my mom's last husband. It was almost as big a piece of shit as Lester Doyle." I take a drink, then press the cold, wet bottle to my hot cheek. "The car lasted longer than the marriage, though."

"How long was the marriage?"

"That one?" I lean my head back against the top of the wooden chair and look out at the silhouette of tree branches against the vivid dusk sky. "Ahh . . . two years, maybe. I don't quite remember, but I know it lasted longer than her marriage to Melvin. She was married to Vince the longest." Light from the transom window illuminates Simon's shoulder and the side of his face. I can't make out his expression, but I don't need to. "Five," I answer the question hanging in the air.

"What number was your father?"

"Two." Of all my mother's men, he's the one I like to talk about least. "I hardly remember him."

"Where is he?"

I shrug in the darkness. "I have no idea. The last I heard, somewhere in Kansas." I tried to find him when I was a kid. Whenever I was sad and lonely, I'd sit on my bed and reach for the phone. "That was about thirty years ago." I remember the sound of my mother and her latest boyfriend's laughter leaching through the thin walls as I reached out to several of my father's relatives in a desperate attempt to reconnect with the most important man in my life. "I used to have fantasy conversations with him in my head. The things I'd say and the things he'd say if I ever found him." But those conversations never came to fruition, and for many years, I blamed my mom. Given Mother's penchant for acquiring men, sometimes while she still had another, it was easy to blame her. "We used to move around so much, I thought he just couldn't find me." I take a long drink, then set the bottle on the porch by my chair. "It never occurred to me that he wasn't even looking." I stand and stretch my arms over my head. For a few seconds, I feel light-headed, and I don't know if I stood up too fast or had too much beer. "Men like him are what I call WADs. Worthless Apathetic Deadbeats. At least that's what I call them in public." I drop my arms and move to the edge of the porch. "In my head, they're worthless asshole deadbeat sons of bitches."

"Bon rein. A man takes care of his responsibilities." Simon gets up and stands behind me, so close I can feel his warm chest against the back of my arm. "I've always been surrounded by a big family. Some should get divorced but stick together for the misery. Some are faithful and others mess around, but every one of them takes care of their kids. Including the ones born outside of marriage." He puts his hands on my shoulders. "They're a pain in the ass and think they have a right to my personal business, but who else is going to give me a kidney if I need it?"

I laugh and look back over my shoulder at him. "If I need a body part, I'm out of luck. There are only two of us and Mom isn't a good donor candidate."

"If you need a body part, cher, you let me know."

I don't think he's talking about a kidney. I turn to look up into his face. "Are you coming on to me, Simon?"

He chuckles. "If you have to ask, I must be getting old."

He's about my age, so he's not *that* old. He has a good business and all his hair. He brought me a fan and beer and made my shitty day better. God knows he's a triple threat when it comes to women — handsome, smooth-talking, charming. "Why hasn't some local girl snapped you up?" I ask.

"You're the expert." His hands slide across my shoulders, and his thumbs brush my jaw.

"Is there something wrong with you?" I mean it as a joke, but it comes out a little breathy, and I want to turn my face into his hand and kiss his warm palm.

He lowers his face and whispers against my mouth, "You tell me."

I hear a little moan, and I think it's me, but I'm not sure. Simon's kiss takes the breath from my lungs, and his mouth works me over, pushing every single thought from my head.

I am not Lulu. I am not an expert.

I am simply a woman being kissed by a man and, thank God, he knows how to do it right.

18

June 18

Hard decisions.
Birds of a feather.
Twisted Twister.

Mom is wheeled out of the big pneumatic doors like the day she got kicked out of Golden Springs, but this time she's pale. Her white, almost translucent skin sets her Renegade Red lips apart, and her eyes look a bit sunken.

She's been gone for five days, and I had the air-conditioning unit replaced this morning before I picked her up. Besides her complexion, there are other changes I notice once we're home. She walks slower and tires quicker. She says she's hungry, but she eats next to nothing. We have to avoid using the word *remember* when she's around. According to my Alzheimer's books (and backed up by Lindsey), some sufferers become irritable when reminded of their memory loss. This behavior can happen at any stage, but we're especially sensitive to the possibility now.

The good news is her UTI is getting better. The bad news is her swearing is getting worse. It's like she has seventy-four years' worth of cuss words stored up inside and she's determined to say every last one of them before she dies.

When Simon dropped by to see how she was doing the other day, she'd looked up from a scrapbook and said, "Holy shit, you're a foxy man."

I hadn't seen him since the night he kissed me senseless on the front porch and jumped in his truck and drove off. I don't know how long I'd stood there staring at the empty driveway before snapping out of it and returning inside. Too embarrassingly long is all I know. Simon is smooth, and I need to watch out for his slick moves. Enough is going on in my life. Especially now that Mom has added swearing to her act.

Lindsey managed to get Mom an appointment with her neurologist only a few days after her discharge. Before we left, I put her hair in a bun and helped her with her lipstick. I try to be optimistic at the clinic, but her mental and cognitive evaluations show a three-point drop since the last time she was tested, shortly after we arrived in Louisiana. Three points closer to end stage. I can't say I'm surprised.

"You're as healthy as can be and pretty as a picture," the doctor tells Mom in a smooth Southern drawl.

She smiles and bats her eyelashes like her old self. "You're a rascal."

Rascal? That's a new one.

"A goddamn rascal."

They both laugh while a little piece of my heart dies. This can't happen. Not now. Not when I've only had four relatively good months with her. I want more good months and more good years.

Along with her new swearing habit, she won't brush her teeth unless Lindsey or I stand in the bathroom and watch her. Suddenly the toothpaste she's used for years burns her gums. We try everything from organic to Sensodyne to Baby Orajel, but she complains about them all and blames Wynonna for the heinous act of stealing all the good toothpaste. "That nasty bitch Wynonna took it. She's a filthy whore and loves to burn my mouth."

"Yeah, nasty bitch," I say, to reinforce that Wynonna is to blame and not me.

"Don't curse, Lou Ann. You were raised better," says the potty-mouthed hypocrite. On the bright side, she doesn't hate me anymore, and we've returned to our equilibrium. At bedtime, I brush her hair while she berates contestants on *Family Feud* and calls Wink "that handsome son of a bitch." She turns the volume up so loud, I swear they can hear it in the next parish. One night, she loses the remote and I have to stand next to the television and change the channels manually.

Most of my mornings are spent painting with Mom and Bob again. After lunch, Mom takes a nap and I head to the attic, where I have become enmeshed in the history of Sutton Hall — the nearly two centuries' worth of recorded births and deaths and receipts for bags of flour, crocks of butter, and casks of Charlie's Fine Whisky. Jasper's gambling ledger was packed away with his gold tie bar and cuff links, and it appears that Simon was right. It was either feast or famine with old Jasper.

The day I brought Mom home from the hospital, I made one of the hardest decisions of my life. I had to choose between Lulu and my mom. Mom's hospital scare made it clear that I can't split myself between the two. They each suffer from the lack of my attention, and I feel guilty neglecting one for the other. But when it came down to it, the choice was clear. Mom is more important, and spending as much time as possible with her is my only priority.

I still have my boss-lady moments, even down here in Louisiana, but Lulu deserves better than I've given her lately. She needs a new voice. Someone young and talented who has her finger on the pulse of the dating world. Someone fresh, but most important, someone who is as excited as I was when I first started the company. The day I chose Mom, I asked Fern to start vetting potential replacements, and since then she's sent me videos by the dozen. No matches yet, so the guest blogging will have to continue for now.

Five days after the neurologist appointment, I force myself to pull a wardrobe steamer trunk from the attic. The canvas is torn and the locks are broken. The only thing holding it closed is a cracked leather buckle. It isn't easy, but I drag it downstairs. It thumps each step of the way, and a yellowed lace sleeve escapes through a crack. I fear the whole thing will bust apart before I get to the parlor.

Raphael hangs upside down from the

grand chandelier in the entry. It's been cleaned and rewired, so there is no danger of electrocution. Sometimes I have to remind myself that that's a good thing. "Shake your tail feathers," he squawks.

That's tame compared to some things that come out of him. Since the day Simon made him talk, the bird hasn't shut up. I'd like to blame Jasper for Raphael's potty beak, but he's added a few more words to his lexicon, courtesy of Patricia Jackson.

"Tony's an asshole."

Okay, maybe me too.

I'm breathing hard by the time I finally slide the trunk into the front parlor. Lindsey looks up from rubbing her belly. "Are you okay?" she asks while practicing her who-who breathing. She's been doing that a lot lately, saying she has to practice so she won't forget to breathe while she's pushing out Frankie.

"I'm fine," I grunt while tugging at the trunk.

"What's going on?" Mom asks as she enters behind me, wringing her hands. She's remembered her lipstick, a rich cabernet that complements her chartreuse dress. Just below her knees, she's pulled on her beige support socks and white orthopedic shoes. "Did Tony bring that?"

"Tony's an asshole," Raphael chimes in.

Mom gasps like always and lectures Raphael on the evils of curse words. I don't even bother to point out her hypocrisy because she'd just shrug.

"I thought you might want to look inside this old trunk," I tell her once she finishes her reprimand.

"What's in it?" Mom stops beside me and stills her hands.

I have a notion of what's inside, but I'm not sure. The buckle finally gives way, and I push the two halves apart. Clothes tumble out and fill the air with the smell of musty old fabric, mothballs, and dust.

Mom puts one hand on the trunk as she reaches for an enormous deep blue hat with a broken ostrich feather and smashed rosettes. She puts it on her head, and I tie the wide ribbon into a bow by the side of her face like she's Scarlett O'Hara. "I love a good hat," she says, and prances around laughing. I take a picture of her in her very large "good hat" and deep red lipstick. "What's that?" She points to the yellowed sleeve, and it turns out to belong to a wadded-up dress with streaks of orange discoloration on the lace and satin. She wants to try it on, but I can tell without even holding it up that it's too small.

331

Instead, Lindsey and I get her into a green-and-yellow-striped skirt and matching jacket with balloon sleeves.

"Put that on, Lou." Mom points a red parasol at the lacy dress, seemingly unable to let it go.

I really don't want to. The dress is yellowed and scratchy and smells like mothballs and old trunk, with just a hint of burnt starch. MISS LILLIAN SUTTON ON HER WEDDING DAY is embroidered on a silk tag. "This belonged to Grandmother. It's her wedding dress."

Mom looks up from a box of gloves. "It's not white."

It used to be. I shake out the mess of a dress, and light from the window picks up tiny glass beads and seed pearls hand-sewn into the lace. This is the dress that Grandmother wore at her first wedding, to my grandfather Louis.

Mom orders me to put it on again, and I reluctantly strip to my underwear and pull the stiff fabric over my head. A row of silk buttons runs halfway down my spine, but the fabric loops are also stiff, and we leave the back open. The chest is tight, and the long lace sleeves are snug on my arms and scratchy against my skin. I run a hand over tiny beads and pearls sewn into the sweetheart neckline and wonder how Grandmother felt in this dress. Happy, excited, scared? Was she madly in love with Louis Jackson? Did she want to run into his arms as he waited for her at the altar?

Mom used to have a black-and-white photograph of Louis in his uniform, but I don't remember exactly what his face looked like. Other than his war hero status, Mom has never really talked about her dad. He left when she was four and died when she was seven, so she never knew him. Grandmother never talked about him either, and I don't know if that was out of respect for Papa Bob or because she'd moved on and forgotten him. Everyone has forgotten. I don't even know where he's buried. It's sad, like he never lived at all.

"I think I found that dress in this photo album," Lindsey says, and brings it to me. She places it on top of the trunk, and it's open to an eight-by-ten photograph taken in a flower garden. Grandmother Lily's floral bouquet is so big it looks like a funeral spray. She's wearing a simple headpiece and a long veil, and if I look close enough, I can see the same lace sleeves and sweetheart neckline. The wedding party is small, with only two family members on each side, and most of them look happy. Gone was the era

of dour-faced photographs. Too bad someone didn't tell the groomsmen that their
joyless expressions were twenty years out of
fashion.

I zero in on the man standing next to
Grandmother, wearing a dark suit and tie, a
white shirt, and a very dapper pocket
square. He's old-school handsome, and his
hair is slicked back from a nasty widow's
peak.

My nasty widow's peak. The one I had lasered off. The one that still grows an occasional stray hair from my forehead. I never
knew my dad or grandfather, and for the
first time in my life, I'm staring at a male
with the same DNA as me.

I show the picture to Mom, and she looks
back and forth from the picture to me.
"That's Momma and Grandmere and
Grandpere." She points to the groom.
"That's my daddy." She moves her finger.
"Jasper and Jed."

"Where's Grandfather's family?"

She shrugs. "Momma didn't know them."

Which I've always thought was strange,
but I seem to be the only one. "Why are
they on the groom's side?"

"School friends."

This time she doesn't lower her voice or
look around when she says, "Jed and Jasper

were gay as a box of sprinkles." Mom shakes her head, and the broken feather falls and hangs off one side. "Momma said Daddy's kin didn't want him to get married."

"Why?"

"I don't know." She digs in a small compartment of the trunk and pulls out earrings, heavy with clusters of rubies and emeralds.

I return my attention to the photograph. My great-grandparents look pleased, Lily and Louis smile pleasantly, but Jasper and Jed look like they're headed to a memorial service instead of their sister's wedding.

Lindsey helps Mom clip on the heavy earrings, which immediately pull at her lobes. "Don't those hurt?" I ask her. She shakes her head and the earrings swing from side to side.

Lindsey takes out her phone and says, "Let me take a picture of both of you."

We walk across the hall to the library, where the lighting is far better. Raphael screams from the chandelier overhead like someone's stabbed him.

"Shut your beak," I say.

"Merde! Shut the fuck up, Boomer!"

I give him the stink eye I've inherited from Mom and slide the doors closed so Lindsey's fear won't cause her to go into early labor.

Mom and I pose in front of the fireplace, our faces dour like Jed's and Jasper's, and almost all the same portraits lining the hall. We play around on the conversation couch; in one pic she holds her hand out like a traffic cop as if to stop the conversation. Then we move near a floor-to-ceiling window and stand within the variegated sunlight. Then, I trade places with Lindsey and snap her in the light, hand on her belly.

"Cup your bump," I tell her as she poses in front of the fireplace. "The other day, I saw a tiny T-shirt that said 'Poop Happens' on it." Lindsey laughs, her eyes bright with joy. "Do you have baby stuff?"

"I have a few onesies and some socks, but I have time to get the big stuff before he's born."

"You get diapers at the birthday party." Mom smiles. "We should give you a birthday party."

I'm sure she means baby shower, but what the hell. "That's a good idea, Mom."

Lindsey rubs her belly and adds, "I can buy Frankie diapers and everything else he needs."

"I think Mom's right." It's too bad Lindsey doesn't have a group of friends or family members to throw her a baby shower. "You need a baby shower."

"No. We don't need a big fuss. I mean, it's not like we . . ." Lindsey blushes and looks down at her stomach.

"You can't speak for Frankie. He might want a big piece of cake."

Lindsey smiles and I snap another picture. "Frankie likes cake."

"I believe that. You're huge!"

I ignore Mom. "We'll need decorations."

"I've never seen anyone as big as you!"

"I've never hosted a baby shower, but it can't be that hard to plan. I'll look on the internet for ideas."

"And games," Mom adds. "A good party has to have games."

Lindsey sits on the couch next to Mom, and I take a few pictures of them together. "Won't it just be the three of us? What kind of games?"

"That game with the dots on the floor." Mom poses with her hands on the side of her face next to the big bow.

"Dots on the floor?" I take several pictures of her looking cheesy.

"You put a hand on one dot and a foot on another."

"Twister?" Lindsey and I laugh. Mom's too old, Lindsey's too pregnant, and I'm too short. Twister isn't fun when you're the short kid.

"Don't invite the Duffys if we're playing Twister." Mom shakes her head. "Rex is a hairy bastard and sheds in the baby oil."

It takes a few heartbeats for that to sink in. Lindsey and I suck in horrified breaths, but Mom is not quite finished.

"What were those people's names?" Mom's brows pull together. "They had a girl your age with really crossed eyes."

"Jodee Pulaski, and her eyes didn't cross if she wore her glasses."

"Lovely couple. Not at all hairy."

"Mom, stop! I don't need to know any of this." I remember that family. They'd seemed so normal compared to mine. The children had been involved in Scouts, they'd gone on family vacations to Yellowstone and Disneyland. They went to church every Sunday. I know because I used to go with Jodee to get saved.

"They didn't want to see Rex's big hairy —"

"Mom, don't say it!"

"— back."

One day, we just never saw them again, but that wasn't unusual. It happened a lot. Mostly because Mom couldn't get along with women for very long. She still can't, but I always thought the Pulaskis stopped coming around because they got tired of saving me on Sundays. I never suspected it had to do with naked Twister.

19

Mom's stash.
The plan.
What's wrong with this picture?

"Hide those someplace where Wynonna
won't find 'em." Mom pulls the earrings
from her lobes and shoves them toward me.
"A spot where no one will find them."

"Okay." I have to fight to keep my eyes
from rolling.

"Damn her." Mom shakes a dramatic fist
as she rises from the sofa.

Lindsey and I make brief eye contact over
the top of her head. Mom has enough
Pirate's Booty to last her several months.
She's stashed it somewhere and can't remember where now. I shove the earrings up
my tight lace sleeve because I don't trust
Raphael not to take off with them if I set
them down.

It's nearing noon, and Mom gets grumpy

around this time every day. Before her bladder infection, her mental and emotional slide started around four in the afternoon. Now it starts sooner. Lindsey and I help her out of the old skirt and jacket, but she insists on keeping the hat. "It's a good hat," she says, and follows Lindsey to the kitchen so she can boss her around. "I want roast beef."

"If you want roast beef, you'll have to make it yourself. I'm making halibut for lunch."

I gather everything and return to the parlor. Raphael is still hanging from the chandelier and screams as I pass, but not like someone's stabbing him this time. No, this scream is filled with terror and happens to sound remarkably like Lindsey's.

"Not funny," I say, but he laughs anyway.

I return Mom's skirt and jacket to the trunk and pull Grandmother's wedding dress over my head. I gather the gloves Mom tossed about and pack them and the dress away. The trunk has lots of little drawers and boxes, some filled with old sewing needles and thread. Others contain old photos of Lily and Louis, lots of random keys, and a stack of letters tied up with blue velvet ribbon. I fan the corners of the envelopes and see they contain letters that were written by my grandparents, post-marked from 1950 to 1953. I toss the bundle on the couch, figuring I can read the letters on nights I can't sleep.

The drawer to the jewelry box is open, and I shut it before getting dressed and heading off to Mom's room to hide the dreadful earrings. Even if Wynonna lived next door, I think it's safe to say the gaudy clip-ons would be safe from her evil grasp.

There are so many places in Mom's room to hide the earrings, and I glance around for a "spot where no one will find them." But it has to be easy for me to remember, like Mom's underwear drawer. Not surprisingly, Mom's beat me to the punch. I find cash folded up with her panties and a long-lost remote control hidden in her compression socks. I wonder what else she's hoarded and find the spare key to the Escalade in a pocket of her jogging pants. She's stashed seven sterling pickle forks with her pajamas, and a thin box of matches from the Belle of Baton Rouge Casino and Hotel in with her bras.

I slip the matches and spare key into my back pocket, doing my due diligence to prevent arson and grand theft auto, and my gaze falls on the brass coal box I found in the attic last month. It's about the size of a small trunk and weighs a ton, and of course Mom wanted it by the fireplace. I lift the lid and discover three bags of Pirate's Booty, two rock-hard bagels, an open sleeve of saltines, half a bottle of water, and a pack of toilet paper. I close the box tight, shocked it hasn't attracted ants. If hoarding pickle forks and toilet paper gives her comfort, I'm all for it.

The hunt for a hiding spot continues, and I pull open a drawer in Mom's bedside chest. It's not a spot that no one can find, but I'm more worried about my memory than about Wynonna's sticky fingers. Inside is Mom's red velvet jewelry box, round and small enough to fit in my palm. When I was a kid, it seemed magical with its colorful jewels, collection of wedding rings, and Great-grandmother's watch pendant. A press of a tiny gold button makes the top flip up.

It's empty. No jewels or rings or watch pendant. Just four red pills. I poke them with my finger and wonder why Mom's bedtime medication is in her nightstand. Lindsey keeps all medications in a lockbox in her bedroom. Mom can't take so much as an aspirin without Lindsey giving it to her, and Lindsey keeps track of everything in her little notebook. At night she transcribes her notes into Mom's electronic medical chart. If anything was missing, anything outside the routine, Lindsey would know it.

Where did these come from?

That day in the cemetery, Mom talked about killing herself with pills. She wanted my help and then got angry when I refused. She was horrible and mad for several weeks, but I thought she'd gotten over it. I thought she'd gotten over her death-with-dignity plan of several years ago, too, but apparently she's never let it go. She can't get her hands on four Flintstones vitamins without someone noticing, so I've rested comfortably in my belief that she has neither the opportunity nor the mental capacity to follow through without my assistance.

I empty the pills into my palm and notice that some of the red coating looks like it's been rubbed off, like the pills sat in water or someone's mouth. Like someone is slipping her medication under her tongue and then slipping it out when no one is looking to create a lethal stockpile. But when? I'm with her at night . . . except when I'm banished or leave before Lindsey gives her the medication. If Mom can hoard bags of Pirate's Booty and toilet paper without notice, I suppose she's capable of hiding little red pills too.

My knees buckle and I drop to the edge of the bed. She's more resourceful than I've given her credit for, more determined than I imagined. Mother is planning to kill herself and she doesn't need me to help her. She's going to do it on her own. She wants to cut her life short but I want more. More time, more memories, more Bob Ross paintings, more nights braiding her hair, and even more twisted Twister stories.

This is so typically selfish of her.

I take a deep breath and close my eyes. An annoying little voice in my head reminds me that I believe people have a right to die. Just not my mom. If that makes me a selfish hypocrite, I don't care. I know she will die from Alzheimer's, but she can't die now. I don't care what Simon said about it not being up to me. God can wait until I'm ready to let her go.

I hear her and Lindsey walk past the door. At some point Mom will notice her pills are missing, but I can't leave them here. I toss the ugly earrings in the jewelry box and replace it in the chest. My heart pounds in my head, and yet I am numb as I wait for Mother and Lindsey to move into the dining room before I slip into Mom's bathroom. I hold the pills over the elevated toilet seat with Mom's new drainage bag hooked to one padded arm.

"Lou Ann," Lindsey calls from down the hall to me. "Lunch."

I hold Mom's life in my palm. All I have to do is tilt my hand and flush. *You want to keep me around until I am just bones and skin and my mouth is hanging open.* She's accused me of wanting her to drool on a bib, too. None of that is true. I love my mom. I know what's best for her. She's been happier since we moved here. Yes, she's lost some cognitive skills, but she has a while yet before the end stage. Just this morning she was laughing and having fun.

"Lou!"

I close my hand. She has a living will and a do-not-resuscitate order. She has the casket and flowers and music picked out for her funeral. She has a right to die. I shove the pills in my pocket. Just not right now.

I join Lindsey and Mom in the dining room as if it is just any other lunch on any other day. It's not for me. Everything is different. The halibut and jasmine rice taste like nothing in my mouth. The food sticks in my throat, and I reach for a heavy silver goblet and watch my mother as I take a drink of water. I watch her take little bites and chew longer than normal. She nods and smiles as Lindsey tells her the latest Frankie news. She swallows and raises a hand to her throat. I watch for her to choke, but she doesn't.

"They ripped out my uterus," she recites word for word the story I've heard all my life. She gets to the part where she almost bled to death giving birth to me and stops. I recognize the lowering of her brows. Her lapse in memory isn't unusual and is no indication that she's slipping any more than the last time.

"You had to have an emergency hysterectomy and couldn't have more children," I remind her. "You always wanted a son." I can feel Mom's pills in my pocket; my emotions are raw. I'm losing my mind again.

"You can have a boy." Mom points her fork at me.

"Me? You know I'm not married."

"Get married." She returns her fork to her plate and scoops up some rice. "It's not hard to get a husband. Especially a shitty husband."

I must be getting used to Mom's potty mouth, because it barely registers. "Maybe it's not hard for you, Mom. You have a passionate nature."

She nods. "And a healing touch."

Yes, but as she's pointed out, she can't

heal herself.

"But don't go for prisoners. They ain't right."

I don't know if Mom's talking from experience, but it makes perfect cognitive sense to me.

"Thanks for the warning." Lindsey chuckles.

I wipe at the red stain the pill coatings left on my palm. I need to talk to her. She needs to know what Mom is doing, but that conversation can wait until Mom takes her nap.

After lunch, Mom and I move to my office for a power planning session. I have to block the last hour from my mind or I'll go crazy. Lindsey thinks she should be in on the baby shower plans, too, but we boot her out and close the door. I pull up an extra chair for Mom, and we sit at my desk so I can write everything down on a yellow legal pad.

"Cocktail peanuts and those butter mints." Mom taps a finger on the legal pad. "Diapers. Lots of damn diapers. Babies poop a lot." Mom laughs, and I tell myself I'm doing the right thing.

I turn on my computer, and we cruise the internet looking for ideas. Mom wants me to write down everything she sees, but I draw the line at a bottle that looks like a boob. It might be just the three of us, but we begin to assemble quite the list.

"Diaper rash ointment," Mom says, and I write down *Boudreaux's Butt Paste.*

I add *cake* and *flowers* to the bottom of the legal pad, and my eye catches a shadow creeping beneath the door.

"Mom," I whisper, and point. "Lindsey's standing at the door trying to listen in."

"Huh." Mom looks but doesn't bother to whisper. "That's her?"

"Shh." I put a finger to my lips. "Say 'dunk tank.' "

"Why?"

"Lindsey's being snoopy, and so she deserves to get a little freaked out."

"Dunk tank!" Mom's looking forward to the party, and her excitement reassures me more than ever that it's not time for her to die.

"Good idea," I say just as loud. "And a Slip 'N Slide."

"Oh, I like the Slip 'N Slide."

Of course she does. "Cornhole. Who doesn't love a good old-fashioned cornhole?" The shadow wavers and disappears.

"Me." Mom's lips purse, and she sits up straight. "I don't like the cornhole."

Well, I guess she has her standards.

Once we've finished our planning, Mom heads to her bedroom for a nap. I wait outside her door, listening for the sound of an opening drawer and the axe to land on my neck. It doesn't happen, and I blow out a relieved breath.

"Are you okay?" Lindsey asks as she passes me in the hall.

Now is the time to tell her. "Yeah." Mom's nurse needs to be informed of what's been happening when she walks out of Mom's bedroom, but I know Mom would feel conspired against and turn Rattlesnake on both of us. "Just thinking about your party." Lindsey would become the new Wynonna. "What do you think of a diaper relay race?" I totally make up. "Instead of a baton, you hand off a diaper."

Lindsey opens her mouth but shuts it again. "Great."

There's no reason to ruin the baby shower. I can keep an eye on Mom, and Lindsey and I can discuss Mom's pill stashing after the party.

For short periods during the rest of the day, I forget the pills are in my pocket. I give Raphael fresh food and water and do laundry. Then something reminds me and I get jumpy, watching and waiting for something to happen.

When Mom goes to bed, I brush her hair and watch her shows and stay with her until she falls asleep. If I'm with Mom when Lindsey gives her her medication and insist on staying until she starts snoring, she can't do anything with her pills.

I shake her shoulder for good measure before I leave her room. She doesn't respond, so I drag myself up the long staircase and shut my bedroom door behind me. My shorts hit the floor as I undress for bed; the pills are still in the pocket. I'll get rid of them tomorrow. No rush. Tonight, I just want to sleep. I am emotionally exhausted, but of course my mind races and I stare at the heavy wooden tester above my head, tossing and turning, thinking of problems without solutions. I still haven't found a Lulu replacement, and Margie thinks it's because subconsciously I can't let go. I don't think that's the reason, although perhaps I am looking for someone just like me and that's not realistic.

After an hour, I give up and turn on the light. I brought the letters I'd found in the steamer trunk upstairs with me and I untie the blue ribbon that binds them.

The first is from Grandmother. I carefully take it from the envelope and unfold the yellowed paper. Her words and handwriting are as flowery as her stationery. She calls Grandfather "beloved Louis" or "darling Louis" or "Louis, my love." She writes that "Patricia is getting to be such a big girl and talks up a storm. Her favorite words are 'gimme dat,' spoken like a barefoot Cajun." She ends the letters with, "Your loving and faithful wife, Lily."

My grandmother's early life sounds just like her — lively and whimsical. With each letter, I can almost hear her voice in my head as she talks about sweet magnolia breezes waking her each morning, listening to the world's most wonderful jazz on Bourbon Street, and handing out books to precious colored children for the Junior League. In one of the letters, she sends a photo of Mom and herself posing with a "hurdy-gurdy man and his petite macaque in Jackson Square." In another, she sends locks of hair from both her and Mom. She writes of missing him and longing for his safe return.

Grandfather's handwriting is perfect. Perfectly spaced letters and words in perfectly straight sentences across the unlined page. He writes the date in the upper left-hand corner and begins with, "To my wife, Lily." He says he misses his "girls and wish I was there to kiss Patricia good night."

Mostly he talks about his duty, the latest in army gadgets, and the magnificent sunset. He ends all his letters with, "Your husband, Louis G. Jackson."

I'm disappointed that the only sense I get of my grandfather is that he was a dud. His letters are formal and relatively boring. He writes of the things he does and sees, but it's like reading a travel guide or *Military Life for Dummies.* The only real hint of emotion is spent on descriptions of places and sunsets and how he "longs for a Sazerac at Arnaud."

I can't imagine my grandmother married to Louis. She seems as flighty as he seems stiff. She writes of love and longing for his safe return. He writes of sunsets and longing for a Sazerac. They seem so mismatched that it makes me wonder if she and Louis would have stayed married if he hadn't been killed. Papa Bob was much better suited for Grandmother and her internal timer.

The last letter from Grandfather is dated November 2, 1953. It's loose and worn in the folded creases as if it was read many times.

My dearest heart,
    This separation is killing me. I long for the days when I am with you again. The

353

memory of the last time I held you in my arms is such sweet torture. It sustains my darkest days, yet makes me long for you all the more. I loathe the world that keeps us apart and the miles that separate our hearts. I do not despair, knowing that you await my return.

Yet, dearest love, if anything should happen to me, know that I shall call to you unafraid. Know that your name is a whisper on my lips. Listen for it and know that I died loving you.

Yours always,

Louis

Wow, my eyes are a little misty. Grandfather wasn't such a dud after all. Beneath that cold exterior, he had a romantic heart. Like me when I started the Lulu blogs. Maybe we have more in common than a horrible widow's peak.

At the bottom of the pile is an envelope. It's empty except for a newspaper clipping, tattered and browned from age. Below Grandfather's military photograph reads,

Jackson, Battle Victim Wife Told He Died a Hero

Mrs. Louis Jackson of St. James Parish was notified that her husband, Major Louis

Gene Jackson, had been killed in Korea on the date of November 24, 1953.

On the thin margin of the notice is written in faded black pen, *Louie. Love of my life. I am demolished.*

That's lovely and heart-wrenching. I know that Grandmother was flighty, but it's good to learn that at one time she did feel something for Grandfather — before she forgot about him and ran off with her first cousin.

I wonder if Louis called out to Grandmother, if her name was a whisper on his lips as he died. My eyes get a little mistier, and I wipe at the corners. He wrote his last letter to Grandmother less than a month before he died. It's romantic and heartbreaking — no wonder Grandmother read it until the creases wore thin. I can't wait to read them all to Mom.

I refold the worn letter and tuck it, along with the newspaper clipping, into the empty envelope so I won't lose anything. My mind flashes to my grandparents' wedding photo, and Jasper and Jed in matching scowls and identical dark suits. I wonder if my grandfather knew the uncles were gay. I imagine not. At that time, homosexuality was against the law, and no one talked about it. It was kept on the real down low. Most gay men got married or were confirmed bachelors with a flair for fashionable pocket squares.

I gaze at all the envelopes lying on my bed, then return my attention to the one in my hand. It's postmarked November 3, 1953, and addressed to Jedediah R. Sutton, Royal Street, New Orleans. I recognize the tight handwriting.

One of these things is not like the others.

I slide the letter and clipping from the envelope and compare dates. I reread everything and my mind spins in circles, but it's ultimately what I *don't* see that stops me.

One of these things just doesn't belong.

Nowhere in the last letter does Grandfather talk about sunsets and camp shovels. He doesn't refer to Grandmother or anyone by name. I hold up the news clipping and take another look at the handwriting in the margin. It's not looping and feminine like Grandmother's. It's thin and slopes severely to the right. *Louie. Love of my life. I am demolished* was not written by Grandmother, and nowhere in any of her letters does she call him Louie.

"Oh my God," I say out loud. The letter wasn't written to my grandmother.

Mom's snores fill my room, and I look at the monitor.

Grandfather "Louie" was as gay as a box of sprinkles.

20

July 13

Mom flirts at the Cheesecake Factory.
A display case of men.
Choices.

We've circled July 25 for Lindsey's baby shower and set out in the red beast for our second shopping trip together. This time I will not be talked into boots and a twenty-dollar trim. First on our list, Party City. Of course, Mom complains about her neck all the way there. She's in a cranky mood, and I wonder if she looked in her little jewelry box and discovered her missing pills. As we get a cart, she throws the stink eye at two loud teens looking at wigs.

"Kids these days."

I grab a cart and test the waters. "Are you going to be okay?"

"My neck's kinked up from your driving."

I've kept my eyes on Mom for a month now, and she hasn't opened the drawer in her bedside table. "I only kinked your neck once." At least not at night.

"Three times."

If something other than a kinked neck were responsible for her mood, she'd let me know. "It's a big car. I can't help it." I defend myself on the way to the baby shower section.

"Lindsey doesn't kink my neck."

I point to a big Mylar balloon in the shape of a baby bottle. "We should get that," I say to distract her.

"It's huge!"

I find the aisle with baby shower supplies and stop at the blue section, where Mother and I argue over the "Beary Cute" party theme or the "Little Peanut" party theme. Mother gets her way, and we go with Little Peanut. The smallest party kit is for twelve people, and I toss it in the cart. I guess we'll be using elephant paper plates, cups, napkins, and plastic flatware for a while. I throw in some blue streamers, tissue pom-poms, and wrapping paper while Mom loads the cart with an *Advice for Parents* baby shower book, an elephant cake topper, and matching favor boxes. I don't know who she thinks we're giving out favors to, but what the hell.

We're having fun, and whatever we don't find today, I can order and have delivered.

I load everything into the back of the Escalade and strap Mom into the passenger side. Next stop, Lakeside Shopping Center and its 130 stores. On the way, I kink Mom's neck only twice. Progress.

I know that Lindsey has mentioned some baby furniture she's ordered, but I thought Mom and I could get her a little bed for when Frankie is downstairs. I pick out a beautiful white wicker cradle that you can take out of the stand and use as a Moses basket. Mom is fascinated with a fifteen-hundred-dollar cradle that detects the baby's sounds and motions and automatically rocks and plays downloaded music tracks. I win this debate, but Mom picks out the blue checked bedding.

We move from store to store, suckers for every cute onesie we see. Believe me, there are a lot of them, and who knew there were so many choices in baby blankets and strollers? Not me, and Mom seems just as confused. I make an executive decision and get the car-seat-and-stroller combo. Mom manages to find a bottle that looks like a boob and a plush elephant with a blue necktie.

"It's like the Dumbo you had as a kid," she says.

Not quite, but that's a mistake that anyone could easily make. "Remember when you used to sing 'Baby of Mine'?"

"No." She scowls and wrings her hands. "I never did that."

Crap. I forgot that "remember" can set her off. "That's right. I got confused," I tell her to defuse the situation. "I used to love it when you sang to me."

She nods and her scowl softens. "I was a good singer."

We're done by noon, and for the first time, I'm glad of the big red beast. With the seats folded down, everything fits in the back.

Mom wants to have lunch at the Cheese-cake Factory. I suggest P. F. Chang's. She wins, of course, and it turns out to be the cherry on top of her day, which has nothing to do with the food and everything to do with our very handsome waiter.

"What's your name?" Mom asks as he takes our drink order.

"Tyson, ma'am."

Just like it says on his name tag. I don't know if Mom really can't read it, or if she's flirting.

"Oohh." Her voice gets low and seductive. "That's a nice name."

Flirting. Tyson is probably twenty-five, looks like a California surfer, and has a

Southern-boy drawl.

"He's so handsome," Mom whispers as he walks away. "And single."

I hardly even think about rolling my eyes. Huge progress. "How do you know? He could have a girlfriend."

She shrugs and takes a sip of her water. "Dating isn't the same as married."

Like that would stop her.

The menu is enormous, and Mom makes me read it to her several times before she decides on a grilled pork chop. But when Tyson reappears with our tea and is ready to take our order, she's forgotten. Maybe. He patiently goes over the menu with her again. "I'm so grateful, Tyson" and "Bless your heart" spill from her flirting lips. "I'll have the grilled pork chop," Mom orders.

I look at the smile on her fuchsia lips, and I'm not sure her memory slip isn't contrived.

"You're damn foxy," she says before he can take my order.

"Thank you, cher."

Lord, Mom practically swoons into a puddle right there in her side of the booth.

I order fish tacos, but I don't get called sweetheart. Of course, I don't call him foxy, either. As I watch him walk away, my gaze falls from the back of his apron to his round behind, and I don't feel an ounce of shame. I am becoming my mother. Either that or I've depleted my willpower to resist temptation. I can't even recall the last time I went on a date — a real date. The kind where you spend two hours getting ready and the anticipation of his kiss steals your breath before he even knocks on your door. The closest I've come to that was the night Simon kissed me on the front porch. That kiss certainly stole my breath; the slow build from hot to hotter and the smooth touch of his lips against mine. My hands on his back, sliding south to his behind. I clear my throat and reach for my tea. I haven't seen Simon since he and his crew finished their work a few weeks ago. The railing and stairs are beautiful, but maybe he can come over and give me a bid for . . . something. Something that doesn't cost an arm and a leg. Like replacing the broken doorknob in the pink bedroom upstairs. That should cost only several thousand.

"Oh, look at him," Mom says, then starts to comment on different men as if the Cheesecake Factory is just one big display case. "Look at that one's muscles."

Tyson sets our plates on the table, and Mom asks him if he is single.

"I'm waiting for the right lady," he says,

and gives her a flirty wink.

"I think he has a big crush on me," Mom whispers as he walks away. "Don't you?"

More like he wants a big tip, is what I think.

"I found some letters Grandmother and Grandfather wrote to each other when he was in Korea," I tell her as I unroll my fork and knife. I haven't mentioned the letters before now because I've been digging deeper for information on Jed. There really wasn't much, until last night when I came across a note that he'd written to his mother, thanking her for the hundred dollars she'd sent him.

Mom takes her eyes from Tyson's behind and turns to look at me. "Daddy was a war hero."

"I know." I'm not a handwriting expert, but Jed's is thin and slopes severely to the right, just like the writing in the margins of Grandfather's death notice. "I'll read you the letters when we get home." I don't know if Grandmother knew that her husband and her brother were lovers, but it is the kind of discovery that could send a woman into the arms of her first cousin. It would explain why we know so little about Louis.

"I don't remember my daddy."

I don't believe Mom knows anything,

because there are two things that Mom has never been able to keep: a husband and a secret. I'm sure Louis and Jed's relationship isn't the only skeleton in the two-hundred-year-old Sutton closet. Not that it really matters, but it is extremely unfair that Grandmother is buried in the sinners' corner while Jed has a tomb with the rest of the family.

"I think you're really going to like hearing your dad's letters."

As it turns out, she finds them as boring as I did.

"He was a war hero, all right." Mom does like Grandmother's, but for the most part, she shows more interest in folding the tiny onesies we bought for Frankie, and I leave the letter to Jed in its envelope. It's best that she thinks of her father only as a war hero.

"What's this one say?" Mom asks, and holds up a tiny shirt with a blue llama on it.

I look up from the stack of letters I'm tying back up with the old blue ribbon.

" 'Ain't No Llama Like the One I Got.' "

We've enclosed ourselves in my office with most of the baby shower gifts. The stroller is still in the back of the Escalade because it's too big to get in the house without Lindsey seeing.

Mom holds up a onesie with a *Star Wars* stormtrooper. " 'Storm Pooper.' "

Mom claps her hands together and laughs, and it isn't until I start to wrap them in Little Peanut paper that I realize just how many poop-themed shirts Mom picked out.

"That one?"

" 'Party Pooper.' " She laughs harder and points at another. " 'Poops I Did It Again.' "

I can see the party now: Mom laughing about pooper onesies, and Lindsey and I laughing at Mom laughing about pooper onesies. Even though it's just going to be the three of us, I think we'll have a good time.

But later, when Mom and I are watching *The Price Is Right,* Lindsey announces, "Jim's coming to the baby shower. I hope you don't mind."

"That's fine. We had to buy twelve table settings," I tell her as I braid Mom's hair.

She hands Mom a sleeping pill and a glass of water. "He might bring his sister." Mom puts it in her mouth and takes a drink. I watch her swallow as I put an elastic at the end.

Lindsey leaves the room, and Mom lowers the volume on the television. "Go get Momma's letters," she says as she wipes cheese dust from her chest.

I hesitate. Did she fake swallow? Is she trying to get rid of me so she can check on her *other* pills?

"Daddy's too. I want to hear them again."

I toss the brush on the bedside chest and walk from her room, pausing just outside the door. My heart picks up a few beats as I wait for the drawer to open and an angry outburst to commence. I give it a good minute, and when nothing happens, I rush to grab the bundle of letters from my desk. Back in her room, we make ourselves cozy against Mom's pillows, and I read her the "good parts" of Grandmother's letters that mention her.

"Read the part where Daddy says he misses me."

" 'I miss my girls and wish I was there to kiss Patricia good night.' "

Mom stares up at the faded gold canopy. Her braid is to one side, and her arms are across her chest. She's so still that if her eyes weren't open and blinking, I might think she'd fallen asleep.

"Good night, Mom." I kiss her cheek and scoot to the side of the bed.

"Daddy was a war hero."

I stop and look across my shoulder at Mom.

"I wish his letters weren't about the war

so much and were more about missing me and Momma."

"Some people just have a problem expressing emotion. Not all men are like Earl with his cactus card," I say, because I'd much rather she talk about Earl than feel sad about Louis's stilted letters.

"He never said he loves us. I would have liked to hear that."

I hate to see my mom sad. "I found another letter from Grandfather that I haven't read yet." I return to sit beside her and pull the letter from the last envelope.

" 'My dearest heart Lily,' " I fudge.

" 'This separation is killing me. I long for the days when I am with you again. The memory of the last time I held you in my arms is such sweet torture. It sustains my darkest days, yet makes me long for you all the more. I loathe the world that keeps us apart and the miles that separate our hearts. I do not despair, knowing that you and my pretty little Patricia await my return,' " I fudge a bit more. " 'Give her a kiss every night for me and tell her that Daddy loves her.

" 'Yet, dearest love, if anything should happen to me, know that I shall call to you unafraid. Know that your name is a whisper on my lips. Listen for it and know that I

368

died loving you and my little girl. Love, Louis.' "

"I never knew." There are tears in the corners of Mom's eyes and I'm glad I embellished. "That's even better than Earl's card."

"I guess some men save up their feelings and write about them all at once."

"I miss Earl," she says through a sigh. "I liked when he took me to dinner, but I'm glad I don't have to eat stuffed peppers at that place anymore. I hate goddamn stuffed peppers."

I smile. "You and me both."

"I'm glad I don't have to listen to crazy people." She looks at me; her eyes are getting droopy. "Except for you."

I laugh and shake my head. I'm not so certain that she's kidding. "You made me crazy."

She yawns and closes her eyes. "I'm glad I don't have to end up like the others. Shriveled up and carted out and folks asking if I passed peaceful. I don't have to get my insides taken out at no hospital." Her voice fades and her chest gently rises as she inhales. We had a good day together. We had a good day yesterday too. She turns on her side, and her mouth gapes open. Her breath catches in the back of her throat and she lets out her first snore of the night. Mom could live for several more years. We have a lot of good days ahead. Someday she'll be too sick, and all our good days will be gone, but she's not there yet. Not when I look into her eyes and I can see her. There are parts of Mom that have faded away forever, but the part of her that brushes her hair a hundred times and puts on her lipstick every morning, the part that loves men and game shows, and the part that loves me, is still there. For all my mother's Alzheimer rages, I know that she loves me.

Shriveled up and carted out like the others.

My vision blurs, and I feel a hard pinch in my chest. I think I'm having a heart attack . . . but I don't fall over or pass out. I just keep standing here by the side of my mom's bed, watching her.

She's going to get sicker. She's worse than when we first moved to Sutton Hall. Most of the time she acts like she isn't aware of her illness, but she must be, or she wouldn't have stashed her pills.

I take a deep breath and let it out. I love her. I don't want her to take her life, but it's not up to me. It's not my choice. I walk from the room and return a few minutes later.

My hand shakes as I open the first drawer

370

in her bedside chest and reach for the jewelry box. It is weightless in my shaky palm, and I spring the top open with my thumb. The ugly earrings are still inside, and I dump them out. I look at Mom, cozy beneath silky gold bedding, snoring like a hibernating bear.

My fist tightens around the little pills I've kept hidden from her.

A sob clogs my throat, and I open my hand, giving her back the right to make the choice.

21

Snips and snails and gruesome tales.

When I told Lindsey we had twelve Little Peanut place settings, I guess she took it to mean that she should fill them all. Precisely at 1 p.m. on the last Saturday in July, Jim rolls up in his Malibu, followed closely by a maroon minivan. The doors to the van slide open and out pour his two aunts, his mother, and three sisters:

Mindy Lee.

Margaret Ann.

Mary Sue.

Jenny Kay.

Janet Lyn.

Jessica.

"Just Jessica?" I ask as I welcome her inside.

"Momma ran out of middle names."

"She has one; she just don' like it," corrects her mother, Mary Sue. "It's Don, like a man spells it. Her daddy was cassed and spelled it wrong on the birt' certificate. It's a long story."

Mary Sue is a more hardened version of her three daughters, with their blue eyes and hair pulled back in varying lengths of brown ponytails. I can't tell the aunts apart and assume they're twins. Curly gray hair frames round faces, and thick glasses rest on their short noses. The only difference I can detect is the color of their Mardi Gras T-shirts.

All six women sit in various chairs I've pulled into the parlor, hands folded in their laps like they're afraid they might break something. Their accents aren't as thick as Jim's, but they sound every bit as Cajun.

The front parlor is awash in blue balloons, streamers, and tissue pom-poms complete with cutout elephants and vases of blue hydrangeas. A WELCOME BABY FRANKIE banner hangs from the balcony above the front porch and a two-tier cake sits on the kitchen table, which we dragged into the front parlor. Or back parlor. Whatever.

I serve blue raspberry punch from one of my great-grandmother's big Limoges bowls. Mom's cocktail peanuts and butter mints sit beside the silver tea service while several bottles of wine chill in crystal ice buckets. Mom and Lindsey and I are all in baby blue — Lindsey in a muumuu, Mom in a tracksuit, and me in a cotton sundress — and all of us in blue sequined headbands.

Mom sits on the chesterfield like she's holding court while Raphael hangs upside down in his locked cage. Both he and Mom have behaved themselves so far, but I know how quickly that can change.

I might be a little out of practice, but I have organized both big and small events. I know how to be the event's attraction and work behind the scenes. The first few years of Lulu, I did both at the same time.

Today I am hostess, photographer, and one-person waitstaff, thanks to the past ten years I've spent making people feel welcome and at ease. I put my skills to work, and by the time I get out the string for How Big Is Mommy's Belly?, the ice is broken, and our guests are much more relaxed. We play Baby Shower Bingo, and I pass out little boxes of Godiva chocolate for prizes. Everyone wins something, but Jim is the big winner of Baby Grab Bag when he pulls out the boob bottle. His face turns red and he quickly leaves the room.

"He's shy, him." His mom shrugs.

His sister Janet Lyn explains further: "I don' tink he's ever touched a real boob in his life."

A chorus of "Janet Lyn!" follows, and I suspect this isn't the first time Jim's middle sister has been inappropriate. There's one in every crowd, and I cut my gaze to Mom sitting next to me, her lips Vermilion Vixen, sipping punch from a Little Peanut cup.

Lindsey's cheeks turn the color of Mom's lips, and I rise to my feet. "It's time for presents!" I place a chair for Lindsey in front of the fireplace and stack gifts at her feet. The first thing she unwraps is a blue-and-white blanket that Mary Sue knitted herself. It's beautiful and warm at the same time. Most of the other gifts are practical, like diapers and baby shampoo, and I slip out of the room and into the library, where I've hidden the bassinet. I sit the little elephant from Mom in the bed and wheel it into the parlor.

When she sees it, Lindsey's mouth drops open. "Oh my gosh!" She puts a hand to her chest, and her huge eyes get a little teary.

"I found that elephant," Mom says. "It's a good one."

"Mom and I thought you could use a little cradle when you're down here with Frankie."

"Thank you." Lindsey looks so happy I just might cry too. "Sorry, Frankie makes me emotional," she confesses, and I hand her a Little Peanut cocktail napkin.

"Happens to everybody," one of the aunts tells her. "It's part of havin' a bebe. Just you wait till labor starts, yes."

Oh no.

"I was in labor fer five days," the other aunt says, and, as if it were a starter pistol, the race is on for the worst birthing horror story.

"Junior tore me up good."

"I ripped every which way."

"Shana gave me back labor. I 'bout killed Bobby Karl."

Wait for it, I tell myself.

"Lou Ann yanked out my uterus."

And there it is. Mom doesn't disappoint and smiles like she came in first place. Poor Lindsey looks horrified, but Mom isn't done. "I almost bled out."

"Who wants cake?" I desperately move behind the table as several hands shoot up.

"You wouldn't think such a tiny thing could tear me up like that."

"More punch?" I hold up an empty paper cup.

"But once I saw her little face, I couldn't stay mad."

376

That's a nice turn.

"She was just the most precious thing. Delicate little face and all that dark hair. Lou Ann was the most beautiful baby I'd ever seen."

"Ahh, Mom." I think she's trying to out-brag everyone else in the room, and I love it. I reach for a big knife as Lindsey holds up the first poop onesie out of a baker's dozen. When I wrapped the thirteen poop onesies, I was almost as amused as Mom. Now, seeing each of those potty-humor baby shirts laid out one by one in public, it's just plain embarrassing for me. Mom and Janet Lyn, on the other hand, laugh so hard they have to hold their sides in pain.

Raphael flaps his wings and squawks at me. "I feel the same way," I tell him.

"Does he talk?" Jessica asks as she stares into the cage.

"Sometimes too much."

"What does he say?"

I turn toward the bird. "Raphael, say, 'Shake your tail feathers.' " Of course, he doesn't, and I shrug. "I guess he doesn't feel like it today." I remove the elephant topper and slice into the top layer of the cake.

"Are you really Lulu da Love Guru?"

"Yes." At least for now.

"I read your book."

"Which one?" I put a piece of cake on a plate and hand it to her. "I've written several."

"It was yellow, I tink, and you wrote about waitin' tree months before you have sex wit your boyfriend."

I stab the pointed end of the knife into the cake plate and wait. This is usually the part where I'm told that my advice sucks because (insert name) ran off with her boyfriend while she was following my rules.

"I followed it and the guy I was datin' dumped me for a salope bonne à rien."

I don't know what that means, but I assume it isn't good.

"I was mad at first, but I'm glad now. They deserved each other."

"Sounds like you saved yourself heartache down the road."

"Yeah." She takes a sip of blue punch from her Little Peanut cup. "How long have you known Lindsey?"

"Almost six months."

"Jimmy really likes her." She turns her head and watches Lindsey rip into more presents. "I hope she's a good person, 'cause my brother is a good guy."

"Lindsey is a very good person." Someone sticks a bow on her head, and she laughs. "Smart too."

"Tony's an asshole." We both turn and look at Raphael. Now is not a good time for his potty beak.

"Who's Tony?"

I shrug. "He learned that from his previous owner."

Jessica and I watch several more bows get stuck on Lindsey's head, and I reach for my phone and take a picture of her looking young and happy and very, very pregnant. Jim returns as I finish cutting the cake, but he's not alone. He's brought reinforcement with him.

"Doctor Simon," Mom calls out as he walks into the parlor.

"Bonjour, ladies."

There's a round of "bonjours," one "How's ya' momma an' dem?" and Janet Lyn's "You been behavin' yaself, boo?"

"Always," he answers.

Mom shoots Janet Lyn the stink eye and pats my empty place on the sofa beside her. "You can sit here."

Lindsey holds up the "Poop Star" onesie to show Jim. "Patricia and Lou Ann got this for Frankie."

He smiles. "Nice."

"Cake?" I ask both men and give Jim the bigger piece because he looks hungry. He might not be, but he's just one of those skinny people you want to fatten up.

As the party starts winding down, I pour cabernet into a Little Peanut cup and take a sip. My finger just happens to swipe across the cake plate and gather a hunk of blue frosting. Yum. Red wine and sugar take me to my happy place. I look over at my mother. She's happy, comfortable in her environment, eating cake, and chatting with "foxy" Simon. Even her eyes are smiling.

It's been nearly two weeks since I returned those little red pills to her jewelry box. Nearly two weeks of watching her swallow her medication. I've given her back the freedom to end her life. It's her choice, and I'm okay with that, but I can't make myself leave until I am certain it won't be the last time I kiss her cheek good night.

I take another swipe of frosting and watch Mom in action as the aunt in the orange T-shirt shows Simon something on her phone. The two of them laugh and Mom gives the aunt the stink eye for daring to encroach on her territory. I wonder what Mom would say if she knew I made out with her boyfriend on the front porch.

"It wasn't the pot dat doomed your marriage. It was the threesome with Rhonda June Farley."

With the tip of my finger in my mouth, I

look over at Janet Lyn and Jenny Kay.

"Oops," Janet Lyn says into the suddenly quiet room. She turns to her red-faced sister. "Sorry, but it isn't like folks don' already know about dat."

Jim makes a sound that is somewhere between choking and wheezing, and his face is back to bright red. I lower my hand and grab a napkin for my sticky finger. I didn't know about Rhonda June Farley, probably because I've not had the pleasure of meeting her, and it appears the other "folks" in the room didn't know either. Mary Sue's mouth moves but no words come out. Everyone's brows are raised up their foreheads, and no one knows quite what to say to fill the awkward silence.

Luckily, I have Mom. "That's how that sort of thing goes sometimes," says the woman with the vermilion lips. She sighs and takes a drink of her punch, oblivious that the attention in the room is now on her. "One person ruins everyone's fun. It's a shame."

Simon's eyes cut to mine. He starts to laugh, and I have to bite the corner of my lip to keep from joining him. "Mais, y'all, did you hear about that break-in at the Speedy Cash?"

"Dat guy was fou fou, yeah," Jim says, but

the room remains silent until Lindsey plops the plush elephant on the top of her belly. "I think I'll name this guy Horton."

"Or Dumbo," someone suggests.

"He doesn't have a hat like Dumbo," a sister argues. "Tantor, after Tarzan's elephant."

"Babar."

"Heffalump."

"Earl's a damn good name." I'm grateful Mom didn't say "Tony" and set Raphael off again.

By the time the party is over, it's three thirty, and I hand out Little Peanut favor boxes filled with small pieces of cake and butter mints. I'm sincere when I tell them, "Thank you, ladies. It was very nice of all of you to give up your Saturday for us." I stand on the porch as the women pile into the minivan. They certainly made Lindsey's day better.

Simon stands on the porch next to me, watching the van pull away. "Mais, that's a load of trouble, no?"

"I appreciate them coming, and I have to thank Jim. It was nice of them all to turn out for a girl they don't know. I'm sure they have better things to do."

"Better than sucking up gossip about your family? I doubt it."

"What could they gossip about?" I wave at them. "We're not interesting."

He laughs at that. "Folks are always interested in who's living out here and if there's anything scandalous goin' on."

"No scandal today, and for whatever reason, I'm glad they joined us. The party would have been boring without them. No labor and delivery horror stories. No one but Mom laughing at all the poop onesies. No one to talk about a threesome with Rhonda What's-her-face."

"Rhonda June Farley," Simon provides.

The van turns and disappears, and I look across my shoulder at him. "You know her?"

"Cher, everyone knows Rhonda June."

I'm dying to ask the obvious question, but I control myself as we return to the parlor. Simon has referred to me several different ways since we first met. I don't know how I feel about "cher." I know I like "tee Lou Ann" more than "swamp rat." "Tee Lou" is better than "fou fou."

"Jim made it sound like y'all were torturing him over here."

Mom's the only one left in the room, and I take her dirty cake plate and cup. "Poor Jim pulled out the boob bottle and got so red, he almost burst into flames," I tell Simon.

"What's a boob bottle?"

"It's in there," Mom says, and points to the baby bag. "It's for trickin' babies."

Simon sticks his hand in the bag and pulls it out. "This tricks babies?" He studies it from all angles like it's a science project. "It doesn't look like any boob I've ever seen."

Again, not going to ask the obvious question.

"I have a glorious bosom," Mom announces.

I could argue, but I won't. "Do you want to write something in the *Advice for Parents* book you got for Lindsey?" I hold it up for her to see. "I can write down a message, then you can sign it."

She motions affirmatively, and I grab a pen. "I want to say . . ." I sit beside her, pen suspended above the page. "Hmm, I want to say . . ." She looks up at the ceiling and yawns. "I want to say, 'I like you more than Wynonna.' "

"That's it?"

"Yep. She never steals my shoes or tries to kill me."

"Any advice about having a baby?"

"No."

"Okay . . ." I write it down, and Mom signs it. She obviously doesn't understand the concept behind the book, but, hey, at least she had something nice to say. I return to the table across the room and grab a garbage bag. "Mom, do you know where Lindsey and Jim are?" I ask as I throw away dirty plates and cups.

"No. Where?"

"No. Do you know — Never mind. It's an hour past the time you usually take a nap."

"I don't need a goddamn nap!"

"Okaaay. Just thought you'd like to know."

She thinks about it for a moment, then scoots to the edge of the sofa. "I need my rest."

Simon holds out his hand for her. "Here you go."

"Thank you, foxy man."

"Have a good rest, Ms. Patricia."

She winks at him. "I'll be good as new."

I drop the garbage bag and walk with Mom from the room, but halfway down the hall she stops. "I forgot something," she says, and retraces her steps.

I can hear her muffled voice and the deep timbre of his laughter. I don't even want to imagine what she might be proposing, but she's smiling and has a Little Peanut party box when she comes back.

"Did you have a good time today?" I ask Mom as we continue to her room.

"Oh yes. That was a good cake," she says,

and sets the favor box on her side table.

"The frosting was excellent." She sits on the side of the bed, and I kneel down to take off her white orthopedic shoes. "You have a birthday in about six weeks. We should get your cake from the same place."

"Carrot," she says. "Carrot cake is my favorite."

Until half a second ago, her favorite has always been angel food with fresh strawberries. I put her shoes to one side and stand. "Do you need anything?"

She lies down on one pillow and puts a hand on her stomach. "Just go out and shut the door."

Rude, but I don't take it personally. When I return to the parlor, Simon is stuffing the last of the wrapping paper into the garbage bag. "You don't have to do that." I pick up the remaining dirty plates and dump them with the used paper.

"Lindsey and Jim just left to look over a car in Slidell that Lindsey found on Craigslist. They shouldn't be gone more than a couple of hours." He ties the bag closed and looks at me. "Is your momma settled?"

"I think so, but with you here, who knows? She might suddenly remember something else." I tie the bag and grab a bottle from the ice bucket. "Wine?"

"Been that kind of day?"

Raphael laughs from his cage. "I'm a lucky son of a bitch."

"That's enough, Ray-feel."

Simon gets the birdcage cover as I fill two Little Peanut cups with a Washington Chablis.

"Good night, Raphael," I say, and hand Simon a blue elephant cup. "Cheers." I tap my cup to his and give my wine a little swirl for good measure before I take a sip. "Mm, that's good."

"I like a good wine but . . ." He looks into his elephant cup. "Do I have to swirl and smell it?"

I chuckle. "No, but my agent, Margie, is a real connoisseur, and it's kind of funny to watch her do her thing. She inhales as she takes a sip and kind of swishes it around in her mouth before spitting it in a bucket."

"Do you do that?"

"No, I'm not a connoisseur. I don't spit." I shake my head. "I swallow."

22

There aren't words.

The double meaning of my words hangs in the air as a red-hot flush works its way up my chest to my cheeks.

"Good to know." There's laughter in Simon's voice, but thank God he's a grown-up. "I'll remember that if I'm ever at a fancy wine tasting."

I clear my throat as if nothing happened and we settle on the chesterfield. "I think Lindsey had a good time."

Simon takes a drink of wine from his elephant cup and sits beside me. "That girl looks like she's going to have that baby any minute."

"Another six weeks or so." I pause a moment to think about that. "I've never lived in the same house as a baby."

"It's gonna be a busy time for y'all. That baby's gonna be screamin' just down the hall from you."

"I know." I groan. "And for such a tiny person, his stuff takes up a lot of space. And he's not even here yet!" I pull my headband from my head and toss it aside. "Can you soundproof that room for me?"

"No, but you're in luck, because lath-and-plaster walls are about two inches thicker than drywall." He points to the ceiling. "But you got some problems upstairs with cracking and deterioration, and that affects the sounds that get through."

"Of course it does," I say through a sigh.

"Jasper always talked about renovating those bedrooms. He had me take pictures of them and the ceiling in the hall. I gave him an estimate, but he never got around to it."

"Maybe he didn't have an arm and a leg to give you." I take a sip of wine. "Or a few other body parts."

"Nah, he just didn't want the upstairs touched." He lifts his cup and takes a big swig. "Especially the big corner bedroom."

"Why?"

"His brother died in that room. Probably other family members too."

I sit up straighter, and the hair on my arms stands up. "In the room across from me? No wonder I hear creepy sounds at night. How many people have died in this house?"

"This is an old house . . . best guess . . ."

"Hard to say."

He laughs. "A cemetery full."

"Great." I turn my body toward him and rest my cup on my bare knee. "Speaking of Jed, did you know him?" If there is any living person on the planet who might know something about his relationship with my grandfather, it would probably be Simon.

"Barely. He was friends with my family and 'em, but he died before I started coming around and working with my parrain."

Damn. "Did Jasper talk about him?"

"Sometimes, yeah."

"Did he mention if Jed had a . . . lover?"

"Mais, no. Jasper was old-school and didn't talk about his personal business." He shakes his head. "Why are you asking about that?"

Instead of answering, I go to the library and grab my grandmother and grandfather's letters. When I come back into the parlor, I say, "I found these bundled together like this." I move across the room to the table and lay them out. "Come look." Once he stands beside me, I say, "These were written by my grandparents during the Korean War."

"What do you think?" I ask after he's had a chance to skim a few.

"I think your grandmere sounds like mine, and your grandpere was uptight and wrote boring letters."

"Exactly! Now read this." I give him the last one. "All the other letters are in envelopes except this one."

Simon lifts a brow as he reads. "I guess he wasn't a stiff all the time."

"I don't believe he sent that last letter to Grandmother."

Simon looks at me, then returns his attention to the letter. "You think he had a side piece?"

"Yes! Jed Sutton."

"Is that your first bottle of wine this afternoon?"

I lean closer to him and point to the different penmanship. "This is Grandfather's handwriting. This is Grandmother's." I slide the empty envelope toward him like I'm a lawyer laying out a case. "The love letter belongs in this envelope addressed to Jed."

"So Jed could give it to another woman."

"No!"

"Mais, wait." He looks at all the evidence on the table before him. "So you think your grandpere wrote this letter" — he holds it up — "to someone other than your grand-mere?"

"Yes."

"And you think whoever scribbled this note" — he pauses to point at the article — "wasn't your grandmere."

"Yes! You got it."

"I'm confused." He shakes his head like he's clearing cobwebs.

I wave at the evidence. "Grandfather was in love with Jed but married my grand-mother."

He rubs his forehead.

"Growing up, all I was ever told about him was that he was a war hero and got a Purple Heart." I take a breath and continue. "I think Grandmother found out, and that's why she would never talk about him again."

"Tee Lou, stop, stop."

I gasp as new thoughts spin around in my head. "Maybe Grandmother wasn't dis-owned by her family as much as she dis-owned them." He just stares at me. I get it. It's a lot to take in at once. "Then, after Jed died, she came back. He deserves to be in the sinners' corner with Grandmother, because I'm fairly sure it's just as big a sin to have an affair with your sister's husband as it is to run off with your first cousin. But he wasn't buried there — either because it would have been a bigger scandal or because he was a man." I throw back the rest of my wine. "What do you think?"

He drops the letter and combs his fingers through the sides of his hair. "I think you make me crazy."

I shake my head. "Well, I don't —"

"I think you do it on purpose," he interrupts, and his eyes are a darker green as he looks down at me. His lids are lowered as if he's suddenly sleepy, and his voice is deeper when he says, "And I think you like it," as he slides his hand across the top of my shoulder to the side of my neck. His thumb lifts my chin and his breath whispers across my cheek. "I think I like it too."

My own breath catches in the back of my throat, and I swallow hard. My mind is racing in all different directions. Then his mouth is just above mine and everything slows to the unhurried brush of his lips and the warm flush of my skin. "This makes things complicated."

He shakes his head and slips his free hand around my waist to the small of my back. "Nothing complicated about it." He pulls me closer. "I kiss you, and you kiss me back if you feel like it. Easy."

That's the problem. It's too easy. Much harder to pull away than to fall into him until I'm in so deep that I don't know where I end and he begins. My head says no, but every other part of my body is screaming *Yes!*

"You're overthinking it."

I'm still Lulu the Love Guru, and that's what I do. I make lists and rules and . . . His fingers brush my back, sending shivers up and down my spine. I am a shameless hypocrite, but I slide my hands up his chest to his shoulders anyway. His muscles harden beneath my touch, and I like knowing what I do to him. I rise on the balls of my feet and say next to his ear, "I don't want to make you crazy, Simon."

"Too late, cher." Then he kisses me. Open-mouthed kisses, hotter than the first time. A flash fire that I breathe in so deeply, I feel it in the pit of my stomach. I know he must stop, but I hope that he doesn't. Not just yet. His hands slide into my hair and he holds my face to his and I never want it to stop. He wants me every bit as much as I want him, and I lose myself in his kiss that lasts forever but not long enough. Against my breasts I feel his deep groan just before he tears his mouth from mine. His labored breath stirs the wild curls resting on my forehead. "If you don't stop me now, we're going to finish this in your bed."

I lick my dry lips as my body wars with my head. It takes me longer than it should to make the decision I've preached for ten years. "I'm going to stop you now." I expect him to cajole or get angry.

"That's what I thought you'd say." He kisses the top of my head.

He sounds so sure, but he doesn't know how much I want to grab his hand and take him upstairs. "I have a three-month rule," I say as much to myself as to him.

He pulls back and looks into my face. "A what?"

"A wait-three-months-before-sex rule."

He grins. "When did we meet, tee Lou? Was it back in March, no?"

"A three-month *dating* rule."

"Seriously?"

"Seriously. It takes at least that long to get to know someone. Some men can't handle it."

He drops his hands and steps back. "I can handle it, but that doesn't mean I like it."

"Patience is a virtue. It's in the Bible."

"I spent twelve years in Catholic schools, tee Lou. I know what's in the Bible." He walks toward the front, or back, or whichever entrance. "Sin on Saturday and confess on Sunday." He opens the front door and asks, "What are you doing next Saturday?"

I laugh and follow him out onto the front porch. "Probably not sinning." I stop at the top step and watch him walk around the back of his truck. "Simon."

He pauses and looks across the distance at me.

"Merci bien," I say, having picked up a little Cajun French here and there. "You didn't have to come today, but I'm glad you did."

"De rien. I had a good time."

"Me too. Almost as good as bobbering."

He chuckles and opens his truck's door. "A good bobber is hard to beat."

After Simon leaves, I take down the party banner and carry everything to the outside garbage cans. Lindsey's been gone for an hour and a half, and Mom's been asleep the whole time, thank God. I would have hated for Mom to walk into the parlor to find me practically wrapped around Simon. I don't know what she would have done. I don't think she honestly believes Simon is her real boyfriend, but he is her "foxy man."

I shake my head as I walk toward Mom's room. She is territorial and I probably shouldn't risk making out with him a second time. Third, rather. I crack open the bedroom door and peek inside. Mom hasn't slept long, but she hates to miss *I Love Lucy* on the Hallmark Channel and I call out, "Mom, it's almost time for *Lucy.*" I walk farther into the room. "Mom, time to get up." Her quilt is thrown back, and she isn't in bed. Her shoes are in the place where I left them. "Mom?" I turn toward the TV and see her on the floor by the hearth. "Mom!" She's on her back, and one leg is bent beneath her as if she crumpled in that spot. I drop to my knees and put a hand on her shoulder.

"Mom?" Her eyes stay closed, sunken into her pale face. I shake her and a small trickle of dark red blood runs from her nose. "Oh God! What happened?" I push two fingers into her carotid artery on the side of her neck. She is cold, her lips are bluish, and I can't feel her pulse. I grab her wrist, but I can't find it there either. "Wake up, Mom!"

I look around, frantic. I can't breathe. I need a phone. I have to call 911. My gaze falls on the bedside chest and I stand up and move across the room. My hands tremble so much, I can hardly yank open the drawer and grab the velvet jewelry box. I'm shaking so hard now I'm coming apart. My heartbeat pounds in my neck and head and I struggle to suck in huge breaths. I'm angry and scared and I can't push the tiny button. "Damn it, Mom!" I get my fingers beneath the lid and rip it open. Four little red pills fly into the air before gently ping-ponging around the hardwood floor.

I race to my office and grab my phone. I try to dial as I run back to Mom's room, but I can't even manage 911. In the few seconds I am gone, hope echoes in my brain. I hope she got up. I hope she's in bed. I hope I'm having a horrible dream, but when I return, she's right where I left her.

"Momma!" I kneel beside her. Her skin is still pale, her eyes sunken, and her lips light blue. The trickle of blood has run down her cheek now. If she didn't kill herself, what the hell happened?

"Don't leave me," I beg, even though I know she is already gone. Nothing will bring her back. "Fuck!" I throw my phone across the room. She has a do-not-resuscitate order. She doesn't want an ambulance or an autopsy. She has it all planned out with Bergeron Funeral Home.

My vision blurs her dark hair and baby-blue tracksuit. The first sob rips apart my chest and turns into a long, painful wail. I fall backward on my butt. My mother didn't kill herself like she planned. She got out of bed for some reason and fell. My cries are loud and uncontrollable and drawn from deep in my soul. I pull Mom into my lap the best I can. Her head falls to the side and blood drips in my lap. I try to speak, but all that comes out is a laborious "Mmmm . . . om." Hot tears roll down my numb cheeks and neck. I pull her closer. Her head rests against my heart, and a Little Peanut party favor box sits beneath her bent leg.

I bury my face in her hair. "Don' . . . leeeeeave me." Why didn't I hear her fall? I should have heard something, but I was making out with Simon. I could have helped her. "Mom . . . ma." My back hurts, but I can't stop wailing.

"Ahhh, baby," I hear. My vision is blurred, but there is no one in the room but me and Mom. "Shhh, Lulu." Something weightless and warm touches my back that I know is my mother, soothing me like when I was a child.

I try to say, "Come back. Don't leave me, please!" It comes out garbled and disjointed.

I feel her around me, calming me as my cries turn to painful hiccups. "Cher, baby of mine."

"Don't go."

There is a hand on my shoulder. This time it's real. "Lou Ann!"

I lift my face and see Lindsey through my

swollen, tear-filled eyes. "My momma's gone."

23

July 30

I'm alone and lost.

I am adrift, no longer connected to anything. A vital part of me is gone. It feels like my heart no longer beats in my chest, yet I am still here. Mother is across the parlor from me. I can see her profile, but she is not here. She stayed with me for the first two days after her passing, but I felt her leave the night I requested an autopsy. I don't know if that is a coincidence, or if she's mad because I went against her wishes, but I don't think I could live the rest of my life not knowing why my mom died. I know Lindsey couldn't. Her guilt was almost as paralyzing as mine until learning Mom suffered a heart attack due to a blood clot that originated from a microbleed in her brain. Even if someone had been next to her and immediately called 911, she likely would have died on the way to the hospital. Lindsey seems comforted by this. I am not. *Likely* only adds to my guilt.

The past five days have passed in flickers of time. I'm in one place, and then I'm somewhere else, and I hardly recall the in-between.

I am dressed in my black suit and new Louboutin heels like the day I took Mom from Golden Springs. The day my life changed, the day my priorities changed. A pillbox hat sits on top of my head, and my lips are Seductress Red in honor of my mother.

Patricia is embroidered in blue on white silk inside the casket; I hadn't realized how opulent the interior draping was the day she picked it out. The shirring and tassels alone are pure brothel, just like she wanted. There are several poster-size photos of Mom about the room. Most of them are black-and-whites of her and my grandmother and great-grandmother. She would have loved the portrait I had colorized of her wearing her blue organza prom dress, which I placed at the head of the coffin, but my favorite is the picture of her wearing the big blue hat with the broken ostrich feather taken the day I pulled the trunk from the attic.

Lindsey and I picked out some of her Bob Ross paintings to display on the mantel above her casket.

Moonlight Sonata plays on the old Victrola, and I sit on the chesterfield where Mother and I talked and laughed and sometimes argued. I can almost smell a lingering trace of Pirate's Booty on the cushions. Lindsey sits next to me. Her eyes are as swollen as her ankles. Raphael is unusually quiet and still, seeming to mourn with us.

There are people here whom I've never met. Some are from Mom's childhood, others are relatives so distant I've never even heard of them before. More than I imagined have come from around the area to pay their respects to a woman they'd never met.

They've brought food and say they're sorry for my loss. They say they know how I feel. I don't think that can possibly be true. Not unless they've experienced a pain so deep it pierces their soul. Not unless they are completely alone in the world and nothing will ever fill the massive hole where their heart once beat.

Simon is here somewhere, but I cannot look at him. He has reached out to me several times, but I cannot see him without being overwhelmed with guilt and shame. While I was kissing him, feeling my body come alive with his touch, my mother's body was doing the opposite just down the hall. It's not his fault, but I blame him just the same.

I look at the pointed toes of my shoes. It's been five days since I walked into Mom's bedroom and found her on the floor. Five days of planning her funeral according to her wishes. Five days of hell and heartache and sleepless nights. Five days of promising God anything for just one more day with her. Just one more day of looking through old albums, painting happy clouds, and watching Wink Martindale. I don't care if that day is spent with her accusing me of trying to kill her or steal her shoes or both.

The funeral director whispers to me that it's time to begin the ceremony. I nod, and he starts with a prayer and Bible verses my mom picked out. He reads the eulogy that I wrote honoring her life. I recall sitting at my computer for hours, but I don't remember what I've written until I hear it from his mouth. It is inadequate, and I am ashamed. I should have said more. I should have described her life in more grandiose terms. If nothing, Mom was over-the-top and grandiose, and my eulogy falls short.

There are no words to describe the agony of seeing my mother in a coffin. It's raw and jagged and burns my eyes with hot tears. How will I live without her? We had our spats and periods of time when we did not speak. Silly and regretful, but I always knew that my mother was just a phone call away.

I make it through the last hymn, and I manage to rise and walk across the parlor. I stand before Mom's shiny white casket, with the gold handles and blue pillow to "match" her eyes. She wears a new blue organza dress and Passion Red lipstick to match her nature.

I kiss her cool cheek and whisper, "I love you always." I am ushered outside so I won't see the lid close on my mother. Lindsey stands beside me, and I lock my knees so I won't buckle on the wooden porch. The first time I stood in this spot, my pump got stuck in a hole while Mom insisted Wynonna stole "the good key." I wish I could go back to that day and do it over. I wouldn't yell at Mom for saying Tony's name.

Lindsey puts her arm around my shoulders, and I turn my face away from Simon and the other pallbearers carrying Mom's closed white casket to the waiting surrey. I don't want to do this. I want to run upstairs and pull the sheets over my head, but I put one foot in front of the other and follow

405

behind the carriage. It's hot and humid, and my footsteps falter on the old cobblestones. Simon takes hold of my arm and steadies me. I am grateful, but I pull away.

It seems to take forever to reach the cemetery. Grandmother's white vault is open, and Mother's coffin is slid inside as we bow our heads in prayer. I'm mad at God. It would be one thing if Mom had actually committed suicide. It's another that she didn't and that God took her anyway.

"Amen," I say along with the others standing around the vault. With that one word, it's over. Mom is truly gone. I am folding in on myself. I do not know how much longer I can remain upright, but I do make it back to the house somehow.

"Can I get you something to eat?" asks a woman from one of the local churches. I don't even know which one, because Mom and I never set foot in any of them.

"No, thank you." I kick off my heels and carry them upstairs to my bedroom. I know the polite thing to do is return downstairs. I need to thank people and make an extra effort to talk to distant relatives. I just can't right now, and I lie down alone instead. I have not slept for more than a few hours here and there for the past five days. I close my eyes, even though I know I will not sleep.

There's a knock on my door, and I hear Simon. "I'm coming in. So cover up if you're naked." He doesn't wait for a response before he walks into my room.

"I'm not naked." I sit up and scooch back against the headboard. "If you've come to tell me I'm rude and bad-mannered for not returning downstairs to chat with the church ladies, I don't care."

He's removed his black suit jacket and loosened his gray tie. "I'm not going to tell you how to behave at your momma's funeral." He sits on the side of the bed as if I invited him. "You look tired."

"I am."

"And mad as hell at somebody."

"I am."

"And I get the feeling that 'somebody' is me." He unbuttons the collar of his white shirt. He shakes his head. "But for the life of me, I can't figure out why."

I lean my head back against the headboard and close my eyes. "I was with you when I should have been with her. I know it's not your fault, but . . ." I shrug and leave the rest unsaid.

"And you think you could have saved her?"

"Maybe."

"Lindsey thinks different."

407

I crack my eyes open and look at him. "Maybe Lindsey wants to think different."

"You really believe that?"

No, but I'm angry and sad and miserable. "My mother got out of bed to stash her Little Peanut box, but she didn't make it." The day after Mom died, I noticed the lid to the coal bin was open. I feel a tiny bit better knowing she rudely shooed me from her room so she could hoard her cake, not because I was annoying her. "She died on the hardwood floor. All alone, while I was down the hall fooling around with you."

"I thought it might be something like that. If you hadn't been in the back parlor 'fooling around' with me, what would you have been doing?"

"I've asked myself that question, and I don't know." I shake my head. "But the answer doesn't matter. It doesn't change anything."

"Mais, locking yourself away does?" He stands and walks to the door. "Your momma was a unique woman. I'm glad I knew her." He pauses long enough to say, "You should try and join the living. It's gotta be better than grieving alone."

Maybe for him, but I prefer to grieve alone. I need to wallow in my misery and guilt, and that's exactly what I do over the next few days. I eat when I'm hungry and spend as much time as I can out on the balcony staring at the Mississippi through the filter of live oaks. Magnolia and wild honeysuckle scent the heavy humid air, and I swim in it until I am dripping with sweat and forced inside.

A week after the funeral, I turn my attention to business, and the decision I've put off making. With Mom gone, my time is free. There's no reason to find a new Love Guru now. Nothing is keeping me from stepping into my Lulu shoes and picking up where I left off. I know the business I built better than anyone, and there's no reason why I can't get the excitement back.

Except that I don't have any desire to get it back. I don't have the drive or heart for it. I don't know when it happened exactly, but over the past six months I fell out of love with Lulu. Out of love with my whole life, really. I've said everything I know to say, and in as many ways as possible, about love and life and dating. I don't have the passion I once did, and I'm okay with that. I open up my fingers and let go. I am relieved and freed enough to look at video hopefuls with a new perspective. Freed to see the excitement and passion in someone else's eyes.

Unencumbered by the heavy burden that has weighed on me for months, I don't take long to find the new Lulu. She is creative and driven and has the spark I've been looking for, and of course, she's gorgeous, with great style. I call Margie with the news, but the fine details will be worked out later. The business will be restructured, but I am the president of Lulu Inc. and will remain in that position. I just won't be involved in the day-to-day, or even month-to-month, decision-making.

When I hang up the phone, I actually feel lighter, and I go to bed knowing I've made the right decision. I quickly fall into a healing sleep that has eluded me since the day Mom died. A deep sleep that is interrupted by someone insistently shaking me awake.

"Lou Ann."

I squint against the hall light flooding my room. "What?" Lindsey is speaking to me, but my head is dull. I just want to be left alone, and I close my eyes. "Go back to bed."

She shakes me again. "My water broke."

"What?" I sit up straight. "What! Are you sure?" It's six days past Frankie's due date and Lindsey has had several false alarms.

"Um . . . yes, Lou Ann, and my contractions are five minutes apart."

"We need to get to the hospital." I throw the covers off my body. "It's Frankie's birthday."

We need to get to the hospital," I throw the covers off my body. "It's Frankie's birthday."

24

September 12

Welcome to your life, Frankie!
Welcome to my new life.

"Here comes a big one."

"Don't tell me!"

I turn my attention from the peaks and plateaus of the monitor measuring Lindsey's vitals to her red face. "Sorry."

Lindsey has opted for a natural, drug-free birth. About two hours ago, she began to regret that decision, but it was too late for one of those spinal taps. She grabs onto the side rail and does her who-who-who breathing, and I'm glad it isn't me in that bed.

Watching the whole birthing process has been a huge learning experience. Lindsey's had so many fingers up her vagina, she should start charging admission. From the safety of my chair next to her bed, I find the whole thing fascinating. When we arrived at the hospital at four this morning, her contractions were four minutes apart. Nine hours later, her contractions are closer and lasting longer, and I wouldn't be surprised if she starts screaming bloody horror like in the movies.

"I have to tell you something," Lindsey says as she takes deep cleansing breaths and the spike on the monitor drops.

"If you want to tell me you're pregnant, I already know."

"Not that. I lied about Frankie's father."

I look over at her. "What?"

"I lied about telling him I'm pregnant."

"Okay." This is kind of a bizarre time to bring it up.

She reaches for a cup of water, and I stand to help. "I don't know who his father is. I just said that because I didn't want you to think I was a slut."

I just look at her, kind of shocked that this is what she wants to talk about right now.

"I had a few wild months after Mrs. Rogan died."

"Mrs. Rogan?"

"My client before Patricia. The Rogan family wanted me to stay in the house and take care of the place until they settled her affairs and put it on the market." She shakes her head. "I lived out my sexual fantasies. I think maybe two or three times."

"Most women do that. It's normal."

"A week. Sometimes twice in one day."

That's not so normal. "Why are you telling me this now?"

"Because I don't want you to be surprised if he comes out part Asian or black or Hispanic or Russian."

Russian?

"Or Swedish."

"He'll come out looking like Frankie. That's all that counts."

"I've felt so horrible for lying to you."

"I really don't think it matters at this point. I don't care. I love you . . . and here comes another one."

"Don't tell me!"

I sit back down in my chair and keep my mouth shut. Or at least I try, but when the doctor comes in and wheels a stool to the end of the bed, all bets are off. I move behind his left shoulder and watch Lindsey grab her bent knees and push. It's not a pretty sight down here in the front row. Kind of disturbing, but exactly where I want to be sitting.

"There's his head," the doctor announces from his catcher's position.

"Where?"

"Right here."

I bend my head down and look right up Lindsey's hoo-ha. "That hairy-walnut-looking thing?"

"Yep."

"Oh my God." It hits me that I am seeing the top of an actual baby's head. I know this is biologically natural, but it's new to me. A few more pushes and Frankie's head pops out like a little purple alien. "Oh my God, Lindsey, Frankie's head's out. I can see his face." The doctor suctions the baby's nose and mouth. Lindsey pushes out a shoulder, and then Frankie just slips into the world and is put on his momma's stomach. Lindsey's bawling and touching him, and he opens his mouth and screams and screams.

"That's my favorite part," the doctor says, and I agree. A nurse hands me scissors to cut the rubbery cord. His color has changed to pink, and he is rolled up in a swaddling cloth like a burrito and placed in his mother's arms.

"Isn't he beautiful?" Lindsey asks through blubbery tears.

"Beautiful." I touch his cheek with the back of my finger. He's the softest thing I've ever felt. He has so much dark hair. "He looks like he's wearing a little toupee," I say, just before I start blubbering too. I've never experienced this kind of awe and sheer joy.

"I'm your momma," Lindsey tells him, and I think of my mother. For the first time since her death, her memory isn't accompanied by pain. I think about her on the day of Lindsey's baby shower, smiling when she beat the other women in the worst-birthing-story competition. I think I'm going to miss hearing about how I ripped out her uterus.

I take tons of pictures, and after a nurse snaps pictures of the three of us, Frankie is taken across the room and put in a little bed beneath a warming light. He weighs in at ten pounds two ounces and he is twenty-three inches long. He looks tiny to me, but I guess that's considered big. At least that's what the nurses tell me. His thick hair is parted on the side like a little old man's, and I think Lindsey can cross Swedish off her list.

The next day, I drive the three of us home and feel bad when Lindsey sucks a breath between her teeth as she gets out of the car. She walks slowly into the house, Frankie in his car seat in one hand and a bag of hospital swag in the other. I follow behind, carrying a gigantic floral arrangement that I can't see over or around. I can only look at my feet and take careful steps. The flowers are from Jim, and the card reads, *To my wonderful girl and little man.* Considering all things, it seems kind of presumptuous to me, but Lindsey cried and didn't ask my opinion, and I'm out of the relationship advice business.

While Lindsey takes a shower, Frankie naps in the cradle Mother and I bought him. Next to his head is the blue elephant named Earl. He's a perfect baby.

The first few days are rough, and I start to think he's less perfect. Frankie doesn't like to sleep at night, and when Lindsey's milk comes in, her boobs are like sprinklers. This makes Frankie very mad. Of course, Raphael has to get in on the act and starts to imitate a crying baby. If it isn't one of them wailing, it's the other, but by the end of the week, Lindsey and the baby have calmed down. Raphael has calmed down too.

When it's just me and Frankie and Raphael in the room, the bird even purrs and shifts from side to side like he's dancing. Frankie's blue eyes get big when he watches Raphael squawk and smiles when the bird opens his beak and bays like a hound dog. Raphael hasn't given up his feud with

Lindsey, but he controls himself when the baby is near.

I love having Frankie around, but I know that he and Lindsey will leave someday. It's only right that she makes her own home. I am not looking forward to that day, but I officially become Frankie's godmother on the third Sunday of his life, which only seems appropriate, since I was the first one to see his face.

I think Mother would have liked Frankie, had they met. He's a handsome little man and a captive audience, right up Mom's alley.

I think about Mom a lot. I still have guilt, but it is less of a companion these days. I remember snippets of our life together — sad, bad, happy, funny — and I don't want to lose those memories. I sit at my desk and turn on my computer, and I am reminded of the day Mom and I used the Google net to search for baby shower ideas.

My first memory of Mom is of sitting on the back of a green velvet couch, brushing her hair and watching Dynasty *through a haze of cigarette smoke,* I write. *I was probably four or five, and I think even back then I knew I had to take advantage of those special times when it was just the two of us. When Mom was between men and I had her full attention.*

I write about my earliest memory of Mom's push-and-pull and about how much I loved her. How much I will always love her.

It takes me several hours to get it all out of my head and into a document I've titled "How I Lost My Mind." I haven't looked at the day planner on my phone since Mother died, but I'm sure it will inspire a new rush of memories for me to write down.

The Louisiana sunlight pours through the library windows, creating a wavy swath across the hardwood floors and round couch. I rise from my chair and stand in that light, looking out at the patchy front yard, where I once stood slapping mosquitoes and sweating in my St. John suit.

It seems like it's been years since I stood next to Mom, both of us looking at the same old estate but each seeing something entirely different. She saw a home, I saw a money pit, and we were both right. Sutton Hall is a two-hundred-year-old money pit, and I can't think of anywhere else I would rather call home.

So much has happened since that day we arrived. Life is so different. I stand in the same place but see a different world. So much has changed.

I am changed. I don't think I was ever a

bad person, I'm just different now. I hope a little better of a person, too. I know I have a hell of a lot more patience.

I hear Lindsey's footsteps, and I turn as she walks into the room. Frankie is strapped in his car seat while his mother lists to the right from the weight on one side. She and the baby are car shopping today, and they're waiting for Jim. Their "friendship" seems to be heading in a more serious direction, but it's none of my business.

"What kind of car are you going to look at?" I take the car seat from her and sit with Frankie on the couch until Jim arrives and the three of them will head out in the Cadillac. It already has the other part of the car seat strapped in the back, and, well, it's more reliable than the Malibu.

"I have my eye on a few different Subarus that are top safety picks by *Car and Driver* magazine."

Frankie is wearing his "Ladies' Man" onesie and socks that are too big. His sleeping cheek rests against his neck pillow.

"Hey, baby." I run my finger across the back of his chubby little hand. "Do you think he needs a haircut?"

"Oh, no. His hair is too beautiful to cut."

He is beautiful and I love him so much — enough to make me think I hear the faint tick of my biological clock. "You could put it in a man bun." Since he came home from the hospital, his thick hair has gotten wavy, and his pink skin has tanned up. With each passing day, he looks more and more like his mom.

"That's crazy."

"No." I point to Frankie's head. "That's crazy. It's even growing down his forehead. I had a widow's peak, and it's not fun." As if he hears me, he sticks out his tongue in his sleep. "See?"

"He could totally rock a widow's peak."

I chuckle as I hear the sound of a car parking in front of the house. It's Simon's white truck, not Jim's Malibu, and it isn't stopping just long enough to let Jimmy out.

I haven't seen Simon since Mom's funeral. For some reason, when he walks into the house with Jimmy, I feel like smiling. I guess that means I'm not mad at him anymore.

"I haven't met this guy," he says, and heads straight for the baby next to me.

"I told ja he has da hands of a football playa. 'Who Dat.' "

Simon bends down on one knee to get a better look. "Un petite cochon."

"Talk about."

At least Jim knows what Simon just "talk about."

Simon lifts his gaze to mine. "How are you doing, Lou Ann?"

Lou Ann? What happened to "tee Lou Ann" or "tee Lou" or "cher"? "I'm good. How have you been?"

"Good. Busy." He points to Frankie. "How's life with the ladies' man, here?"

"Better now that he sleeps." I look up as Lindsey walks toward me and says, "I don't know when we'll be back." She picks up the car seat. "Do you want me to pick up anything for you while we're out and about?"

"No, I'm good. Don't worry about me."

"Okay, but call if you think of something," she says as she heads out of the library.

"Hold up a minute, Jimmy." Simon stands and waits until Lindsey and the baby are on the front porch. He takes Jim aside and talks to him, but I can't understand a word either of them says. I can gather it's about Lindsey and the baby, and things get a little heated when Jim raises his voice and angrily leaves the room.

"Is he okay?"

"He'll calm down." Simon sits next to me and watches Jim through the window. "He just didn't want to hear what I had to say."

"About?"

"About playing at being a daddy. It's all

fun and games now, but if he's not real sure this is what he wants, he needs to walk away before that baby gets used to him in his life."

"It sounded as if he didn't like your advice."

"No, he did not." He places his elbows on his knees and continues to look out the window. "He said that I should know him better than that, and if I don't, I should . . . fuck myself. The little crotte."

I burst out laughing.

"You think that's real funny?" He looks over his shoulder at me.

"Very."

"Get your laugh out, and when you're done, I'll take you fishing."

"Are you asking or telling?"

"Whichever works for you."

"You know I don't like to torture innocent fish."

"Yeah." He stands and offers me his hand. "That's why I rigged a pole with a new pink bobber just for you."

Some men bring a girl flowers. Simon brings a new pink bobber. I take his hand and rise to my feet. I can't think of anything better than a pink bobber. "Same alligator deal as before?"

"Same deal." He keeps my hand in his and we walk from the library. "I'll wrestle gators, but it's going to cost you."

"How much?"

"You know I'm not cheap, tee Lou."

"Is it going to cost me an arm and a leg and a few other body parts?"

He laughs and drops my hand to open the front door. "We can probably barter something."

It's good to hear his laugh again. "Are you going to take advantage of me because I'm a woman?"

He raises a brow as we step outside and into the Louisiana sunlight. "Are you coming on to me, cher?"

I walk past him and say over my shoulder, "If you have to ask, I must be getting old."

ACKNOWLEDGMENTS

A special thanks to my agent, my rock, and my friend, Claudia Cross. It's been a wild twenty years.

Lauren McKenna for believing in me. Your enthusiasm for and insights into Lulu were invaluable and our conversations priceless.

David. For the best three words of my day: "Baby, I'm home."

ABOUT THE AUTHOR

Rachel Gibson is a *New York Times* and *USA TODAY* bestselling author of more than twenty-five novels, including *The Art of Running in Heels* and *Just Kiss Me.* She has received the RITA Award, the Golden Heart, the National Readers Choice Award, and more.

The employees of Thorndike Press hope you have enjoyed this Large Print book. All our Thorndike, Wheeler, and Kennebec Large Print titles are designed for easy reading, and all our books are made to last. Other Thorndike Press Large Print books are available at your library, through selected bookstores, or directly from us.

For information about titles, please call:
  (800) 223-1244

or visit our website at:
  gale.com/thorndike

To share your comments, please write:
  Publisher
  Thorndike Press
  10 Water St., Suite 310
  Waterville, ME 04901